"He's not
with hunger

He reached
could resist.
tion of his solid, muscular body molding itself to her
own as if it belonged there, when he kissed her.

Her eyes widened in surprise and she whimpered in
protest, intending to pull out of his embrace, but his
mouth on hers soon banished all rational thought . . .

Titles by Leslie Brannen

HEALING HEARTS
LOVE HEALS ALL

Love Heals All

Leslie Brannen

JOVE BOOKS, NEW YORK

LOVE HEALS ALL

A Jove Book / published by arrangement with the author

PRINTING HISTORY
Jove edition / December 1997

The Putnam Berkley World Wide Web site address is
http://www.berkley.com

ISBN: 0-515-12188-6

A JOVE BOOK®
Jove Books are published by The Berkley Publishing Group, a member of Penguin Putnam Inc., 200 Madison Avenue, New York, New York 10016.
JOVE and the "J" design are trademarks belonging to Jove Publications, Inc.

PRINTED IN THE UNITED STATES OF AMERICA

10 9 8 7 6 5 4 3 2 1

In loving memory of my mother,
Julia Trahan.

She is missed.

LOVE HEALS ALL

1

THE UNOPENED LETTER, FOLDED AND STUFFED IN THE back pocket of Catherine Wills's trousers, seared her hip like a branding iron. She hoped it contained good news, or her future looked bleak.

But the letter would have to wait.

She cantered her black mare down the sweeping tree-lined drive leading to the Coopers' sprawling horse farm. The warm May breeze lifted the wide brim of her brown felt hat and pressed her father's old shirt against her lithe body. Her mare's hoofbeats shook the ground and rumbled like thunder heralding an approaching storm.

As Cat approached the two-story wood frame house, two large, short-haired mongrels, sons of Cat's own dog, came charging across the lawn to investigate the trespasser. She ignored their frenzied barking and rode on.

When she reached the stable yard, she dismounted quickly and unhooked her medical bag from the saddle horn. After turning her hot, lathered mare over to one of the grooms for cooling, she entered the stable and paused until her eyes adjusted from daylight to dimness. She breathed in the unmistakable fragrance of clean straw and horse before hurrying down the long corridor to Gustavus's stall.

Jace Cooper and his son, Michael, stood deep in conversation outside the closed stall door. Jace, a tall, lean man with a bold blue gaze that never failed to appreciate any woman within whistling distance, rubbed his jaw, a sure sign of worry.

Michael sensed her presence immediately and turned. His cool blue eyes warmed in welcome, but his handsome, chiseled features remained as set and worried as his father's. "Willie. Glad you could come so quickly."

"I came as soon as I could," she said, setting down her medical bag.

"I appreciate it," Jace said. "If anything happens to this horse, my wife'll hang me."

Everyone in Little Falls, Missouri, knew that his wife, Clementine, doted on her flashy Hanoverian carriage horse, and loved driving him at a fast, showy trot around the countryside.

Cat looked over the stall door at seventeen hands of listless chestnut horse lying flat on his side like a slain giant from a child's fairy tale, his long legs and neck extended straight out.

"How long has he been like this?" she asked the men with her usual crisp efficiency.

"Since this morning," Michael replied.

"And how often does he lie down?" was Cat's next question.

"Every five to fifteen minutes."

"When he does get up," Jace added, "he walks around the stall and paws at the floor. Sometimes he turns his head to look back at his flanks, then he lies down again."

Cat fell silent, her mind collecting the symptoms in an attempt to determine the horse's illness. As Little Falls's unofficial veterinarian since her parents moved away, she hadn't lost any animals. There was always a first time.

She looked at the men. "Has he been passing manure?"

"Not much," Michael said. "And they've been dry."

Cat thought hard and fast as she took the stethoscope from her medical bag. She opened the stall door, and murmuring soft, soothing words to the horse, cautiously stepped inside.

Gus snorted and lifted his head, his liquid brown eyes filled with pain, but made no attempt to rise. Her presence appeared to calm him.

Cat stroked his neck, noticing that at least he wasn't sweating as he would with colic. She listened to the full, steady thudding of his heart, relieved that the pulse wasn't the rapid, feeble beat that presaged death. She carefully touched his abdomen, which was full, but not distended with gas. When the horse barely flinched, she nodded in satisfaction.

"It's not colic, is it?" Jace said.

Cat shook her head. "No. The large intestine is impacted."

Having worked around horses all their lives, Jace and Michael knew as well as Cat that an impacted intestine could prove fatal if not recognized promptly, or treated correctly.

Jace swore a blue streak and grasped the edge of the stall door so hard his knuckles turned white. "Did you catch it in time?"

"I won't lie to you, Jace," Cat said. "It's too soon

to tell. I'll know in twenty-four hours, after I administer a physic."

Cat left the stall, and told Jace to bring her a bucket of water and Michael a quarter pound of table salt. When the men returned ten minutes later, Cat mixed the salt with a pound of Epsom salts, and added them to the water. Then Jace urged Gus to his feet so Cat could give him the physic to drink.

"I don't have to tell you to give him as much water as he wants, right?" she said to Jace, who nodded. She also prescribed an enema every hour, and an abdominal rub. "I'll look in on him tomorrow."

Having done her best with the horse, Cat turned her attention to Michael, her closest friend since childhood.

Cat could easily understand why people often mistook them for brother and sister when they were together. Both were tall, with similar dark, unruly hair, fair skin, and piercing blue eyes. The closeness in their ages also made them seem like siblings. Now twenty-two, Michael had been born in 1866, just one year before Cat.

Lately, however, Cat had begun to experience disturbing feelings for Michael that were anything but sisterly.

"You might as well visit while you're here," Michael said.

Suddenly Cat remembered the letter. Her mouth went dry. Butterflies fluttered in her stomach.

Michael raised one dark inquiring brow. "Something wrong?"

"Walk outside with me."

They left Jace tending to Gus, and walked out of the barn into the bright sunshine. Cat strode over to the corral fence and leaned against it.

Her heart hammering, she reached into her back

pocket and took out the letter. She smoothed it with trembling fingers. "This came in the morning mail. It's from the Chicago College of Veterinary Medicine."

"What's it say?"

"I haven't opened it yet." Cat coughed. "I'm sure it's bad news, like all the others."

She took a deep breath, tore open the envelope, and removed the letter. The crisp white sheet crackled as she unfolded it. Her avid gaze devoured the neat, uniform words printed by one of those newfangled typewriting machines.

She only needed to read it once.

Hot, disappointed tears stung her eyes. She looked up at Michael. "Here." She thrust the letter at him. "Read it for yourself."

While Michael read, Cat balled her hands into fists and jammed them into her pockets. Frustration and anger simmered to a boil, igniting the volatile temper inherited from her Irish mother.

"I don't know why I want to go to veterinary school so badly," she said. "My father warned me that they don't accept women. But did I listen? Of course not. I kept writing letters to one school after another like a damn stubborn fool, begging them to let me in, and getting the same answer."

She wrinkled her nose and mimicked the starchy old geezer she imagined took such glee in refusing her request. "We don't admit women. It doesn't matter if you have more experience than most of the men who come here. Go back to baking pies and sweeping floors like a good little girl." She threw up her hands in disgust. "Why did I even bother?"

Michael gave her shoulder a comforting squeeze. "Because you're the kind of person who fights to make her dreams come true no matter what the odds."

He understood her so well.

She took off her hat and ran a quick hand through her mop of short black curls. "Do you think they wouldn't let me in because I'm not smart enough?"

Michael carefully refolded the letter and handed it back. "I don't think intelligence has anything to do with it, because you're as smart as a whip."

"Maybe I'm not as good a vet as I think I am."

Michael grasped Cat's shoulders, forcing her to look him straight in the eye. "Now, hold on just a minute, Catherine Wills. Don't you let some old stuffed shirt make you doubt yourself. There isn't a farmer for miles around who isn't beholden to you for saving some animal that would've died otherwise. You're a damn fine vet and you know it."

Cat sighed. "I wish I could convince these college folk."

"They won't let you in because you're a woman, and only because you're a woman."

"There's got to be *something* I can do to make them change their minds."

"Even if you went to Chicago and pounded down their doors, they *still* wouldn't let you in."

Cat kicked at the earth with the toe of her boot. "You're right, Cooper. My mother always told me that there are some things in life you can't change, so you may as well accept them and move on."

Problem was, she didn't know where to move next.

While Michael went off to do the rest of his morning chores, Cat headed for the house.

Disappointment warred with anger at the unfairness of the college's rejection. She wanted to kick something—anything—hard.

Cat had always yearned to be a veterinarian like her parents. Her mother, Maddy, had used her extensive knowledge of herbs to heal both the citizens of Little Falls and their livestock until the day Dr. Paul Wills came to town. Though he had an impressive medical degree from Harvard University, Cat's father preferred doctoring animals to people. After he and Maddy married, they both shared the veterinarian duties, and as soon as their daughter could understand and take direction, they let her help.

For Cat, like her mother, experience had taken the place of formal schooling in veterinary medicine. But unlike her mother, she was not content. She yearned to know beyond what her parents could teach her. And for that she needed veterinary school.

Unfortunately, the schools were not cooperating.

Now Cat felt as though her legs had been shot out from beneath her. She was adrift, with no light to guide her through the changes turning her life upside down.

She hoped Clementine Cooper could offer some direction. Ever since Cat's parents had left Little Falls for New York City, Cat had grown to rely on Clementine, her mother's close friend, for advice.

Cat walked up the porch steps, paused to pat the dogs, then went inside. She found Michael's mother sitting in the parlor, contentedly darning one of her husband's shirts, and looking as perfect as always.

Ever since Cat could remember, she had always stood a little in awe of Clementine Cooper's ability to look fresh and polished. Every dark hair remained in its simple chignon, even when she went out driving on a breezy day. Clementine always carried an ivory-handled sunshade to preserve her milk white complexion. Though she preferred stylish gowns with bustles from a fancy St. Louis dressmaker, even her everyday wear of a plain shirtwaist and a black skirt looked elegant on her slender form.

Clementine looked up at Cat, turned pale, and rose. "You've been to see my Gustavus? How is he?"

Cat gave her a reassuring smile. "I don't want to make any promises, but I think he's going to be fine."

Clementine closed her eyes and sighed. "Thank God. If anything happened to my baby..." She opened her eyes and studied Cat. Like Michael, his mother read people as well as Cat read animals. She sat back down on the settee and indicated that Cat should join her. "And how are *you* faring?"

"Not so good." Cat took the letter out of her pocket and handed it to Clementine. She sat down. "Another veterinary school rejected me. They were my last hope."

Clementine's brow puckered in a scowl as she read the letter. When she finished, she handed it back to Cat. "I'm so sorry, my dear. I know you had your heart set on vet school."

"I was counting on it." Cat folded the letter and stuffed it in her pocket. "But now it's not going to happen, and I don't know what to do."

"You don't really *need* schooling, do you? You're a vet already. What you don't have in book learning, you make up for in experience."

"But I know I could be an even better vet if I went to school."

"Perhaps you should join your parents back East."

After much agonizing, Cat's father had accepted a position as head of the New York Humane Society. He and Maddy had wanted their only child to come with them when they left in February, but Cat had declined, saying that she wanted to stay in Little Falls until she left for school in the fall. Though her parents had been disappointed, they agreed that at twenty-one she was old enough to live her own life.

She wrinkled her nose. "I'm just a country girl at heart. I don't think I'd be happy in the big city without some purpose, like school."

"Your mother seems to like New York, but I'm sure that's because she's with your father."

Cat snorted. "Mama would be happy living on the moon if Papa was with her."

Clementine smiled. "I feel the same way about my husband." She patted Cat's hand. "I wouldn't worry about your future. You've got the boardinghouse."

Cat had taken over running the boardinghouse her mother had inherited from Augusta Sims when the elderly lady passed on just last winter.

"And you're able to practice veterinary medicine," Clementine added.

Cat let out a glum little sigh. "Who knows for how long, now that Dr. Kendall's come to town."

Clementine raised her finely arched brows. "He'll be doctoring animals like your father?"

"That's what I understand," Cat said.

"I can't see where he'd have much call for that. You're the best vet for miles around, and everyone knows it."

"Several of the farmers have been going to him. I guess they prefer a man caring for their livestock." Cat shifted in her seat. "Maybe he'll take over all the vet work, and I'll be out of a job."

"Surely not."

But even Cat could see the uncertainty creep into Clementine's eyes as she considered that possibility. She picked up her sewing. "What about marriage, and children?"

Cat blinked. "Marriage? I can't say that I've given it much thought."

Clementine smiled, deepening the lines at the corners of her eyes. "I think you'd make some man a fine wife. You're pretty, smart, and you have a kind, generous heart. I'm betting you'd make a fine mother as well."

Cat felt the heat rise to her cheeks. "First I have to meet the right man before I start thinking about marriage and a family."

Clementine finished her stitch and snipped off the thread with her sewing scissors. "None of Little Falls's eligible bachelors strike your fancy?"

She fell silent, picturing every one of them in her mind. "Can't say that they have."

Clementine patted her hand again. "Don't worry, dear. I'm sure there's a man out there who's just perfect for you."

After leaving Clementine, Cat wandered over to the corral, where she found Michael putting a spirited blood bay stallion he was training through his paces.

Both horse and rider made a magnificent picture. Michael sat tall and straight in the saddle, his right hand resting lightly on his thigh, his left holding the reins. Beneath him, the restless stallion rolled the bit and danced in place, eager to do as he pleased. Michael reined him in swiftly, asserting his own dominance. The stallion recognized his rider's superiority and quieted down.

Michael kept the stallion standing for several minutes, then urged him into a walk with imperceptible signals. They circled the corral and stopped by Cat.

She stood on the fence and stroked Dancer's glossy arched neck. The Coopers didn't own this horse; they were training him for a wealthy railroad man from St. Louis.

"You've worked wonders with him," Cat said. "He

wouldn't sit still for anything three months ago."

The stallion snorted and pawed the earth, but didn't try to bolt or unseat his rider.

Michael beamed in approval. "We've all been working with him every day. I guess something finally sank into his thick skull."

"Can I try him?"

"He may look tame, but I think he's still got a few nasty tricks up his sleeve."

Cat glared at him. "If there's one thing I can't stand, Cooper, it's somebody telling me I can't ride."

"Now, don't go getting all prickly on me," he said. "I know better than anybody just what a good rider you are. But I also know this horse better than you. And I don't completely trust him yet."

She gave him a teasing smile. "Worried about me?"

He grinned back. "Yeah, you could say I'd feel bad if you broke your neck."

"Come on, Cooper. Just let me ride him around the corral once or twice. I'll stick to that saddle like glue no matter what he does. I promise."

"Willie—"

She leaned forward. "You're supposed to be my friend. You know I'm just as good a rider as you." When he still hesitated, she added, "Or are you afraid I'll show you up?"

His gaze turned frosty. "You don't play fair, Willie."

"No, I don't, do I. Why don't you let me ride him as a reward for treating Gus?"

Michael sighed. "Okay, I give up." He swung down from the saddle and held the stallion's head. "I can't believe I'm agreeing to this."

Cat climbed over the fence. "You know nothing will happen to me, that's why."

She extended her hand and let the stallion nuzzle

her palm, then she blew gently into his nostrils. "That's a good boy." She stroked his face and scratched his forehead, watching him close his eyes in equine delight. She murmured endearments.

When the stallion stood calm and still, Cat mounted him and settled lightly into the saddle.

Michael handed her the reins, worry creasing his brow. "Just around the corral a couple of times, that's all. And if he even feels like he's going to—"

"I know, I know."

Cat touched her heels to the stallion's sides and started walking him, his gait as smooth and flowing as running water. They hadn't gone halfway around the corral when she urged him into a trot that barely lifted her out of the saddle. He responded to heels, knees, and hands without hesitation.

Michael stood beside the fence, out of her way, his nervous, worried eyes locked on her. "That's enough, Willie. Don't push your luck with him."

She had to feel this glorious winged horse run. She just had to.

Cat leaned forward and clucked him into a canter as smooth as the slide of a rocking chair.

Without warning, the stallion shied.

Cat went flying.

She heard someone shout her name before she hit the ground and night fell.

Cat opened her eyes. Night had miraculously turned into day. Something hard surrounded and supported her, something harder pillowed her head.

Michael's shoulder. She could see the strong line of his jaw. His clean, masculine scent filled her nostrils. She was lying on the ground and Michael was holding her. And muttering what sounded like a prayer.

Then his hand brushed over a breast. Her nipple

tightened in response, jolting her into full-blown consciousness.

"What in the hell do you think you're doing?" she snapped.

"Sorry." His fingers touched her ribs, exploring gently, and stopped. "I'm checking for broken bones. If I don't find any, I'll break your damn-fool neck myself."

Cat heard the relieved expulsion of breath, and saw his throat work as he swallowed hard. He looked down at her, his cool blue eyes bright and angry. He uttered an oath, then his mouth swooped down on hers, his lips hard and smooth and punishing.

Cat's eyes flew open as a sweet, liquid warmth hit her middle like a kick to the gut, igniting her senses with a quick, fierce snap. She closed her eyes and kissed him back. God, his mouth felt good.

When they parted, she stared up at him, breathless and dazed. In all the years she'd known him, Michael had never kissed her full on the mouth like that, with such passion.

"Why'd you kiss me?"

"That was just a little hello kiss to welcome you back to the land of the living after I'd given you up for dead."

Nothing more, nothing less.

"You needn't worry." She struggled to rise. "I'm fine."

"Stay put, damn you," he growled.

Cat stayed put. "I didn't break anything, Cooper. I've been thrown before. I know how to fall."

"Quiet." His gentle, unsteady hand patted her arms, her legs, everywhere, and didn't stop until he was satisfied. "You're damn lucky, Willie."

"I just got the wind knocked out of me, that's all."

"I knew I never should've let you ride that sneaky

son of a bitch." His voice shuddered with guilt.

"Just stop it right now." She stared up at him. "I won't have you blaming yourself," she said sharply. "It wasn't your fault. I insisted."

"It was my fault for listening to you."

Her heart gave a queer little lurch at the tenderness in his voice. She reached up and touched his cheek. "How sweet. You were worried about me."

He gave a derisive snort. "For about two seconds. Can you stand up?"

"Yeah."

Michael rose first, and helped her to her feet. He gripped her arms when she swayed. "Maybe the doctor should look at you."

Cat took a deep restorative breath. "I don't need any doctor. I'm fine."

Michael released her reluctantly. Her shoulder would be stiff and hurting tomorrow, but she'd had worse falls.

She glanced at the stallion standing nonchalantly at the far end of the corral, looking quite pleased with himself.

"You know I've got to get back on him," she said to Michael.

He swore a blue streak that would've done his father proud. "The only way you're getting back on that horse is if I lead him around."

"Fair enough." Cat dusted off her britches and looked around. "Do you think anyone saw what happened?"

Michael smiled grimly. "We'll find out at dinner."

Later, when Cat and Michael went inside for the noon meal, Jace didn't blister his son's hide for letting Cat ride Dancer, so she knew he hadn't seen her thrown.

She exchanged relieved looks with Michael.

After dinner, Michael said, "Do you want to get back to town?"

Cat rose. "Sure. I seem to remember you challenging me to a race from the Beatty place to the boardinghouse gate."

"I did," he said. "Get ready to eat my dust."

"That'll be the day."

Cat thanked Clementine for dinner, said good-bye to Jace, then hurried after Michael before he rode off without her.

2

Dr. Horatio Kendall stood on his wide, shaded veranda and ran a nervous hand over his balding head. He paused to collect his thoughts before rereading the disturbing letter he had just received from his youngest son.

Drake was in trouble.

Again.

Dr. Kendall scowled and shook his head. At least Drake hadn't fallen under another woman's spell. His father remembered all too vividly the opportunistic Irish parlormaids who had attempted to trap the wealthy, unsuspecting Drake into marriage. First one had gotten herself pregnant, followed shortly by another in a different family's household. All either of them had gotten out of Dr. Horatio Kendall were too-generous cash settlements to keep their mouths shut, and their little bastards out of sight.

No. Drake's latest misfortune had something to do with the Paul Revere Bank, his place of employment.

Former place of employment. Drake had been dismissed, but his letter didn't say why.

Dr. Kendall wondered why Drake's two older brothers, who also worked at the bank in positions of some authority, hadn't prevented this catastrophe. Hadn't they remembered their father's lectures about the importance of family loyalty? Obviously not.

He also wondered why Drake was coming out to Little Falls. Surely his brothers would find him another position with some other Boston firm. They had in the past.

The doctor looked down the dusty, unpaved Main Street of the small Missouri town he had moved to just three months ago, taking over Dr. Paul Wills's practice. For a man born and raised in Boston, he felt at home here. He liked standing on his veranda and hearing nothing more than the occasional clopping of hooves and the sweet trill of birdsong at daybreak. He appreciated the sincere friendliness of its inhabitants after the hypocrisy of Boston. He'd miss seaside summers in Manchester-by-the-Sea and attending Symphony, but he was looking forward to local celebrations such as Independence Day and the autumn Harvest Festival. Though he already missed his tailor, the Dobbs's Mercantile provided all necessary, if not luxury items, of haberdashery he required. Even his visits to the women of One-Eyed Jack's had been convivial and most satisfactory, the best two dollars he had ever spent.

He frowned. He was fifty-seven and ready to appreciate the slower, simpler pleasures of small-town life. But whatever would a sophisticated young man like his son *do* here? Well, he'd learn Drake's intentions when he arrived. According to the letter, that could be any day now.

The faint rumble of hoofbeats distracted him. He

shaded his eyes and looked to the left. Two riders silhouetted against a rising dust cloud galloped recklessly toward town. They drew closer and closer, revealing two determined men leaning low over their horses' necks.

The pair raced closer and closer. Dr. Kendall pursed his lips in disapproval as he recognized the matching black Thoroughbreds charging neck and neck. He had seen them racing down Main Street many times since his arrival. The taller rider was Michael Cooper, but his trouser-clad companion was not a man at all.

The imposter was none other than Dr. Wills's tomboy daughter.

Dr. Kendall shook his head sadly. Didn't the young woman realize the untold damage she was doing to herself by repudiating her basic feminine nature? She never wore a dress. She boldly strode around town in trousers and a man's shirt, the long sleeves always rolled up to her elbows, letting the sun brown her arms like some common field hand. She doctored animals, risking a bite, a scratch, a kick in the ribs. She played cards with her boarders every evening. She even called herself Cat, as a man would nickname himself Bill or Sam.

She reminded him painfully of his headstrong former wife, Belinda, a nurse he had married because they shared a passion for medicine. Unlike Dr. Kendall's beloved first wife who had died five years ago, Belinda brazenly thumbed her nose at convention, not caring whom she offended or hurt as long as she did what she pleased. Finally, she caused a scandal and ruined both her husband's medical career and her own when she divorced him.

The riders bore down on him like a runaway train. Catherine Wills shouted something, and her horse surged ahead in a burst of speed, flattening her hat's brim against the crown and pressing her shirt against her small breasts. Dr. Kendall felt the ground shake as they sped past and waved, the rising dust stinging his eyes and making him cough.

He sighed sadly as Catherine Wills sent pedestrians scattering. Someone needed to teach the hoyden proper, ladylike behavior. Evidently everyone in Little Falls overlooked her shocking, unfeminine conduct, but Dr. Horatio Kendall knew that nothing good could come of it.

With a shake of his head, he turned and walked back inside.

Cat and Michael slowly walked their horses back to the boardinghouse to cool them down.

"So you were going to make me eat your dust," she said.

"I would have, too," Michael retorted, "if I had kept Rogue back and saved his strength for the finish, like you did with Rascal."

"Excuses, excuses."

He grinned. "There's always a next time. And next time, I'll win." His grin faded. "It feels odd to see the new doctor in my grandparents' house."

"I feel just as odd seeing him in my father's office."

"What can we expect? My grandparents moved to St. Louis, and your parents to New York City. Can't leave their house and office empty."

They stopped in front of the boardinghouse, dismounted, and tied their horses to the hitching post. Cat was just about to open the gate when a feminine voice called Michael's name. She turned to see Sally Wheeler, the schoolteacher's daughter who lived across the street, mince down her front steps, her long skirts held out of the way in her right hand.

Cat said to Michael under her breath, "I wonder

how long she's been lying in wait for you."

Michael's expression darkened like an approaching storm.

Sally sashayed across the street and headed their way. A pretty young woman with buttermilk skin and gossamer spun-gold hair that glinted in the sun, Sally wore a pink dress that flattered her shapely hourglass figure and made her look as sweet as frosting on a cake.

"Come to think of it," Cat whispered, "I've never seen that getup on her before. She must've bought it just for you."

"Just you wait, Cat Wills . . ." Michael muttered between clenched teeth.

Sally gave the horses a wary look and a wide berth. She greeted Cat politely, then turned up the warmth of her dazzling smile when she said to Michael, "Were you planning on spending the evening in town?"

"Yes, I was," he replied.

"He's eating with us," Cat piped up. "Ida May's fixing her beef stew."

A line of pique appeared between Sally's brows. "That's too bad. I—that is to say, my mother and I— were hoping you'd join us for supper." Sally took a step closer to Michael and twirled one golden ringlet around her finger. "We're having fried chicken, mashed potatoes, and biscuits."

Michael's favorite meal.

"We just had chicken for dinner at the Coopers'," Cat said. She looked over at Michael. "You wouldn't want to eat the same thing twice in one day, would you?"

"Maybe I would," Michael replied. He looked back at Sally. "Thank you kindly for asking me, but I did accept Cat's invitation to eat at the boardinghouse tonight. Perhaps another time."

Sally thrust out her plump lower lip and became the picture of feminine dejection. "I was so looking forward to your company this evening."

Cat stroked her mare's face. "Life's just chock-full of disappointments, isn't it?"

Michael cast her a warning glance, then said to Sally, "How about Sunday, after church, if your mother wouldn't mind going to the trouble?"

Sally's bright smile rivaled the sun. "I'm sure it wouldn't be any trouble at all. Not for *you*."

Michael smiled back. "I'll see you Sunday then, after church."

They said their good-byes. Sally turned and headed back to her house. Cat opened the squeaking front gate and waited for Michael. Together they walked up the brick walk.

"I know what Sally Wheeler wants for supper, and it's not fried chicken," she said in a teasing singsong voice.

"If I want to have supper with Sally Wheeler, that's my business," he snapped. "And I don't appreciate your putting words in my mouth. I can speak up for myself."

His sharp tone took Cat aback. "Sorry. Just trying to keep you from being hog-tied and branded."

He placed a hand on her shoulder. "I know. But there are just some decisions a man has to make for himself. And who to keep company with is one of them."

Cat jammed her hands into her pockets and counted bricks to hide her hurt. What had gotten into Michael? He had never been so testy with her before. And all because of that brazen little snip Sally Wheeler.

Cat knew that every eligible female in the county considered Michael a fine catch. He was kind, personable, thoughtful, and since he'd one day inherit the lucrative Cooper horse farm, he'd always provide well for his family. His dark, roguish good looks and those melting blue eyes didn't hurt, either.

Cat understood that attractiveness because she also found him irresistible. So irresistible that she suspected she was falling in love with him. Not that he had given her any cause. He never flirted with her. He never looked at her with the intense, speculative gaze he often bestowed on other women. And the only time he'd kissed her passionately was this morning, and he'd dismissed that as a casual "hello kiss."

As they climbed the porch steps, Cat decided that Michael Cooper was a lost cause. Someday he'd marry, and she'd even lose him as a friend.

The minute Cat and Michael walked into the parlor, a raucous voice screeched, "Midnight dreary . . . weak and weary . . . nevermore . . . nevermore."

Cat walked over to the sunny window, where a bright-eyed black crow cocked his head to the side as he sat on a perch in his huge cage. "Has Edgar been a good boy today?"

"Nevermore," he replied.

The loquacious Edgar Allan Crow had been left behind when his owner, an actor with a down-at-the-heels theatrical troupe passing through Little Falls on its way to fame and fortune in the gold fields of Colorado, had disappeared into the night owing Cat two weeks back rent.

The crow was not the only stray that adopted Cat. A haughty long-haired feline that Maddy Wills had named Ulysses the Second lay languidly like a fluffy feather boa along the back of the horsehair sofa, his inscrutable green eyes trained patiently on the birdcage. Somewhere in the house lurked Bounder, Cat's mongrel dog, awaiting the birth of her tenth litter of puppies.

Cat headed for the kitchen, with Michael not far behind. She found Ida May diligently stirring a pot on the stove.

Ida May Reese had lived at the boardinghouse ever since Cat could remember. A wiry, nervous woman in her midfifties, Ida May had moved to Little Falls after she lost her family in the Civil War, and supported herself by sewing. Now she cooked and cleaned in exchange for room and board.

"Something smells mighty good," Cat said, carefully sniffing the fragrant steam rising from the stew pot.

Michael kissed Ida May on the cheek. "How's my favorite cook?"

She beamed indulgently at him. No woman could resist Michael. "Don't let Belle hear you say that."

Cat reached into her back pocket, took out her wrinkled letter, and set it on the table for Ida May to read. "Another vet school turned me down."

"I know it's disappointing," Ida May said, "but your father did warn you."

Cat looked around the kitchen. "Have you seen Bounder? She should be having her pups any minute now."

Ida May put the lid back on the stew pot and set down her wooden stirring spoon. "I haven't seen that rascally mutt since dinner." She shook her head. "You should've gotten a male dog like Zeke." She sighed. "Now *there* was a dog."

Zeke had been Cat's mother's beloved coonhound, now buried beside the shaded sycamore where he used to tree his feline nemesis, the first Ulysses. To Ida May, everything in the past had been so much better than the present, as she often reminded anyone who'd listen.

Ida May wiped her hands on her apron. "Then you wouldn't be riding around half the county, trying to find homes for all her puppies every spring and fall."

Cat slipped her arm around the older woman's waist for a quick hug. "Oh, don't be such a cross-patch, Ida May," she teased. "I know you'd miss that dog more than anybody if something happened to her."

Ida May's pursed lips twitched into a smile. "Maybe I would."

"Let's see if we can find her," Michael said. "Maybe she's in the shed."

They walked outside together, through Maddy Wills's overgrown herb garden, and out to the squat wooden shed where one of Cat's boarders now used the dark building to develop his photographs.

Cat knocked on the door. "Denny, are you in there?" When no one answered, she opened it a crack and peered inside. She listened. A faint whimpering made her grin, and she turned to Michael. "Bounder's had her pups."

He smiled back and followed her inside.

Cat paused, letting her eyes become accustomed to the shed's dimness and her nose to the sharp odor of photographic chemicals. The table in the center, where her mother had once prepared her herbal rem-edies and now Denny developed his photographs, gradually took shape. Seconds later, Cat could discern the bottles lining the shelf on one wall. She looked around. There, in a quiet, shadowed corner, lay Bounder on an old scrap of blanket she had dragged across the floor to make a comfortable nest for herself and her newborn pups.

"Bounder," Cat said softly, crossing the room. "You're a mama again."

Bounder, a brown-and-white short-haired mongrel with upturned ears that flopped over comically at the ends, lifted her head, whined in greeting, and wagged her long, skinny tail.

Cat knelt and gently lifted one of the pups that had been forced out of the chow line by his more aggressive littermates, and stroked his head with her forefinger. "Look at this little feller. He's no bigger than a rat and his eyes are closed, but he's still as cute as a button." She put him back when Bounder gave a worried whimper.

"How big's the litter this time?" Michael asked, peering over Cat's shoulder as she gave her dog a reassuring pat.

Cat quickly counted the nursing pups. "Only eight." Last fall, there had been twelve, though one had died. She looked up at Michael. "Who do you think fathered them?"

Michael hunkered down beside her and absently stroked Bounder under the chin. "Judging from their black markings, I'd say it's got to be Heck's dog."

Heck Hechinger owned the livery stable.

Cat nodded. "Just like the last time. And the time before that."

"I guess that makes Bounder and old Buck mates for life," Michael said.

Mates for life. Cat suddenly became aware of Michael crouched so near that his soft shirtsleeve brushed her bare arm, making her shiver.

"Like husband and wife," she said, breathing deeply. He smelled of freshly laundered, sun-dried clothes, leather, and his own clean, spicy masculine scent underscored by the faint tang of sweat. Intoxicating.

"Something like that."

Cat looked over at him. In the shed's weak light, Michael's pale blue eyes looked dark and mysterious framed by thick black lashes a woman would envy. His sensuous, chiseled lips were slightly parted, and Cat wondered what he'd do if she leaned over and kissed him full on the mouth rather than on the cheek as she usually did. She felt a queer clench deep inside, and she quickly looked away as heat flooded her cheeks.

She couldn't resist asking, "You ever think about getting hitched?"

"Sometimes. You ever think about it?"

"Sure." It was now or never. She took a deep breath and blurted out, "Lately, I've been thinking of marrying _you_."

Michael burst out laughing. "You're joking, right?"

"No, I'm not joking. I think I'm falling in love with you."

His laughter died. He walked over to her and placed his hands on her shoulders. "Cat, you only _think_ you love me because I'm the only man you've ever been close to. You're mistaking friendship for love. They're quite different, believe me."

She stared at his lips and remembered their weight and texture against her own, the way they expertly stirred her body. "But you kissed me after I was thrown."

"I kissed you because I was relieved you weren't hurt," he said gently. "I kissed you in the heat of the moment, not because I desired you as a woman."

Cat blinked hard and tried to salvage her battered pride with a smile. "You're right, Cooper. I was only joking. Like you said, it was a 'hello kiss.' "

"A casual kiss between friends. So, if you could

have your pick of any man in the county, who would you marry?"

Cat lifted one shoulder. "Haven't really thought about it."

Michael's eyes twinkled. "Of course you have. All women think about it."

"How do you know?"

"I've been around. I hear them talking among themselves when they don't think any men are listening."

Cat took a deep breath and blurted out, "You ever lain with a woman?"

She suspected he had. According to rumor, Michael had inherited his father's way with the ladies.

Michael's expression grew shuttered and disapproving. "I know we're close friends, Willie, but there are just some things a man doesn't talk about. What I do with women is none of your business."

"I'll bet it first happened when you turned eighteen." Cat rose so she could lean her backside against the narrow windowsill. "You and your parents went to St. Louis to visit your grandparents, and when you came home, you were different."

Curiosity flickered in the depths of his eyes. "How?"

"Just changed, that's all. I could tell. You started looking at women differently, like you knew some deep, dark secret about them that no one else did. You started flirting with them, too." Except her. He never flirted with her.

"I was growing up, Willie. Changing from a boy to a man. That's all you saw."

She folded her arms. "I'll bet Jace took you to a St. Louis whorehouse."

Michael turned a guilty shade of pink and Cat grinned.

"Well, I'll be . . . does your mother know?"

"It's not exactly something a man shares with his mother." He glared at her. "Or a woman he thinks of as a sister."

Stung, she stepped away from the window and made a production of looking around for a box or a basket. "I'd better bring the pups inside, where they'll be safe."

"Why don't you wait a couple of hours?" Michael suggested. "Let Bounder get used to having people around them first."

"You're right." She leaned over and looked at the puppies again. "Which one do you want?"

"Oh, no, you don't, Catherine Wills. We have two, and two's plenty. You'll have to find homes for them somewhere else."

She looked over at him and grinned. "I think the new doctor needs a dog, don't you?"

3

A LIGHT GRAY HAZE OF ACRID CIGARETTE AND CIGAR smoke floated near the ceiling at One-Eyed Jack's. The buoyant tinkle of piano music grew faster and louder, vying with the low rumble of conversation for dominance. A few men stood drinking at the bar and laughing too loudly with three of Jack's girls. Others played cards at the round tables scattered throughout the room. Michael sat alone.

After supper at the boardinghouse, he had played three hands of toothpick poker with Cat and Denny, the photographer, until nine o'clock. Cat and Denny didn't want to play a fourth hand, so they both retired for the night. Michael, still feeling restless and edgy, decided to visit Jack's.

He sipped his cold beer. His conversation with Cat in the shed kept replaying in his mind. Her pointed questions about women had made him uncomfortable, and he didn't know why. Usually he would deflect her curious comments with some teasing remark that always left Cat grinning.

She had never before told him that she suspected he'd visited a St. Louis whorehouse.

Jace, after catching Michael stealing a kiss from a neighboring farmer's daughter during one Harvest Festival, had administered a stern lecture about a young man's wild oats and how their indiscriminate sowing with respectable young women often led to a reluctant trip down the church aisle at the business end of a shotgun. The following week on a trip to St. Louis, Jace had dropped off his son at a whorehouse.

Michael had never felt so awkward and embarrassed. His pretty young instructress had been flattering, patient, and very thorough. He discovered he enjoyed the whispers, the touching, the dizzying heat.

He'd had his share of women since. Mostly sporting gals. And a neighbor's needful, obliging young widow, until she married again and moved away.

"What's a handsome young fella like you sitting here all by himself?"

He rose. "Evening, Ruby."

Ruby Desire, Jack's "hostess," was not the prettiest woman in the saloon. Her drab, mouse brown hair lacked an appealing shine, and one front tooth bore a slight chip where a drunken, half-crazed patron had once backhanded her and sent her crashing into a table. But her enticing body compensated with an ample bosom forever threatening to spill out of the artfully low-cut satin bodice of her short burgundy silk dress. Her generous, gently flaring hips always caught a man's gaze as they wiggled suggestively with every step.

Michael had patronized her frequently when she first arrived in town, but his interest in paid-for pleasure always waned. Ruby accepted the fact that their time together was strictly business, and didn't take offense when he stopped accompanying her upstairs.

If she ever harbored thoughts of anything permanent between them, she never shared them with Michael.

Now he enjoyed nothing more than her conversation. She knew people inside and out, and had an appealing dry sense of humor.

He pulled out a chair. "Care to join me?"

"Always a pleasure." She gathered her skirts with a practiced hand and sat down, the silk whispering promises.

Michael signaled for Jack to bring Ruby her favorite drink, a tall, watered-down whiskey, for it was only ten o'clock, and she had business to conduct.

She no longer tried to lure him upstairs as she did the other men. She didn't lean forward and take a deep breath to render him incapable of reason, or coyly walk her fingers up his arm, or nudge his foot under the table. Instead, she rested her pointed chin in the palm of her hand and studied Michael out of world-weary brown eyes.

"You look like a man who has woman trouble," she said.

Michael smiled wanly. "Is it that obvious?"

"No. I just know what to look for." Jack set Ruby's whiskey down in front of her, pocketed Michael's money, and went back to the bar. Ruby sipped her drink. "Is that schoolteacher's daughter making a pest of herself?"

"Sally? She invites me to dinner now and then, but I wouldn't say she makes a pest of herself."

"Neither do ants at a picnic." Ruby shook her head. "You'd better watch yourself with Miss Sally Wheeler. She may look all sweet as sugar, but inside, she's about as harmless as a bullet to the brain. You start accepting too many dinner invitations, and people will say you're courting her. She'll make a few assumptions of her own."

"Sally can have her pick of men."

"But she wants you."

"I doubt that."

Ruby rolled her eyes. "Lord, give me strength. . . . Half the women in this town are after you, and the other half are either married or too old to care."

Michael scowled. "I'm getting sick and tired of hearing what a great catch I am."

"Handsome as the devil and kind to boot, the hard-working heir to a successful horse farm . . . yes, I can see why no women would want a worthless no-account like you."

"Cat doesn't."

Ruby's eyes widened. "That beanpole in britches?"

Michael's face grew warm. "She's not a beanpole."

"And I suppose you've seen her without her clothes."

Only once, when they were children. Michael was pretending to be Dr. Wills and Cat his patient. Then her mother walked in on them.

"Ruby—"

"Don't get sore. I know when to quit." She studied him carefully. "So that's the way the wind blows. You want to marry Cat, but the little fool doesn't want to marry you."

"She's not a fool."

Ruby shook her head. "Oh, dearie me, I knew it. You're a goner. Might as well marry her and put the rest of the women in this town out of their misery."

"I never said I want to marry Cat."

Ruby placed a hand over his. "You can try to kid yourself, but don't try to kid old Ruby. If you want her, what's stopping you from going after her?"

He leaned back in his chair and shook his head. "That's some imagination you have. Cat and I grew up together. We're close friends, that's all."

"All the more reason to want her," Ruby said. "Friends often make the best lovers. A man knows what he's getting."

Michael sipped his beer. "I don't want to marry Cat."

"You keep saying that. You trying to convince me, or yourself?"

"I wouldn't have to keep saying it if people would take me at my word."

"You two are so close it's like you're glued together. Racing your horses. Staying overnight at the boardinghouse. Everyone's bound to think something more's going on."

He had to admit that lately, he couldn't stop thinking about Cat. He'd be grooming the horses and listening for Rascal's hoofbeats. If Cat didn't come out to the farm that day, he'd wonder what had kept her, and wind up making a special trip in to town just to see her.

He also noticed things about her that he hadn't paid much mind to before, like the clean, blue-black sheen of her hair when the sun hit her curls just right, and the way she sucked on her lower lip when she was deep in thought. And he loved listening to Cat's rich, robust laugh that bubbled up from deep inside her like spring water. But that didn't mean he was sweet on her. He was around her so much, he was bound to notice such things eventually.

"Ever think about why you spend so much time together?" Ruby asked.

"I enjoy her company. She's smart, and she makes me laugh. Half the time, she knows what I'm thinking before I do." He placed his elbows on the table and leaned forward. "And she's the only person who doesn't keep reminding me what a great catch I am."

Ruby looked deep into his eyes as if she were a

fortune-teller peering into her crystal ball. "You do want Cat, but you're afraid she doesn't want you."

Michael drained his beer glass in one deep swallow. "That's bull, pure and simple."

"Cooper, my boy, how long have we known each other?"

"Three years. Ever since you came to Jack's."

"We're friends, right?"

He nodded.

"I'm only riding you so hard because I don't want to see you make a mistake and pay for it the rest of your life.

"I know." But even as he reached out and squeezed Ruby's hand, he knew that a confidence shared with her would be a betrayal of Cat.

Ruby glanced over at the bar. "I see a look of disapproval in Jack's eye, so if you'll excuse me, the night is still young, and I've got to earn my keep." Just as she was about to rise, Michael stood and held her chair for her. She smiled flirtatiously. "Unless, of course, you'd like to come upstairs with me. On the house, for old time's sake."

They both knew he wouldn't, but she always hoped and offered.

As always, Michael smiled, and whispered, "Thank you for the generous offer, but some other time."

She paused, growing serious once again. "Remember what I said. Close friends often make the best lovers. But don't wait too long to tell her your feelings, otherwise she may find someone else."

He took her hand and kissed it. She glided over to the bar where several men stood drinking alone, and joined a handsome dark-haired one. She placed a hand on his arm, looked up at him as though he were the only man in the room, and whispered in his ear. He looked her up and down, grinned, and nodded.

Michael watched as Ruby and her eager customer headed upstairs.

He finished his beer and left.

Cat lay in the velvety darkness of her first-floor bedroom, her door left ajar so she could hear Michael coming in.

She hated it when he went to One-Eyed Jack's. Though she never frequented the saloon, she knew what went on upstairs between Jack's girls and his customers, the same things that must have happened in the St. Louis whorehouse. Curiosity and jealousy consumed her like fire whenever she wondered if Michael availed himself of their hospitality.

She knew all the girls by their exotic names— Azalea, Cleopatra, and Ruby—for each of them had gone to Cat's father for doctoring at one time or another. Cat had always found them to be personable. That was before she started wondering if Michael ever accompanied one of them upstairs.

Cat had tried, in the shed this afternoon, to get him to admit that he had been with one of the saloon girls, but he hadn't said yes, and he hadn't said no. When Michael wanted to keep something from her, he could be as tight as a clam.

Cat sat up, molded her pillow into a more comfortable shape, then turned on her side. Where was he? It had to be past midnight.

The front door opened. Cat held her breath and listened. The door closed. Familiar footsteps crossed the parlor and paused in the hallway. Then Cat heard Michael slowly climb the stairs to the spare bedroom.

When his footsteps died away, she breathed a sigh of relief. He wouldn't be spending the night at Jack's. To her knowledge, he never had. But he was a young, red-blooded man with needs.

"What's wrong with me?" Cat lay back and stared at the ceiling. "Why do I care where Michael Cooper spends the night?"

But she did care. Lately, the thought of Michael with some other woman made her steam with jealousy. Drove her crazy. She wished her mother was still here so they could sit down together over a cup of coffee and have a long talk about men. Maddy would tell her what to do. Writing her mother a letter just wasn't the same as a face-to-face talk.

Why was she wasting her time? Michael had told her over and over again that he couldn't think of her as more than a friend.

This unrequited love business sure was hard on a woman.

She closed her eyes and finally fell asleep.

The following morning, Cat awoke to the mouth-watering aroma of flapjacks cooking on the griddle. She washed and dressed quickly in clean trousers and shirt, then headed for the kitchen.

"Morning, Ida May." She paused to pat Bounder lying on a blanket and nursing her hungry pups in a warm, cozy corner of the kitchen. "Where is everybody?"

Ida May, standing at the hot stove, expertly turned a flapjack while Ulysses sat nearby, flicking his tail and licking his chops. "It's past eight o'clock, lazy-bones. The men have all come and gone. I'm surprised you didn't hear them tromping through the house. Denny went to photograph the new Evans baby."

Cat looked around expectantly. "And Michael?"

Ida May stacked several steaming flapjacks on a plate and handed it to Cat. "He said he had to get back to the farm. He fed Rascal for you before he left."

Cat took her plate to the table and sat down, trying

to hide her disappointment. "He could've woken me up."

Ida May poured herself a cup of coffee and sat down across from Cat. "He said he looked in on you and saw that you were dead to the world, so he figured you needed the sleep."

Cat broke off a piece of flapjack and fed it to the waiting Ulysses, who had switched his allegiance in the hopes of receiving a tantalizing tidbit. "Considerate of him."

Either that, or he was trying to avoid her. No, that couldn't be the reason. They were friends. Friends enjoyed each other's company. They didn't try to avoid each other.

Ida May added sugar and milk to her coffee. "How are you and the new doctor getting along?"

"I don't see him that often, but I'd say just fine," Cat said.

Ida May's faded eyes took on the faraway look that warned those around her that she was about to pay a lengthy visit to the past. "I remember when your father came to Little Falls. He was the town's first real doctor."

Of course Cat knew the story of her parents' meeting by heart, but she patiently held her tongue and let Ida May retell it as if for the first time.

"Sparks flew between those two from the moment they met," Ida May said, smiling. "Your mother had been doctoring the good citizens of Little Falls and their livestock with her herbal remedies long before your father came along. She had no objection to his doctoring people, but she drew the line at his taking over her veterinary duties." Ida May rolled her eyes. "Oh, the rows those two would have!"

"Dr. Kendall is old enough to be my father," Cat said between forkfuls of flapjacks washed down with coffee, "so I don't think any romantic sparks are going to be flying between us. And as far as him taking over my veterinary duties, I don't see that happening yet."

Ida May sipped her coffee. "Did you know that Dr. Kendall's youngest son is coming here to live with him?"

Cat raised her brows. "Do tell. Where'd you hear that?"

"Dr. Kendall told the Reverend Dawlish, who told his mother, and Francie gave me the news just last night."

Cat should have guessed. Francine Dawlish and Ida May were both members of the quilting circle, a group of ladies who met weekly to sew quilts to raise funds for various church and civic projects. They knew everything going on in Little Falls before anyone else.

Cat finished her flapjacks. "I wonder why he didn't come out here with his father, if he's intending to stay?"

"Maybe he just got tired of big-city life."

Cat rose and took her plate over to the sink. "Guess we'll learn his reasons when he gets here."

Ida May looked wistful. "His name's Drake, and he's only twenty-eight. It'll be nice for the single girls to have another eligible bachelor in town."

So they can all leave Michael alone, Cat thought.

She washed her plate and dried her hands on a towel. "I'll be over at the livery stable, checking on Heck's bay to see if she's still lame."

Ida May rose. "And I'll be cleaning up."

"Thanks. See you at suppertime," Cat said, and strode out of the kitchen.

As she passed the dining room door, she glanced inside and noticed several of Denny's photographs scattered across the table. She stopped and went to look at the collection of sepia-toned prints freshly mounted on pasteboard.

She smiled in childlike delight at the one of her and Rascal. Cat was surprised the image looked so sharp and clear. She could have sworn that her restless mare had nodded her head just at the crucial moment Denny's flash light had gone off. But she hadn't, and there stood Rascal and her proud mistress, frozen forever in time.

She liked the one of Heck Hechinger standing straight and tall and proud at his anvil, his hammer in one hand, tongs and horseshoe in the other. And another of the quilting-circle ladies seated as stiff as a collection of tombstones around their latest creation. When Cat came to a small one of the two-month-old Shaughnessy baby lying in his tiny coffin, she sighed and sadly shook her head. Then she thumbed through the rest.

Her eyes widened when she came to the last and largest photograph. There stood Jack behind his bar with a polishing cloth in hand, his black eye patch turned toward the camera, giving him a sinister air that belied his gentle nature. Leaning up against the bar was none other than Miss Ruby Delight.

So Denny was expanding his subject matter beyond babies and respectable family folk to include photographs of saloon girls. He certainly had captured Miss Ruby's personality as she brazenly lounged against the bar, displaying her outthrust bosom and long legs beneath that short flounced skirt as if they were goods for sale in Dobbs's Mercantile. Her frank gaze held both a challenge and a promise.

Is this what drew Michael to One-Eyed Jack's?

Cat sighed. She looked down her shirtfront. She had no bosom to speak of. Her legs were lean and shapely from riding, but nobody ever saw them, so what good were they? Her straightforward gaze usually revealed exactly what was on her mind, never holding a challenge or a promise. If that's what it took to interest a man, Michael would never stop seeing her as a friend and start looking at her as a woman.

She placed the photograph at the bottom of the pile, where Ida May wouldn't see it, then she went off to examine Heck's bay.

The morning stage rolled past the livery stable in a thunder of hoofbeats and a cloud of dust just as Cat finished examining the rest of Heck's horses.

Cat squinted and waved her hand in front of her nose to dispel the dust that stung her eyes and tickled her nose with the threat of a sneeze. She walked down Main Street on her way back to the boardinghouse.

She should have known that Teddy Granger and Buster Blick were up to no good. She glanced across the street and noticed the little hooligans in a huddle at the alley entrance between the laundry and the mercantile, where the youngest Dobbs boy stood listlessly sweeping the boardwalk in front of his father's store and dreaming of freedom.

A few seconds later, Teddy and Buster separated. Cat stopped and watched them.

When Teddy sauntered past the laundry, he suddenly turned, drew back his arm, and threw something. The Dobbs boy yelped in pain and whirled around, his homely face contorted in outrage and promising swift retribution. Teddy stuck his thumbs in his ears, wiggled his fingers and made a rude face. The Dobbs boy swore and ran after him with his broom upraised, leaving the mercantile unattended just as the boys hoped.

Buster gave a furtive glance up and down the street

before dashing into the store. He reappeared a minute later, his pockets bulging.

"Hey, Buster!" Cat cried, running across the street. "Stop right there."

Buster gave a guilty start and tore off with Cat in hot pursuit.

Instead of dashing down an alley, Buster ran toward the stagecoach, which had pulled up in front of the post office so the driver could deliver the mail pouch and discharge his passengers.

"Help!" Buster screamed, glancing back at Cat as he ran. "Help me! Please!"

Nice try, Buster, Cat thought as she lengthened her stride, *but it's not going to work.*

Along the boardwalk, the commotion caused people to stop and stare. Several stagecoach passengers turned and watched as Buster ran toward them.

"Help!" he hollered. "She's gonna kill me!"

Cat was just about to get her hands on the little thief when one of the stagecoach passengers, the tallest man Cat had ever seen, suddenly stepped in front of her and blocked her way like a stone wall.

"Hold it right there."

"Get out of my way!" Cat snapped, and swerved to go around him.

He grabbed her arm, stopping Cat in her tracks.

She whirled around, spitting mad at the stranger's gall, and struggled to break free of his iron grip. "Let go of me, you fool, before he gets away!"

"Go pick on somebody your own size," the man said, grabbing Cat's other arm as well to restrain her. "He's only a boy."

Cat glared up at his handsome, determined face. How dare he manhandle her. "That *boy* just robbed the mercantile."

When her struggles were to no avail, Cat drew back

her foot and kicked him with all her might.

The man swore and doubled over, one hand clutching at his bruised shin, but the other still stubbornly holding on to Cat.

"Let me go!" she snarled, and tried to kick him in the other shin.

He was too quick for her. One arm snaked around her waist, and before Cat could draw another breath, he lifted her off her feet and effortlessly tucked her underneath his arm.

"Put me down!" she screamed.

4

"I'LL PUT YOU DOWN IF YOU PROMISE NOT TO KICK ME again," replied the exasperating masculine voice.

His arm surrounded and squeezed Cat's middle like a barrel hoop and she gasped for breath. "I promise not to kick you again." She didn't, however, promise not to scratch his eyes out.

The oaf set her down with surprising gentleness, then released her.

The minute Cat felt solid ground beneath her feet, her Irish temper ignited like a match to tinder and sizzled along her skin, heating her rage to boiling.

"Who in the devil's name do you think you are?" She planted her hands on her hips and tilted her head back to look up at him, for the stranger was even taller than Michael. A good half foot over six feet by the looks of it. Her furious gaze raked him up and down. She itched to kick him again.

"Listen here, city slicker. That 'boy' you let get away is the town troublemaker. In fact, he and his accomplice just robbed a store. I would've caught him if you hadn't stopped me."

The giant casually folded his arms across his broad chest, his brown eyes glinting with that infuriating amusement as they roved over Cat from head to toe. Then he grinned. "I'll be damned. You're a woman."

"Any fool can see that," she snapped, suddenly caught off guard by the warmth in his voice and the intensity of his stare.

His full lips twitched in an effort to damp down a smile. "Oh, I think I can be forgiven for assuming that someone who's dressed like a man is actually a man."

"That didn't give you the right to hoist me up like a sack of oats."

His handsome countenance turned contrite. "No, it didn't, and for that I apologize." He took off his hat, revealing thick blond hair the color of a sun-streaked wheat field just before harvest. "But what else was I supposed to think, Miss—?

"Wills. Catherine Wills."

Recognition lit his face. "Are you any relation to Dr. Paul Wills?"

"He's my father."

"Well, I'll be . . . then you must be the granddaughter of Dr. Barnabas Wills."

Cat regarded him suspiciously. "Where'd you hear about my grandpapa?"

Those brown eyes danced with amusement. "He's been a good friend of my father's as long as I can remember. I'm Drake Kendall."

So this was Dr. Horatio Kendall's youngest son. Sun-god handsome. Well dressed. Charming.

He put his hat back on. "Do you know my father?"

"Little Falls is a small town. Everybody here knows everybody else."

"I'm sorry I manhandled you, Miss Wills, but try

to see the situation from my point of view. A child comes running down the street, chased by a man—or someone I assumed to be a man. Naturally I thought the boy was in danger."

What he said made sense. Cat felt her anger cool and subside. "I suppose anybody not from these parts would've jumped to the same conclusion."

His eyes twinkled and he extended his hand. "No hard feelings?"

The minute Cat grasped his long, cool fingers, she felt a queer little jolt skitter up her arm. "No hard feelings, Mr. Kendall."

Without warning, he drew her hand to his lips and kissed it, his gaze boldly holding hers. "Please. Call me Drake."

The warmth of his lips as they brushed the back of her hand made Cat feel funny inside. A hot blush flooded her cheeks. She pulled away as if burnt. "I don't know you well enough to call you that."

"I'm sure you will," he replied with another smile.

The stagecoach driver swaggered out of the post office and bellowed that the stage would be pulling out in ten minutes. He proceeded to unload Drake Kendall's two huge bags from the baggage compartment and lug them onto the boardwalk. The onlookers dispersed and went about their business, now that the confrontation between Cat and the giant had ended peacefully.

Kendall looked at her. "Can you tell me where my father lives?"

"The old Boswell house, that big white one down the street, with all the shade trees. Or he could be in his office." She pointed in the opposite direction, to the building where her own father had practiced medicine for over twenty years.

Drake Kendall smiled and tipped his hat. "Thanks,

Catherine Wills. I'm sure we'll be seeing more of each other."

Why did it sound like a promise?

"Maybe," Cat said.

She wished him good day and went off to report Buster and Teddy to the sheriff, unaware that Drake Kendall never took his eyes off her.

Drake watched the tall, lanky hellion stride off, his attention captured by a shapely backside that even her loose-fitting trousers couldn't conceal. He had seen his share of women's backsides, but never one displayed so publicly in britches. He wondered why Catherine Wills's family allowed her to parade around in such provocative attire.

Too bad. Beneath that mannish outfit dwelled a budding beauty. The deep, soft blue of her eyes and her full, rosy lips taunted him as much as her delicious backside.

The stagecoach rolled off to its next destination. Drake looked up and down the straight, unpaved street. He scanned the storefronts on both sides. A bank, a post office, a sheriff's office. Dobbs's Mercantile and One-Eyed Jack's. His father's office and Hechinger's Livery. Some nondescript buildings badly in need of painting squeezed in between.

He curled his lip in disgust and contempt. Was this all there was?

He should have stayed in Boston and taken his chances.

He looked for someone to carry his luggage. When no porter stepped forward, Drake effortlessly picked up the heavy bags and started walking.

A minute later, he came to the—what had Catherine Wills called it?—the old Boswell house. The sprawling wood-frame structure painted a clean bright white and surrounded by several trees outshone the others on the street, certainly befitting Dr. Horatio Kendall's status as a wealthy Easterner. Drake carried his bags into the cool shade of the long, wide veranda and set them down. He rang the doorbell and waited.

Seconds later, the door opened. A woman wearing a white apron stared up at him. "Yes?"

Drake smiled and tipped his hat. "I'm Drake, Dr. Kendall's son. He's expecting me."

She smiled back, and opened the door. "I'll tell the doctor you're here."

Drake entered and set his bags down while the housekeeper disappeared down the hall. He glanced to his right, into the parlor. Not as elegant as the Beacon Hill house, but comfortable. Living here would be tolerable. But first he had to convince his father to let him stay.

Drake heard light, quick footsteps coming down the hall. He turned and studied his approaching father.

For a man who had spent the last two years enduring crushing professional and personal blows, his father looked remarkably well. Oh, bitterness and disillusionment still hardened Horatio Kendall's aquiline features, but his color was better, and his intelligent brown eyes now glimmered with enthusiasm.

"Hello, Father." Not sure of his welcome, he didn't step forward or extend his hand.

"Son." His father extended his hand. "How was the trip out here?"

Relief flooded through Drake. He shouldn't have worried. His father had never let him down before, and he wouldn't now. He understood. Always.

"The train ride was endless," Drake said, "but heaven compared with that rickety stagecoach. I thought the train ran through Little Falls."

His father shook his head. "The railroad bypassed Little Falls years ago."

More than the railroad had bypassed this hole in the wall.

"Take your bags upstairs to the second room on the right," his father said. "When you've unpacked, come downstairs and we'll have dinner."

"Dinner? Don't you mean luncheon?"

"We call it dinner out here."

He didn't have to add that after this *dinner*, they'd talk about Drake's reason for coming to Missouri. He could still read his father like a book.

He was about to suggest that the housekeeper take his bags and unpack for him, then thought better of it. Too soon to make demands. Drake hoisted his own bags and headed for the stairs. He couldn't wait to tell his side of the story.

Later, his father escorted him into the dining room and asked, "Is your room satisfactory?"

"It's very comfortable."

His father seated himself at the head of the table. "I thought you'd like it."

Actually, he didn't. The bed was so short, he'd be sleeping with his feet dangling over the edge of the mattress. Was it too much to ask that his father remember his youngest son's great height, and find him a suitable bed?

The housekeeper served the soup.

"You're looking well, Father," Drake said. He tasted the soup. Not the cuisine he was used to, but palatable. "Life out here seems to agree with you."

"Picking up stakes and moving west was one of the smartest things I've ever done." Horatio sipped his soup. "If Barnabas Wills hadn't told me his son was giving up his practice and moving to New York, I'd still be back in Boston, licking my wounds."

A day didn't pass that Drake didn't curse the elder Dr. Wills for putting that particular flea in Horatio Kendall's ear. His father decided that a one-man practice in a small Missouri town was just what he needed to put the painful past behind him.

A part of Drake couldn't blame him. Horatio Kendall's very public divorce from his much-younger second wife had rocked Boston society and shattered his family. The whispers and the surreptitious glances were bad enough, but to have the ensuing scandal ruin a long and distinguished medical career . . .

"When the board at St. Luke's passed me over and appointed Mason head of surgery," his father said, "I thought my life was over. But here, I've discovered it's just beginning."

"They wouldn't have passed you over if Belinda hadn't divorced you," Drake muttered. Selfish bitch. "Mustn't let any scandal taint the sacred St. Luke's."

"I never should've married her," Horatio said. "You and your brothers were right. You warned me she was too young. You said she was nothing like your mother." He sighed. "But I thought that since she was a nurse, she'd understand what my medical career meant to me. I should've realized that her own ambition would take precedence over mine."

"Would it have killed her to wait until after you were selected head of surgery before she divorced you?" Drake said. "We all begged her to wait, but she wouldn't. She thought only of herself." And the lover her own age that she couldn't wait to marry.

"It's finished," his father said curtly, the old pain flaring in his eyes. "I don't wish to hear Belinda's name mentioned ever again."

The housekeeper returned to remove the soup bowls and to set a platter of fried chicken in front of Horatio.

Drake prudently changed the subject. "Did I mention that I've already met Dr. Wills's daughter?" Her guileless blue eyes and trim backside still tantalized him.

His father beamed, the pain in his eyes replaced by delight. "A charming young lady. It's so unfortunate that she chooses to traipse about the countryside dressed like a man."

Drake helped himself to a drumstick. "Surely she doesn't wear that appalling clothing all the time."

"In the three months that I've lived here, I've never seen her wear anything else," his father said.

Drake's brows rose in surprise. "She never wears dresses? Not even in church on Sunday?"

"Never. She stands in the back. And that's not all she does."

While Drake ate, his father indulgently enumerated Miss Wills's shocking transgressions. She rode astride like a man, racing her horse up and down Main Street. She played cards every night in the boardinghouse she owned. She was the town veterinarian, and spent most of her time doctoring animals.

"In spite of her tomboyish behavior, I must confess that I do like her," Horatio said.

Drake gnawed his drumstick down to the bone. "Doesn't anybody in town object to her disgraceful behavior?"

"Not that I can see. They're all used to her, especially since she's a damn good vet. The farmers and ranchers around here will overlook anything to keep their livestock healthy."

"Now that you're here, I'm sure that'll change."

"What do you mean?"

"Didn't you agree to take over Dr. Wills's veterinary duties when you took over his practice?"

His father shifted in his seat. "If I hadn't agreed to

it, Wills wouldn't have sold me his practice."

Drake recalled the time his brother Ethan's dog had become ill, and their father brought the animal to a vet for treatment. Drake had asked his father since *he* was a doctor, why did they have to bring the dog to someone else? Because animals had their own doctors, his father replied.

"Have you treated any animals yet?" Drake asked.

"A few, and they all got better," he said defensively. "Even though treating animals is beneath a physician of my considerable skills, it's not as hard as I thought it would be." He shrugged. "I'll do what must be done, and excell at it."

Drake privately felt that his father had bitten off more than he could chew, as he had with Belinda, but he held his tongue.

Just as the housekeeper came to clear away the plates, the doorbell rang. She went to answer it. When she returned, she told Dr. Kendall that a medical emergency awaited him in his office.

Horatio rose and flung down his napkin. "We'll talk about the Paul Revere Bank when I get back."

Drake froze. His father knew! Damn that Ethan for squealing on him.

Dr. Kendall flew out of the room to tend to his patient, leaving his son to anticipate the worst.

Drake didn't have long to wait. His father walked through the door twenty minutes later, summoned Drake to his study and closed the door. Drake knew he was in trouble when Horatio seated himself behind his desk, and said, "Sit down."

The doctor leaned back in his swivel chair and passed a hand over his balding head, a bad sign. His brown eyes darkened to onyx. "I understand you're in trouble again."

Drake leaned back in his own chair. "I'm sure

Ethan told you his version of what happened." His oldest brother always had resented him as their mother's favorite.

"A letter from him arrived the very day I received your telegram from St. Louis. He said he wrestled with his conscience for weeks before writing it, but—"

Drake snorted in derision.

"—he felt that I must be told." His father regarded him sternly. "Drake, Ethan says you embezzled money from the Paul Revere Bank. Is this true?"

Drake leaned forward. "I needed the money to pay off some gambling debts. You were on your way out here, so I couldn't ask you to help me out. Ethan and Win refused to lend me any more money, so they left me no other choice." Drake rose and paced the study. "What else could I do, Father? The men I owed money to were hounding me, even threatening to kill me." He had a flash of inspiration. "They even swore they'd harm Ethan's family if I didn't pay up. What else could I do?"

"Did you tell this to Ethan?"

"You know Ethan. He would've claimed I was just making up stories to save myself."

"So you stole." Disdain dripped from each word.

"I planned to give it back as soon as I could." Drake returned to his chair. "But then an auditor discovered what had happened."

His father turned white. "You fool! You could've been arrested. You could've gone to prison." He shook his head. "And brought more shame to the Kendalls."

Anger sent Drake bolting from his chair to tower over his father's desk. "That's all you care about, isn't it? The precious Kendall name. You don't give a damn what happens to me."

Horatio rose and faced him. "That's not true, and

you know it. I can think of two instances in particular when your family rallied around you."

Drake clenched his teeth. Leave it to his father to throw his indiscretions with those Irish maids in his face. "Unlike your precious Ethan and Win, I'm not perfect, Father. I make mistakes."

Accusations of favoritism always silenced Horatio. The anger dissipated. "None of us is perfect." He sat back down, calmer now. "Ethan did come to your aid, didn't he?"

Drake sat back down. "He convinced the bank president not to press charges."

"I'd say your brother saved your hide."

"He kept me out of jail, but he refused to save my job. I was dismissed. And he wouldn't use his connections to help me find another one." Drake couldn't keep the sneer out of his voice when he said, "So much for family loyalty."

Drake remembered that final confrontation in Ethan's office all too well. His pompous, sanctimonious brother placed the width of his mahogany desk between them and informed him that "the family" was sick and tired of sweeping his problems under the rug. Oh, Ethan could save Drake's job, but he thought it was high time his baby brother suffered the consequences of his actions. As of the moment Drake walked out the door, the Kendalls washed their hands of him. He would be on his own. After all, Drake was twenty-eight years old. Time he stopped floating through life and settled down.

Drake had wanted to grab his brother by the lapels, pull him out of his chair, and punch him in the pompous, sanctimonious face.

His father ran his hand across his head. "Why didn't you stay in Boston and look for another job?

Any of my old friends would've been willing to help you."

Drake picked an imaginary piece of lint off his trousers. "I decided to follow your example and come west, Father, to the land of opportunity."

Horatio looked stunned. "And what occupation do you intend to pursue here in Little Falls?"

"When I got off the stage, I noticed a bank down the street. Maybe I can work there."

"Don't even consider it, Drake," his father said.

Drake rose and went over to the window. "All I'm asking for is a place to stay until I decide what to do." He turned. "Is that too much to ask of my own father?" When Horatio made no reply, Drake added, "For heaven's sake! All I'm looking for is a second chance." He played his usual trump card. "Mother would've given me one."

Horatio rose and faced him, guilt slumping his shoulders. "I know she would've. And so will I." He placed his hand on Drake's shoulder. "No matter what you've done, you're still my son. You can stay with me for as long as you like."

Drake tried to look suitably grateful. "Thank you, Father. I knew you wouldn't let me down."

The older man smiled wanly. "Come on. I'll show you around the town. Such as it is."

"I've had a long day, and I'm really tired. If you don't mind, I'd like to rest."

"Take all the time you need."

Drake lay on his bed, his feet resting on a chest he had dragged from its place against the wall to the foot of the bed, to extend its length. Recalling the conversation with his father made him scowl at the ceiling.

What was eating at the old man anyway? Whenever Drake had come to him with some problem in the past, his father always took care of it without complaint. Now he was acting as if Drake's presence here was a big imposition.

"You'd think the old man would be happy to see his own flesh and blood," Drake said aloud.

Whether his father liked it or not, he was here to stay—at least until the next big opportunity presented itself.

He rose and went to the window. He surveyed the dusty, unpaved street and nondescript houses below in disgust. Little Falls didn't look like a town of big anything, much less opportunities.

A boy cantering a sleek, coal black horse slowly down the street caught his attention. He paused to study the rider more carefully.

The "boy" turned out to be none other than Catherine Wills.

Drake grinned. "Why, that little hellion . . . she fooled me again."

He watched her ride past the house. She stared straight ahead, unmindful of him standing at an upstairs window. He admired her profile, from her straight nose to her boyishly slim body and long leg, for she rode astride.

He wondered if Miss Wills had a man in her life. Her grandfather had said she wasn't married. Drake smiled to himself at the prospect of getting to know her better.

Maybe Catherine Wills would be his next big opportunity after all.

The following morning, Cat took several of her dog-eared veterinary journals over to Dr. Kendall's office.

The minute she stepped through the familiar door and into the hallway, she felt the homesickness wash over her. If she listened carefully, she could almost hear her father's deep, impatient voice diagnosing someone's illness in his surgery, and offering treatment. A vision of her mother, her green eyes and freckled face glowing with enthusiasm as she prepared her herbal remedies in the kitchen, flitted next through Cat's mind. A third benign ghost, herself as an energetic, noisy little girl, came running down the stairs with the black, long-eared coonhound, Zeke, tagging at her heels, his nails clicking on the bare wood floor. They rushed past her and vanished through the closed front door, only the well-remembered sound of high-pitched, girlish laughter lingering.

Cat shook off the feeling. The house belonged to someone else now. Time to bring these ghosts out of the past and into the present.

She knocked on the surgery door. "Dr. Kendall?"

"It's open," came the faint reply.

Dr. Horatio Kendall sat behind his desk, writing, his pen scratching in the room's silence. Engrossed in his work, he didn't look up to see who had entered his surgery, giving Cat a few seconds to study him.

He didn't bear the slighest resemblance to his tall, handsome son. Dr. Kendall was much shorter, only Cat's height, and slight of build. Any golden hair he might have possessed in his youth was almost gone. What little remained had turned gray and wispy around a shiny bald crown. His features appeared sharper and more aquiline than his son's, making him look more distinguished than handsome.

Then he looked up. When his dark brown eyes met Cat's gaze, the resemblance became so apparent, Cat wondered why she hadn't noticed it immediately.

"Yes, Miss Wills," he said, smiling warmly. "What can I do for you?"

She smiled back as she approached his desk, and

wished him good morning. "I'm through with these veterinary journals, so I thought I'd pass them along to you."

She set them on one corner of his desk.

"Why, how thoughtful of you. I'll read them as soon as I have the opportunity."

"I figured you might find them useful, seeing as how you're sure to be called on to take care of some farmers' animals as well as the farmers."

"That's why I'm here," he said.

"You come highly recommended by Grandpapa Wills. He told my papa you were one of the finest doctors he'd ever known."

Dr. Kendall's gaunt cheeks turned light pink. "I'm flattered." He indicated one of the chairs across from his desk. "Make yourself comfortable."

Cat sat down and leaned back in the chair. "I just wanted to tell you that I think there's plenty of business for two vets to handle in Little Falls."

Dr. Kendall raised one gray, bushy brow. "So you still intend to practice, even though I've taken over."

"Yes, I do. I know I don't have any formal schooling, like you, but my parents taught me everything they know, and I have been the town's unofficial vet for years."

The doctor rose from his desk and walked over to the window overlooking Main Street. "To be honest with you, Miss Wills, I don't approve of anyone practicing veterinary medicine without formal schooling."

Cat drummed her fingers against the chair's arm. "It's not that I haven't tried to get into school. None of them will accept women."

"I know."

"That's not my fault."

"Veterinary schools don't admit women because

they feel women aren't suited to such dirty, dangerous work."

Cat bristled. "I'm living proof that's not true. I'm a good vet. I've saved more animals than I've lost."

He turned around. "You shouldn't lose any."

Cat rose. "Well, I didn't come here to argue with you, Dr. Kendall. But I still intend to keep on being a vet as long as the farmers want my services."

"I can't stop you, but I'd urge you to reconsider, and leave the vet work to me."

Cat jammed her hands into her pockets. "As I said, I think there's enough work for both of us."

Then she wished him good day, and left.

5

Cat had just finished turning Rascal loose in the corral and was heading back to the house when Denny appeared in the shed's doorway and motioned to her.

She veered left to join him. "More pictures?"

His hazel eyes twinkled as he stepped aside and held the door open. "Wait'll you see these."

A whipcord-thin man in his early thirties, Dennis Dunleavy lived and breathed photography. He combed his curly auburn hair and shaved only because Cat or Ida May reminded him. He often forgot to eat. His rumpled clothes usually exuded the faint, sour odor of chemicals. But he had a true gift for putting people at ease and making them reveal their true selves for his camera. As Ida May liked to say, "That boy can squeeze sugar out of a pickle."

Cat stepped inside the shed and waited while Denny preceded her to the long table where he mounted his photographs. He pushed aside the paste pot and took a moment to spread the pictures out, then stepped back.

Cat took one look at the pictures, blushed to the roots of her hair, and stepped away. "Dennis Dunleavy! That's Cleopatra from One-Eyed Jack's, wearing nothing but her *unmentionables*! And you took that picture upstairs, in her *bedroom*!"

He smiled. "But the boudoir is where Cleo works. I just photographed her getting ready for work, that's all."

"You'd better not let Ida May see these," Cat muttered, "or she'll have a fainting fit and want me to throw you out."

All of the photographs were of the saloon girls. Cleopatra stood beside her brass bed, one knee drawn up to the mattress. Another showed Azalea reclining across hers. A third had captured Ruby Delight sitting in a grinning man's lap, her arms around his thick neck, his gaze on her ample bosom. To Cat's relief, the man wasn't Michael.

"You disappoint me, Cat," Denny said. "I thought you understood what I want to accomplish."

"I know you want to photograph life in Missouri before it disappears forever, but to go up to a saloon girl's *bedroom*, and take pictures of her in her *unmentionables* . . .*" Cat shook her head. "Most folk around here would call that indecent."

"All the girls agreed to pose for me. I didn't have to twist their arms."

Cat wondered if he had paid them and in what coin, but held her tongue. None of her business.

Denny had arrived in town shortly after Cat's mother inherited the boardinghouse from Miz Sims. Maddy Wills had taken to him immediately, especially when he touched her heart with his tales of his early years spent slaving at grinding, monotonous factory work to support himself while he scrimped and saved to buy a camera and a dream.

With the great Civil War photographers as his inspiration, he headed west.

Denny rearranged his work on the table and studied each one. "I'm preserving these women's lives for posterity, so that many years from now, somebody will look at these photographs and wonder what these women were like."

Cat leaned her hip against the table edge and crossed her arms. "I'm not so sure any of them will want what they did recorded for posterity, especially if they marry and become respectable."

Denny's hazel eyes twinkled. "You mean they wouldn't want their grandchildren to find one of these hidden away in some trunk in the attic?"

"Could prove embarrassing to Grandma."

Denny rifled though more photographs until he found another one. "Let's take this one of you and Rascal. A hundred years from now, don't you think someone looking at this photo will wonder who you were, and why you dressed in britches instead of a dress?"

Cat thought for a moment. "I hope someone tells them that I was a vet, and britches are more comfortable for doctoring sick animals."

"Just like I hope someone will tell them that Ruby Delight's husband sold her favors to his friends when she was only sixteen, and after someone shot him in a brawl, she had no alternative but to keep doing what she did best. Or starve."

Cat raised her brows. "I never knew that about Ruby."

"Not many people do."

Did Michael?

Cat moved away from the table. "Ida May was

right. You sure can squeeze sugar from a pickle."

Denny laughed softly. "People tell me their secrets because I'm genuinely interested in their lives, and I really listen, that's all." He collected his pictures. "Now, if you'll excuse me, I want to show my masterpieces to the girls."

Cat led the way out of the shed and went back to the house, while Denny headed off to One-Eyed Jack's.

Cat found the boardinghouse empty.

"Where is everybody?" she asked Bounder, who rose and left her whimpering brood for a moment to pad across the kitchen and greet Cat with a wagging tail and a lick of her hand. Cat stroked the dog's head, then checked on the pups. "Must be quilting circle day for Ida May."

She poured herself a glass of cold water, fished a molasses cookie out of the earthenware jar, and headed for the parlor to relax for a few minutes.

Just as she walked through the door, Edgar Allan Crow shrieked, "Cat!" She knew he wasn't referring to her, but the opportunistic Ulysses, who was balancing precariously on the windowsill and poised to spring at the birdcage.

Cat stamped her foot and shouted, "Scat! You leave that bird alone."

Ulysses leaped off the windowsill and streaked out of the parlor.

"Weak and weary," Edgar said, unruffling his feathers as he settled down on his perch swing.

"I'll bet." Cat set down her glass, crumbled off a piece of cookie and fed it to him.

The squeak of the front gate distracted her, and she looked out the window. There, walking up the brick walk, was none other than Drake Kendall.

"Well, I'll be," she whispered.

Cat stepped back behind the curtain and peered out at her unexpected visitor. He was so tall, he looked as if he could reach up and pluck a stray cloud right out of the sky. But he wasn't heavy. No paunch hung over his belt. He moved with confidence and a light step, not lumbering like many men of such a great height.

As the man approached the porch steps, Cat noticed he was carrying a small paper bag. She stepped even farther back so he wouldn't see her watching.

First came footsteps on the stairs, then on the porch. Next a knock on the door.

"Just a minute." Cat gobbled up the rest of her cookie and washed it down with a sip of water. She set down her glass, opened the door, and propped her hip against the doorjamb. She crossed her arms and tilted her head back. "Why, Mr. Kendall."

He had already taken off his hat and kept his head bowed slightly so it wouldn't bump the porch ceiling. "Miss Wills," he said with a smile.

If Cat hadn't already been dazzled by his golden hair, the smile would have blinded her. "What are you doing here?"

"I've brought you a little peace offering." He held out a small paper bag.

Cat moved away from the doorjamb, unsure whether to take the bag. "Peace offering? For what?"

"For the ungentlemanly way I treated you when we first met."

"Oh, that." She waved her hand in a dismissive gesture. "It's forgotten. You didn't have to bring me anything."

"But I did. Go on, take it. They're lemon drops from the mercantile." His brown velvet gaze held hers.

"The boy behind the counter said that they were your favorite."

Cat felt the heat rise to her cheeks. Damn the Dobbs boy for telling a complete stranger about her weakness for lemon drops!

She took the bag. "Thank you kindly."

"It's not much. I wanted to bring you a dozen hothouse roses or a box of chocolates as I would to a Boston lady, but I've discovered that there are no such amenities in Little Falls."

"The only flowers around here grow wild in the spring and summer," Cat said. "And as for chocolates . . . you'd have to go all the way to St. Louis for those. But lemon drops are just as good."

He smiled again. "Aren't you going to invite me in?"

She remembered her manners. "Come on in and set a spell."

The minute Cat and Drake Kendall crossed the threshold, Edgar started jabbering away, Bounder trotted out of the kitchen to inspect the caller, and Ulysses reappeared to leap up on the back of the sofa, where he sat with his long plumed tail curled around himself and stared out of curious green eyes.

Kendall extended his hand for the dog to sniff. "This is quite a menagerie you have here."

"Just a few strays I've taken in," Cat replied, stroking Ulysses. She introduced the animals, then said, "Bounder just had puppies and I have to find homes for them. I'll let you have your pick of the litter."

Kendall held up his hands in protest. "The first and last time I brought a puppy home without my father's permission, he tanned my hide and made me bring it back." He smiled. "I wouldn't care to repeat the experience."

Cat smiled back. "Hard to imagine anyone tanning

your hide now that you're a grown man." She couldn't think of too many men who would want to tangle with this giant.

"That wouldn't stop my father," he said.

Cat suddenly found herself at a loss for what to do next. He was the new doctor's son, and he had come all the way from Boston. She should make the effort to be sociable. But there was something about Drake Kendall that made her nervous. Maybe it was his overpowering size, or the intense way he kept looking at her, as though he were trying to see into her soul.

What would her mother do? Why, she'd offer him refreshment.

"You care for some of Ida May's molasses cookies? She just baked a fresh batch this morning."

"I'd like that."

Cat took his hat and set it atop the piano along with her bag of lemon drops, then led the way into the kitchen. "Have a seat."

Instead, he followed Bounder over to where her puppies lay sleeping together in a pile. He knelt on one knee to inspect them. "They are handsome."

Cat filled the kettle with water. "You can pick one out now, and take him home later, after he's been weaned."

Kendall rose and walked over to the kitchen table. "I hate to say no to such a pretty saleswoman, but I must. I'm a guest in my father's house."

"I understand."

Did he really think she was pretty? Cat hid her embarrassment by making a production out of placing the kettle on the stove, then opening the cupboard. She stood on tiptoes to reach the teacups.

"Allow me."

Drake Kendall had come up behind her. Before Cat could sidestep out of his way, he stretched his long arm high over her head to retrieve the cups. She froze lest any sudden movement cause him to drop them. She felt the warmth of his breath on the top of her head, and his shirtfront brush her shoulders as he reached. She held her breath. Her pulse raced. She swallowed hard. All she had to do was step back, and she'd bump up against his broad, hard chest.

Why was this man—a complete stranger—flustering her so? Maybe because her own father had once done the same to her mother, and they had wound up married.

The second cup and saucer retrieved, Drake Kendall brought them over to the table, blissfully unaware of the effect he was having on Cat.

She placed several cookies on a plate. "So you're from Boston."

"I've lived there all my life," he replied.

"You have any brothers and sisters?" Cat felt his gaze on her as she poured hot water into the brown china teapot, spilled it out and added three teaspoons of tea leaves.

"Two older brothers," he replied, his rich voice suddenly cooling. Then it warmed again. "I know you're an only child."

Cat smiled. "Grandpapa Wills must've told you that."

"He also told me that he wishes you had gone to New York with your parents so he could see more of you."

She turned, touched. "Did he really?"

Kendall's mouth was full, so he nodded.

Suddenly Cat felt as though this man sitting in her kitchen wasn't such a stranger after all.

The water came to a boil, and Cat added it to the teapot. "I've only seen Grandpapa Wills three times in my life, but we write to each other when we're not busy. Little Falls is so far away from Boston, and his arthritis keeps him from traveling."

"That's a shame," Kendall said. "Families should be close."

Cat brought the teapot over to the table, her nervousness gone. "So what brings you all the way out here? You just visiting, or do you intend to stay?"

"I heard the West was a land of opportunity," he said, "and I'm here to seek my fortune."

"What'd you do back in Boston?"

"I worked in a bank."

Cat poured the tea. "My best friend's grandfather is a banker."

Kendall raised his brows as he accepted a cup. "Does he own that bank on Main Street?"

"Sure does, though now it's just a branch of his bigger bank in St. Louis." Cat paused. "Maybe he'd give you a job, if you're looking."

Drake's smile died and his expression became shuttered. "I don't want to work in a bank anymore. I want to try something different, where I can be my own man."

"I can understand that. I'm a veterinarian myself."

Drake Kendall wrinkled his aristocratic nose. "Why does a pretty young woman like you want to spend her time slogging through barnyards and risking her life treating sick animals?"

Cat stared at him in surprise. No one had ever questioned her desire to be a vet. Her parents just assumed that their daughter shared their passion and would want to follow in their footsteps. The local farmers always called on her when their livestock was sick. None of the townspeople thought her occupation odd, or if they did, they wisely kept it to themselves.

"I guess we're more open-minded about women out here," she said.

"I guess so." Drake Kendall sipped his tea. "In Boston, we gentlemen put our ladies on pedestals. They are the weaker sex, after all."

"Weaker sex?" Cat scoffed. "Guess you've never seen a woman spend a whole day behind a mule, plowing a field."

He curled his lip disdainfully. "No, I haven't, and I hope I never do. Women shouldn't plow fields. They should adorn a home with their beauty and refinement."

A woman as adornment. Cat tried to see herself "adorning" anything, and failed. The closest example she could think of was Sally Wheeler. She shuddered at the thought of turning herself into that simpering pink confection.

She almost spoke her mind to Drake Kendall, then remembered what her mother had told her about not arguing with company. The man was a guest.

"Like I said, we're more open-minded out here." She minded her manners and picked up the teapot. "More tea? Cookies?"

He finished the last cookie and shook his head. "They're delicious, but if I eat any more, I'll spoil my dinner—excuse me, *supper* I think you call it."

Cat smiled. "You'll be talking like the rest of us before you know it."

"Speaking of the natives, I'd like to ask a favor of you, Miss Wills."

"Call me Cat. Everybody does."

"And my friends call me Drake." He paused. "As I'm new in town and don't know anybody, would you mind showing me around and introducing me to people?"

Cat rose. "If you have some time, I can take you around right now."

She emptied the teapot and quickly rinsed the

dishes, acutely aware of Drake's eyes on her. Then they left the boardinghouse together for his tour of Little Falls.

Drake was a man used to commanding attention wherever he went, partly because of his great height and striking good looks, and partly because of his supreme confidence. He liked attention. Craved it. Saw it as his due.

That afternoon, the citizens of Little Falls did not disappoint him. The women smiled and batted their eyelashes, the men regarded him with respect.

As he followed Catherine—he found it impossible to think of her by that absurd nickname—through one business establishment after another, meeting people she had known all her life, Drake found his spirits lifting and his optimism returning. Maybe there were more opportunities in this hole in the wall than he had originally thought—at least until something better came along.

He glanced down at Catherine walking beside him, matching his long stride with her own. Beneath those cropped curls and mannish clothes dwelt a feminine young woman. He also sensed a sensual, passionate nature hidden as well. He enjoyed awakening such passions in women. Cat's only annoying flaw was her independent spirit, but that could be squelched easily enough.

A challenge.

That's what he needed.

And Catherine Wills was going to provide it.

The following morning, Cat was on her way to the mercantile to buy some thread for Ida May when she heard the unmistakable sound of someone groaning in pain.

She paused and looked down the narrow alley. At first glance, the passage seemed empty. Only several kegs stood near a doorway at the farthest end.

There it was again, a low moan.

Cat walked down the alley.

To her surprise, Teddy Granger sat doubled over in pain, wedged between the barrels, his skinny arms wrapped around his middle. A dime novel lay on the ground beside him.

Cat knelt down. "Teddy, what's wrong?"

At the sound of Cat's voice, the boy started and looked up at her, his dirty face pasty beneath the grime, and his blue eyes wide with the fear of a trapped animal staring down the barrel of a hunter's gun.

"I didn't do anything wrong, Miss Cat. I didn't."

She placed a calming hand on his arm. "I'm not accusing you of anything," she said quietly. "I just want to know what's wrong."

"My—my stomach aches," he said, and groaned pitifully.

At first Cat was ready to dismiss the cause of his pain as the result of stuffing himself with all the candy he and Buster had filched from the mercantile. But she remembered her father telling her about the difference between a simple inflammation of the stomach caused by overeating, and more serious abdominal pain.

Although Cat had little regard for Teddy because of his unabashed penchant for thievery, she nonetheless felt sorry for him. A hardened criminal at the tender age of eleven, Teddy lacked a father's firm guiding hand. His downtrodden mother worked from dawn until dusk as a laundress to support both herself and her wayward son because her good-for-nothing husband had deserted them when Teddy was only six. While her labors put food on their table and clothes on her son's back, they sapped her energy to provide much in the way of moral instruction.

"Where does it hurt?" Cat asked gently.

"Way down here." Teddy indicated his lower right side, way down by his thigh, far away from his stomach.

"Did you tell your mother?"

He shook his head and grimaced. "I don't want to bother her when she's working."

"I'm going to take you to Dr. Kendall's office and have him examine you." Cat rose and extended her hand. "Can you get up and come with me?"

"I—I'll try." The boy grasped Cat's hand with his grimy paw and hauled himself to his feet, where he swayed and groaned again, hunched over like an eighty-year-old man.

Cat placed a supporting arm around his shoulders and led him out of the alley.

When she arrived at Dr. Kendall's, she had Teddy sit in one of the chairs outside the surgery door. Luckily, no one else appeared to be waiting.

The doctor came walking down the hall from the direction of the kitchen, carrying a steaming cup. "Is there something I can do for you, Miss Wills?"

"Teddy here has a bad stomachache," she replied, casting a concerned glance at the boy, whose face was creased with pain.

Dr. Kendall's sharp, aquiline features softened. He set down his cup and knelt by Teddy's chair. He patted the boy's knee with a gentleness that surprised Cat, for he had impressed her as a stern man, not given to emotional displays. "Been eating too many sweets, have we, lad?"

Teddy didn't even try to smile.

"I think Teddy's malady is more serious than a case of too many sweets," Cat said.

The doctor rose and glowered at her. Before she knew what was happening, he grasped her arm and pulled her down the hall, out of Teddy's earshot. "A little sensitivity, if you please, Miss Wills. We don't want to scare the lad half to death."

"I'm sorry," she whispered, taken aback. "I didn't mean to frighten him."

Dr. Kendall gave her a forgiving smile. "I know you're used to treating animals that lack our ability to reason. We can say anything in front of them. But human beings are capable of understanding, so we must be very careful what we say. Especially around young children who are so easily frightened."

Before Cat could comment, Dr. Kendall returned to Teddy's side and knelt down so he was at eye level with the boy. "Now, there's nothing to be frightened of, young man. I'm going to take you into that room right over there, and you're going to lie down on my big table." He smiled, and almost looked as handsome as Drake. "Why, my table is so comfortable, I'm sure you'll think you're in your own bed, and fall asleep."

Teddy managed a wan smile.

Dr. Kendall escorted Teddy into the surgery. He emerged five minutes later and said to Cat, "Where is the boy's mother? Why isn't she here with her son?"

"Mrs. Granger works in the laundry," Cat explained. "Teddy knows he's not supposed to disturb her when she's working."

The doctor's warm gaze chilled. "Get her here. Now." He lowered his voice to a whisper. "If I'm right, the boy has appendicitis, and I'll have to operate right away."

Or he'll die, Cat thought. "I'll get Mrs. Granger right now."

She hurried to the laundry to inform his mother that her son's life could be in danger.

Luckily for Teddy, Dr. Kendall performed an operation and successfully removed the inflamed appendix before it burst.

As Cat sat with the weeping, terrified Mrs. Granger in the waiting area, she couldn't stop thinking of Dr. Kendall's sensitivity and patience when dealing with the sick. He was going to be a change from Cat's own father, who could be brusque and testy when treating his two-legged patients.

Even though Dr. Kendall disapproved of Cat encroaching on his territory with her own veterinary work, she liked him. But she wasn't about to give up and let him take over. He'd just have to get used to sharing the duties.

When Teddy was out of danger, Cat went home reassured that Little Falls was indeed big enough for both her and the new doctor.

6

THE HAMMER CAME DOWN HARD ON MICHAEL'S THUMB. Excrutiating pain almost blinded him. He jerked his hand away, bellowed and doubled over, then swore so loudly Jace and Curly stopped and stared.

Jace looked down from the barn roof where he and Curly, the groom, knelt nailing boards in place on the new addition. He removed several nails from between his pursed lips. "You okay, son?"

Michael swore another blue streak. "Damn hammer."

Curly pulled a red bandanna out of his back pocket and mopped gleaming beads of sweat from his ebony face. He grinned. "Don't you go blaming that poor hammer."

"Tell me you didn't crush a finger." Jace sounded odd. "Your mother will kill me if you did."

Michael stared down at his red, throbbing thumb. "Naw. It just hurts like hell." He could kick himself for not keeping his mind on the job, but he had a good reason.

He hadn't seen Cat in four days.

Two days sometimes passed between visits, but never this many. If Cat didn't stop by the farm on her way to performing her veterinarian duties elsewhere, Michael saw her when he rode into town. Now, with construction of this new addition to the stables keeping Michael busy as long as daylight lingered, he barely had enough strength to crawl into bed after supper let alone ride into town.

He knew something was wrong. Cat never neglected her four-legged patients. She would certainly have ridden out by now to check on Gustavus. But she hadn't.

The slow clopping of hoofbeats coming down the long drive followed by the dogs' barking caused Michael to look up expectantly. His spirits sank down to his boots when he saw not Cat and Rascal, but the Coopers' own buggy with Belle, the housekeeper, at the reins and the dogs following her.

She had returned from town. Maybe she'd seen Cat.

Michael squinted up at his father. "My thumb is killing me. I'm going to have Belle take a look at it."

Jace nodded and pounded in another nail with one swift stroke.

By the time Michael walked from the stables to the house, Belle had disappeared inside. He found her in the kitchen, unpacking a box of supplies.

"I've had an accident," he said as he came through the door.

The black woman raised her brows. "You still standin' on your own two feet, so it can't be that bad."

"It sure hurts."

She took his hand and examined his red, swollen thumb. "What'd you do to it?"

"This thumb had the misfortune to get between my hammer and a nail."

Belle winced. "Don't look like you broke nothing. Have a seat and let me see what I can do."

Michael unpacked sugar, buttons, a paper of sewing needles and several spools of thread from her box with his good right hand. "How's everything in Little Falls?"

She filled a basin with water. "The same as the last time. Why you askin'?"

"Just curious." When he finished, he sat down. "Dad's been keeping me so busy building the new addition that I haven't had a chance to get into town myself." He smiled. "A man's got to let off steam sometime."

Belle slanted him a glance as she rummaged through her medicine box. "About the only news I heard was that one of Dr. Kendall's sons come to town."

"I thought they're all back in Boston."

Belle brought a tin of an herbal ointment Cat's mother had taught her how to make and a roll of bandages over to the table. "Not the youngest. I seen him myself when I was in the mercantile." She took Michael's hand and immersed it in the water, ignoring his gasp of pain. "I was standing by the window, waiting for Tessie to get through helping another customer, when this giant walked by."

Michael raised his brows. "Giant?"

"Taller than your daddy even. Tallest man I ever seen in all my born days." Belle gingerly bathed the thumb's swollen, sensitive flesh. "Must be a full half foot over six feet. Like I said, a giant." She patted the thumb dry and inspected it. "There's blood under the nail, but I can't do anything about that. As I was sayin', this man was handsome. He was so good-looking, he even made an old married lady like me feel as fluttery as a schoolgirl."

"Belle Ritter, I'm surprised at you, a respectable married lady lusting in your heart after some single gent."

Her dark eyes sparkled flirtatiously. "I may be married, but I ain't dead."

Michael roared.

"Cat seemed to appreciate him, too," Belle said.

His laughter stuck in his throat like a fish bone. He coughed. "Cat?"

"She was with him." Belle patted the thumb dry. "They was chatting away like old friends."

Michael cleared his throat. "I didn't know she'd met Dr. Kendall's son."

"According to Tessie, Cat was one of the first. Seems this Drake—funny name for a feller—mistook Cat for a boy when she was trying to catch a couple of little thieves. Lifted her right off her feet, he did."

The throbbing ceased. "I'll bet that didn't sit well with Cat."

"Not at first." Belle gently dressed his wound with ointment. "According to Tessie, who heard it from Ida May at yesterday's quilting circle, Mr. Drake Kendall apologized to Cat for mistaking her for a boy, and he even brung her lemon drops."

Lemon drops. Cat's favorite. "Who told him about the lemon drops?"

Belle finished bandaging Michael's thumb. "That too tight?"

Not that he could feel it. He shook his head.

Belle added, "According to Tessie, Drake Kendall came into the mercantile and asked for the name of Miss Catherine Wills's favorite candy."

Michael thanked her and rose. Suddenly the huge, airy kitchen seemed to shrink, the walls closing in on him. He had to get outside.

"That girl is sure causing a stir," Belle said, gathering her medical supplies.

"What do you mean?"

"Tessie said that ever since this Drake Kendall arrived, Cat's been showing him around town. She even took him with her when she rode out to some of the farms."

So that's where she'd been for the last four days, showing the doctor's son around.

"Isn't that just like Cat," he said, "making a stranger feel welcome. Especially a city slicker from Boston."

"She surely has been busier than a bee in summer," Belle agreed, her watchful eyes never leaving Michael's face. "But she should take care."

"Why should she?"

"You know folks. They see Cat and this Drake fellow always together, they gonna start saying that they're keeping company. Before you know it, folks'll have them marching down the aisle."

"Cat?" Michael pasted on a smile. "Nobody's going to make her do anything she doesn't want to do." He kissed Belle on the cheek. "I'd better get back to work before my father comes looking for me."

He turned and strode out of the kitchen.

Belle stood at the sink and watched out of the window as he walked away. She shook her head. "Some men need a nudge, and others need a good swift kick in the pants to make them see what's right under their noses."

She returned to the table to put away the rest of her supplies.

Hammers pounding echoed the pounding in Michael's thumb and in his head. He felt dazed and disoriented, as though some tornado had picked him up and set him down in a foreign country where he didn't recognize the people or speak the language.

He hadn't met this Kendall fellow yet, but already he didn't like him. Not because he was rumored to be tall and good-looking. Michael felt no threat there. The source of his resentment was Kendall's smooth, big-city ways.

When Belle had related how the doctor's son had gone to the mercantile to learn the name of Cat's favorite candy, then sweetened his apology with lemon drops, Michael's blood boiled. Level-headed Cat was a country girl at heart, and an innocent in the ways of men. She might not be immune to such practiced flattery. She could get hurt.

Over his dead body.

If Ruby were here, she'd tell him that the reason he was feeling so protective of Cat was because he was sweet on her himself. Not true. He just hated the thought of a friend hurt by some city slicker who'd go back to Boston and leave her with a broken heart.

When Michael reached the stables, he shaded his eyes against the hot noonday sun and looked up at his father, still hammering away at the roof. "My hand's still sore," he said. "I'm going to stop work for the day and ride into town."

Jace stopped hammering and removed the last nail from between his lips. "Go ahead. I'll have one of the men take over."

Michael turned and headed for the corral to saddle up Rogue.

No sooner did he finish tightening the cinch than the sound of hoofbeats and dogs barking caused Michael to look up. Rascal came cantering down the drive with a familiar rider on her back.

Michael blinked twice, fearing Cat would disappear like a puff of smoke. She didn't. She grinned and waved, slowing Rascal to a walk as she approached him.

"Howdy, stranger," he said, unhooking the stirrup from the saddle horn. "Long time no see." Had only four days passed since he had last seen her? She looked different, like someone who'd been away for a long time and suddenly returned.

Cat halted her mare and dismounted. Her blue eyes sparkled as she walked over to extend her hand for Rogue to nuzzle. "I know I should've ridden out sooner to check on Gus, but I haven't had a minute."

"You don't need an excuse to visit," he said. "You know you're always welcome."

Her gaze fell to his bandaged thumb. She pulled off her gloves and reached for his hand. "What happened?"

The minute her warm fingers touched his, Michael felt something stir inside. He squelched the feeling and told her what had happened.

Cat snorted in derision. "I'd kiss it and make it better, but I'm sure you're saving that honor for Sally."

"Her lips are softer, anyway," he retorted with a wicked grin.

"You ought to know."

"I do."

That brought a faint blush of anger to Cat's cheeks, but she deftly changed the subject. "Maybe you'd better let Dr. Kendall take a look at your thumb. You might've broken something and not know it."

"Belle tended it." He tried to keep the annoyance out of his voice and failed. "It'll be fine in no time."

Cat's eyes widened in surprise. "Suit yourself."

She took down her medical bag from the saddle horn, plunked her hat on it as if it were a coatrack, and rolled up her shirtsleeves. She ran her fingers through her hair, tousling her curls. "Has Gus gotten any better?"

"Yes, he has, no thanks to you."

She arched a brow. "What's that supposed to mean?"

"Didn't you say you'd look in on him the next day, to see if your physic had worked?"

Cat looked stricken. "I'm sorry. I know I should've. But I had other things to attend to."

He had punished her enough. "No harm done. The physic worked. He's better."

She gave a sigh of relief. "Good."

Michael headed for the Hanoverian's stall, and Cat fell into step beside him.

The minute Gus heard them approach, the big horse poked his head over the door and whickered softly.

"He does look better," Cat said, extending her hand and letting him nuzzle her palm.

Watching her, Michael wondered how anyone could mistake Cat for a boy. Sure, she wore her father's old shirts and those baggy trousers. But if anyone watched her, really *watched* her, they could see that she moved too gracefully for a boy. And her hands, with the long, tapered fingers now stroking Gus's nose, felt too soft and smooth. No boy he had ever seen possessed such huge blue eyes always so quick to reveal her every mood, or those perfect rosy lips, the lower lip slightly fuller than the upper one.

"How's my big, strong baby?" she crooned to the horse, her voice as light and lilting as music on a summer's night, a sweet feminine voice that Michael never tired of listening to. In response, Gus nuzzled her cheek in an equine kiss. "I love you, too, you old reprobate."

"Well, what's the diagnosis?" Michael said, staring

down at the ground. Something about watching her whispering in Gus's ear and stroking his face so tenderly made him uncomfortable. "You know my mother. She wants to drive him, and she's getting impatient."

Cat opened the stall door and went inside to examine him. When she finished, she said, "Your mother can drive him any time she wants."

"She'll be glad to hear it." He watched her give Gus one final pat and admonish him to be a good boy, then she turned and came to Michael's side.

"I thought I'd ride back to town with you and stay the night," he said. "Mind if I bunk at the boarding-house?"

"Have I ever minded? Even though you're going to Sally Wheeler's for Sunday dinner tomorrow."

He grinned. "Want to come along? I'm sure Mrs. Wheeler won't mind setting out another plate."

Cat rolled her eyes. "Five minutes of Sally's company is more than I can stand."

"You sure you don't mind my staying over?"

"I said I didn't."

With this Kendall fellow suddenly in the picture, he wasn't sure of his welcome.

"You never know when you might need to rent out that spare room," he said.

"Two boarders are plenty for anybody to handle." She put on her gloves and smoothed them out. "Now, are you coming back to town with me?"

"Lead the way."

He wouldn't miss meeting Drake Kendall for the world.

"I haven't seen you for four days," he said, staring straight ahead as they rode down the dusty road leading back to Little Falls. "What's been happening in town?"

Cat glanced over at him. "Lots of fireworks at the boardinghouse. Denny took some pictures of the saloon girls in their unmentionables, and got careless. Ida May found them."

Michael burst out laughing, causing Rogue to fling back his head at the startling noise. "The girls at One-Eyed Jack's let Denny photograph them in their unmentionables?"

A faint blush stained Cat's cheeks. "They sure did. I told him to keep those pictures under lock and key, because most folk would think them indecent. But you know Denny. He says he's just recording their lives for posterity."

Michael didn't need Denny's photographs to show him what Ruby looked like in her camisole and pantaloons, but prudently held his tongue.

Cat shook her head. "Ida May turned so red, I thought she was going to have an apoplectic fit. She wanted me to throw Denny out on his ear, but I calmed her down."

"Ida May's a practical woman," Michael said. "No matter what she may think of Denny's work, he always pays his rent on time."

"Lord knows the boardinghouse has seen its share of deadbeats over the years."

They rode in a comfortable silence broken only by the soft creaking of saddle leather and clopping of hooves on the hard, dry road.

"So," Michael said, "tell me about Dr. Kendall's son."

Cat looked at him. "Who told you about Drake?"

So they were already on a first-name basis after knowing each other for only four days. His thumb throbbed.

"Belle," he replied. "She went into town today and stopped at the mercantile."

"Tessie must've told her."

"Nothing gets by Tessie." Michael patted Rogue's neck. "So, what's this Drake Kendall like?"

"He's a nice man." Cat told him the story of their inauspicious meeting, corroborating Belle's version. "He even came to the boardinghouse to apologize and bring me a peace offering."

Why did she sound amazed?

"Lemon drops," he said.

Cat smiled wryly. "I'm sure Tessie told everybody."

"Just about." Michael breathed deeply of the sweet spring air underscored with the pungent aroma of horse. "So what's he doing in Little Falls, and how long's he staying?"

She told him the doctor's son had been feeling hemmed in by big-city life, and when his father came west, he decided to join him. "He hasn't said how long he'll be staying."

With any luck, Drake Kendall would be on tomorrow's stage.

Guilt made Michael shift in the saddle. He was being unfair and petty. He hadn't even met Kendall, and already he had formed a negative opinion. He decided to reserve judgment.

"Belle tells me you've been showing him around," Michael said.

"Just to introduce him to a few folks and make him feel welcome."

How like her. "I'm sure he appreciated it."

"He did."

As they continued their ride into town, Michael talked of his father's plans to expand the stables and buy more horses. Cat expressed her fears that the incorrigible Teddy Granger and Buster Blick were headed down the primrose path to a life of crime. Michael asked if she had heard from her parents lately, and Cat replied that she owed her mother a letter. They were discussing possible homes for Bounder's latest litter when the outskirts of Little Falls finally appeared over a slight dip in the road.

Michael halted Rogue. "Want to race?"

Cat eyed his bandage. "I couldn't do that. It'd be like taking candy from a baby."

Michael grinned. "Just because I banged my hand, don't make the mistake of thinking you're going to win, Miss Wills."

She smiled back, her blue eyes dark and gleaming with the spirit of friendly competition. "Tell you what. I'll give you a head start, and I'll still beat you."

"That's what you think."

Rogue and Rascal, sensing their riders' excitement and knowing that a race was imminent, pawed the earth and danced in place.

"What's the finish line?" Cat asked, reining in her impatient mare with one hand and settling her hat more firmly on her head with the other.

"The livery," Michael replied as Rogue took a hesitant step forward, eager for his master's signal to run.

Michael leaned forward in the saddle, clicked his tongue and touched his heels to Rogue's sides. The gelding bounded forward as if shot from a cannon.

All thoughts of Drake Kendall disappeared in the sheer exhilaration of the race. With a powerful animal running smoothly beneath him and the wind whipping tears from his eyes, Michael's spirits soared.

Seconds later, he heard Cat thundering up behind him. He smiled to himself as he slowed Rogue just a fraction, for he knew Cat's favorite strategy of letting Michael set the pace while she reserved her mare's strength for the final burst at the finish line.

Let her catch up with him, and then they'd see who was going to win this time.

Seconds later, Rascal edged alongside of Rogue. Michael risked a glance at Cat, and saw her leaning low over her mare's neck, her expression intense. But she made no attempt to pull away from Rogue.

They raced neck and neck, neither one willing to make the first move.

The Dawlish house appeared on their left. Michael got ready. As soon as they reached it, he would make his move.

Just as Rogue galloped past the Dawlish's front door, Michael gave him more rein and nudged his sides with his heels. Rogue lengthened his stride at the command, running even faster and pulling away from Cat in a burst of speed.

Michael galloped past his grandparents' former house that was now Dr. Kendall's. So intent was he on the race that he barely noticed the tall man standing on the porch.

Michael raced down Main Street. Several pedestrians saw him coming and wisely did not cross the street. No wagons or carts blocked his way today.

There was the finish line just ahead.

The minute Michael raced by Hechinger's Livery, he sat back in the saddle and slowed Rogue, turning him around so Cat could see the triumphant expression on Michael's face.

To his surprise, she wasn't behind him.

Frowning in puzzlement, Michael stared down Main Street.

Cat and Rascal were nowhere to be found.

7

WHERE HAD CAT GONE? SHE ALWAYS FINISHED A race. Always.

Panic grabbed his throat. What if something had happened to her?

Michael's worried, searching gaze found her. He breathed a deep, shaky sigh of relief that shook him all the way down to his boots. She had stopped by his grandparents' house and was talking to some man taller than Rascal.

Belle's giant.

Cat had stopped racing so she could talk to Drake Kendall.

Michael slowly cantered back the way they had come. As he drew closer to the conversing pair, he tightened the reins, bringing Rogue up short and causing the gelding to arch his neck and fight the bit, parading in a show-off strut.

Cat glanced at Michael, then said something to Kendall on the other side of the white picket fence. Kendall turned, stared at Michael with the unflinching, appraising look of one man sizing up another. Then he dismissed him with a small, condescending smile.

Michael ignored the insult and said to Cat, "You okay?"

She looked puzzled. "Why wouldn't I be?"

"You didn't finish the race. I thought Rascal might've gone lame, or tripped and thrown you."

Cat patted the mare's lathered neck. "Rascal's fine, aren't you, girl?" She dismounted. "I just stopped to talk to Drake. Michael, this is Dr. Kendall's son. Drake, this is my good friend, Michael Cooper."

Michael stayed mounted, but drew his horse close enough to the fence so he could extend his hand to the other man. "Kendall."

Kendall shook hands, but he didn't smile, and his brown eyes remained cool. "Cooper."

"Michael is the man I told you about," Cat said, oblivious to the tension running like a tight wire between the two men. "Our families have known each other forever."

"I seem to remember your grandfather mentioning the Coopers," Kendall said. He looked at Michael. "Your family owns a horse farm outside town?"

Michael nodded, dismounted, and faced Kendall across the fence. "We breed some of the fastest horses in the state."

"Do tell," Kendall said, obviously unimpressed.

"Cat and I have known each other ever since we were children," Michael said.

He had to admit that the doctor's son possessed enough golden-god looks and the dynamic, sophisticated presence of an older man to turn the most level-headed woman into a walking, talking mooncalf. Although Michael had met only a few such men, there was something about Drake Kendall that sounded loud warning bells.

Michael mentally shook himself. He had only just met the man, and he didn't like him. Or trust him. No, he wasn't being fair. He should give Kendall a chance.

Cat said, "I'd better go and cool Rascal down."

Michael nodded to Kendall. "I'm sure we'll be seeing more of each other."

"You can count on it," Kendall replied.

Cat said good-bye, and led her horse away. Michael and Rogue fell in step beside them.

When they were far enough down the street so Kendall wouldn't overhear, Cat pulled off her hat and swatted Michael on the shoulder. "What's wrong with you?" she hissed. "I've never seen you act so rude. If looks were bullets, Drake would be dead."

Michael's wretched thumb began to throb. "You scared the life out me, Willie. One minute you were behind me, the next you weren't there. I had visions of you lying on the ground with a broken neck. Then I turned around and there you were, big as life, talking to some man over the fence."

"I don't see what you're all fired up about. It was only a race."

"*Only* a race? I've never heard you call the Fourth of July race *only* a race. I thought we were practicing so you could win this year."

The town's Fourth of July celebration featured a horse race that attracted the best riders and the fastest horses from three neighboring counties. Michael had won last year, with his father coming in a close second. Cat placed fourth.

"I was practicing," Cat said. "I didn't think stopping to talk to Drake this one time would make any difference."

"You're right. It won't." Michael reached over and tousled her hair. "I intend to beat you anyway."

She smiled at him. "Not this year, you won't."

"That's what you said last year and look what happened."

"Care to make a little wager?"

"Naw. That'd be like taking lemon drops from a Cat."

They continued their good-natured squabbling until Drake Kendall disappeared from view.

Drake lingered at the fence for a moment and watched Catherine Wills and Michael Cooper lead their horses up the street.

He could tell Cooper didn't like him, but he was used to inspiring envy in lesser men. Besides, the feeling was mutual.

He grudgingly admitted that Catherine's friend possessed a dark, bold Byronic handsomeness, and he did cut a dashing figure on horseback. Insignificant, but obviously a highly prized commodity among the unsophisticated female population of farm country. Ultimately, Drake dismissed him as nothing but a country bumpkin who wouldn't know the difference between a Chopin nocturne and "Oh, Susannah." He'd bet anything that Cooper hadn't even scraped the manure off his boots before coming to town.

Content with his own unchallenged superiority, Drake walked back to the house and into his father's study. He sat down to read a week-old St. Louis newspaper, but his thoughts wandered to the photographs he had glimpsed yesterday at Catherine's.

When he had gone to call on her, he heard the old lady boarder shrieking like a banshee. He came running to her assistance and found her furious and red-faced, sputtering about "filth and damnation" as she stared at what looked like large playing cards fanned out on the kitchen table.

The minute she realized he had come into the room, she hurriedly collected them, but not before Drake had caught a glimpse of the objects she was trying to hide.

They were titillating photographs of scantily clad women.

The old lady slipped the pack into her apron pocket, and when she finally stopped fuming and composed herself, she muttered something about "that Denny leaving his filth around for God-fearing folk to find." When Drake told her he was calling on Catherine, she replied that Cat had ridden off to the Wright farm to tend sick cattle, but she would return later that afternoon.

Drake went home, but he couldn't stop thinking about those photographs.

They still aroused him. Tempting visions of that one saloon girl sitting on a patron's lap, her voluptuous bosom nearly spilling out of her camisole, flitted through his mind. He closed his eyes and moaned as he felt himself grow painfully hard.

When he finally got himself under control, he flung aside the unread paper, rose and went to the window. Those pictures had reminded him that he mustn't neglect his carnal desires while in Little Falls. He had denied himself far too long. A visit to One-Eyed Jack's would remedy that situation.

He wondered if Catherine and her "close friend" were lovers. The farm boy certainly treated her with a lover's possessiveness.

Drake slowly paced the study. No, Catherine Wills may have been familiar with rutting barnyard animals because of her work, but he sensed she herself had never coupled with a man.

It was time she did.

A plan took shape. He stopped his pacing, astonished by his own brilliance. He would take the tomboyish Cat, a veritable rough lump of coal, and transform her into a sparkling diamond, a paragon of refined and elegant femininity. Once she became a true lady, she'd never lower herself to doctor animals again. She'd leave the veterinary duties to Drake's father, who would be so appreciative, he'd order his two older sons to welcome their younger brother back to Boston. And find him another suitable position.

Drake smiled. He would turn Catherine into a lady to get back in his father's good graces, but he would seduce her for his own pleasure.

Perhaps if she pleased him enough, he'd even marry her and make his father's fondest wish come true by settling down.

Several days later, Michael relaxed at his corner table in One-Eyed Jack's and savored his cold beer.

He scanned the room. A few tables stood empty. Several men drinking at the bar had elbow room to spare. Cleo and Azalea drooped like thirsty flowers over their drinks. Not much action at Jack's on a Wednesday night.

Michael had just come from the boardinghouse, where Cat had tripped all over herself to keep from asking him about his Sunday dinner with Sally Wheeler and her mother. After their own supper, no one wanted to play cards, so Michael strolled over to the saloon.

He watched Ruby make her entrance. Tonight she lacked her usual verve and finesse. She walked rather than glided down the staircase, and leaned heavily against the bannister to steady herself. For once, she looked as though she didn't give a hoot who noticed her long, splendid legs beneath the short and saucy gold satin dress.

Ruby approached his table. Even paint and powder couldn't conceal the dark circles beneath her eyes or make her sallow skin glow. Michael rose.

"Slow night," she said, her teasing voice listless as she sat down.

He took his seat and studied her. "You don't look so good tonight, Ruby."

"Kind of you to notice." She closed her eyes and let out the breath she had been holding against some internal pain. "You'll have to forgive me if I'm not my usual bright and sparkling self tonight." She glanced over at Jack behind the bar. "The boss won't like it, but I'm going to call it a night."

"If Jack gives you any trouble, send him over to me."

Gratitude momentarily eased the weariness from Ruby's pinched features. "Ah, Cooper, how'd I ever let you get away?"

He knew better than to answer her.

The appearance of Drake Kendall in the saloon doorway momentarily distracted Michael. Cold, hard dislike shot through him. He couldn't help it. Not wanting to give Kendall the satisfaction of catching him staring, Michael looked around Jack's instead, to gauge others' reaction to the city slicker.

Jack's eye narrowed while he mentally measured the depth of the stranger's pockets. Cleo and Azalea perked up and stared, mentally measuring another part of his anatomy. The other men measured his mettle against their own. Most looked away.

Michael sipped his beer. "Have you met Drake Kendall? The doctor's son."

"Haven't had the pleasure, though I do business with his father on a weekly basis."

Michael raised his brows. "Can't fault the doctor's taste."

Ruby glanced back over her shoulder to where Kendall stood. He stared at her as if he'd seen her somewhere before, winked and let his gaze fall to her breasts. Ruby tugged at her bodice to cover a little more flesh. "I know all about his kind."

"Spoiled rotten? Full of himself?" Michael drank his beer. "And he's headed our way."

"Lucky us."

Kendall sauntered across the room as if he owned it, stopped at their table and towered over them, his great height casting them in shadow. "Good evening, Cooper." He removed his hat and smiled down at Ruby. "Ma'am."

She tilted her head back so she could look up at him. "Ruby Delight's the name. Welcome to One-Eyed Jack's, Mr.—?"

"Drake Kendall. I arrived a couple of days ago from Boston."

"I know your father," Ruby said. "Intimately."

Surprised flickered in the depths of Kendall's eyes, but that didn't deter him. He placed a proprietary hand on Ruby's bare shoulder. "If you'll excuse us, Cooper, I have some business to conduct with this little lady."

A look of resignation flickered across Ruby's tired features, and she took a deep, shuddering breath, marshaling all her energy to rise.

"The lady's mine for the evening," Michael said.

Ruby's dark eyes widened, but she stayed put.

Kendall's smile froze in place. He rested one hand on the table and leaned toward Michael. "It's early. Her kind can surely satisfy two paying customers in one night."

"Tonight it's just me. No one else."

Kendall straightened.

Ruby reached over and lifted his hand from her

shoulder. "You heard the man. I'm not available tonight."

White-hot fury twisted Kendall's face into an ugly mask. "I say you are." He grabbed Ruby's wrist and jerked her to her feet. "We're going upstairs. Now! Cooper, you can have her when I'm finished."

Michael jumped up so fast, his chair crashed back against the wall with a resounding bang.

"You deaf," he growled, "or just plain dumb? I said that the lady's mine for the evening."

From his threatening height, Kendall looked Michael up and down. "Who's going to stop me?" He turned and started to drag Ruby off.

Michael's heart raced and a great roar of anger welled up from deep inside. He was probably going to regret it in the morning, but he rounded the table and grabbed Kendall's shoulder. "I said, let her go!"

Before Michael could blink, Kendall dropped Ruby's wrist, whipped around with surprising agility for such a big man, and threw a punch. Michael ducked just in time and swung back, hitting Kendall in the stomach. With a woof of surprise, he folded over, giving Michael the chance to sock him in the face. When his fist connected, he thought his own knuckles would burst through the skin.

He stepped back.

But not fast enough.

Kendall's left fist shot out of nowhere, catching Michael a glancing blow high on the right cheekbone. Pain lacerated his face. Stars danced before his eyes. He staggered back against the table, pushed himself off, and flew at Kendall.

The giant came crashing down like a fallen tree, with Michael falling on top of him.

Suddenly hands grabbed his shirt and shoulders, pulling him off his opponent.

"Break it up, you two," came Jack's gruff command from somewhere off to his right. "I don't want my place busted up. If you want to fight, take it outside, or the sheriff'll let you cool off in jail."

Michael stood there breathing hard, with hands restraining him. Two men helped Kendall to his feet. He glared at Michael while he wiped the blood trickling from the corner of his mouth.

"Had enough?" Michael asked, breathing hard. God, he hoped so. He had endured enough pain for one day.

Kendall nodded reluctantly.

"Then apologize to the lady."

Kendall bit off every word resentfully. "I'm sorry for foisting my unwanted attentions on you, Miss Delight."

Ruby inclined her head in acknowledgment.

Kendall shook off the men who held him and staggered away like a whipped dog. Jack's patrons went back to their cards and drinking. The piano player launched into a sprightly tune.

Ruby placed a hand on Michael's arm. "I'd offer you one on the house if I weren't feeling so poorly. But I know you wouldn't take it."

"Oh, I think I've gotten myself into enough trouble for one evening." Wait'll this got around.

Drake Kendall staggered out of the saloon and leaned against one of the overhang's support pillars to catch his breath and stop the spinning in his head. His jaw ached and throbbed. The warm, metallic taste of iron made him want to retch.

Laughter wafted out of the saloon.

His cheeks burned. So the bumpkins were laughing at him, were they? Well, Cooper was going to pay for humiliating him, and pay dearly. A plan formed in his mind.

He stepped into the darkness and headed for the boardinghouse.

Cat sat on the porch swing, gently rocking and petting Ulysses, who lay curled in her lap. She had lost all track of time. Michael wasn't back from Jack's, and Ida May and Denny had already retired. Across the street, the lights went out in the Wheeler house.

"Wake up," Cat whispered to Ulysses, shaking him.

The cat rose and stepped off her lap, pausing to give her a disdainful green-eyed stare. He jumped down from the swing and sauntered back into the parlor, his plumed tail flicking.

Cat rose and leaned against the porch railing so she could look up at the stars. The night air smelled sweet and grassy, with a cool breeze blowing.

Michael occupied her thoughts. He sure had been testy when she stopped racing last week to talk to Drake. But he was always so polite to Sally Wheeler no matter how silly she was. Cat sighed in frustration. He saw her as nothing more than a friend, and he always would.

The front gate squeaked, followed by slow, measured footsteps.

Cat peered at the towering masculine shape walking up the path. "Drake?"

He climbed the porch steps and stepped into the weak rectangle of light from the open door.

Cat took one look at his bruised, cut jaw and dirty, disheveled clothes and gasped. "What happened to you?"

"I got in a fight at One-Eyed Jack's." He sounded tired and deflated. "I know it's late, but would you mind if I came in for a minute? My father is going to be furious with me, and I don't want to face him just yet."

"Come to the kitchen. Let's see if I can patch you up."

He followed her, his footsteps slow. Once in the kitchen, Cat poured water into a basin and fetched disinfectant and salve.

She sat Drake down and used a clean cloth to dab at the raw cut on his jaw. "Any teeth loose?"

Drake poked at his teeth with his tongue, winced, and shook his head.

"This should be a colorful shade of purple by tomorrow," she said. "When you get home, put some ice on it to reduce the swelling." She gently dabbed the salve onto the cut, then stood back and surveyed her handiwork. "What happened?"

He took a deep breath, propped his elbows on the table, and cradled his head in his hands. "I behaved like an ass. I approached this saloon girl about"—he blushed—"you know. Conducting business. When she refused, I became rather insistent."

Cat frowned and crossed her arms. She might not approve of the girls' line of work, but she didn't hold with treating them like dirt.

He looked up at her out of soulful eyes, as contrite as Bounder when she got caught getting into mischief. "I know it wasn't gentlemanly of me, but I was lonely. I miss Boston and all my friends. I thought a little female companionship would take the edge off." He groaned. "I don't blame Cooper for hitting me."

Cat's eyes widened. "Michael did this to you?"

Drake looked away. "I deserved it."

Cat sank down into the nearest chair. "I can't believe Michael would do something like this. He's not a violent man."

"It was my fault. I didn't know he and Ruby . . ." He shrugged. "He said she was his for the whole night."

Cat felt a hot knot of jealousy twist in her gut. So there was something going on between Michael and Ruby. Every time she teased him about it, he always told her his relationships with women weren't any of her business.

"Don't blame Cooper," Drake said.

"Oh, but I do," Cat replied. "Michael should've known better."

Drake pushed back his chair and hauled himself to his feet. "Time for me to go home and face the music." He reached for Cat's hand to kiss, though he winced when his lips brushed her knuckles. "You've been splendid. Thank you for patching me up. And for listening."

Cat showed him to the door and wished him good night. Then she returned to the porch swing and waited for Michael.

8

For the second time that night, the front gate squeaked open, followed by slow, hesitant footsteps. Cat could almost hear Michael creak and groan as he stiffly climbed up the porch steps. He paused, blinking as if the diffused light from the parlor window were as bright as the sun. He swayed and grabbed one of the overhang's support beams to steady himself.

Cat felt like strangling him as she rose from the swing and folded her arms. She had never seen such an awesome swelling as the one closing Michael's right eye into a slit.

"What are you doing back here so early?" she snapped. "I thought that you and Ruby would be keeping company for the entire evening."

He shook his head to clear it. "Where'd you get that notion?"

"Drake Kendall," she retorted coldly. "He came here about half an hour ago so I could patch him up after you beat the stuffings out of him."

"Cat, I—"

"Inside," Cat snapped, suppressing the desire to swat him herself. "I don't want all of Rose Street to hear what I've got to say."

She marched into the parlor, her simmering anger beginning to boil. Though the birdcage was covered for the night, Edgar Allan Crow sensed the tenseness in the room and rustled around. Ulysses, draped across the back of the sofa, raised his head and stared out of startled green eyes. Even a worried Bounder came into the parlor to whimper and sit pressed up tight against Cat's leg. She gave the dog a reassuring pat and sent her back to her pups. Then she turned to face Michael.

"I'm not spending the night with Ruby," he said gently.

She knew he wouldn't lie, but it didn't make any difference. "I don't give a damn who you spend the night with, Michael Cooper."

"I only said that to keep Kendall away from her. It didn't do any good. The bastard started dragging her off, and when I tried to stop him, he—"

"I don't care who started it." Cat felt anger roaring through her veins, whirling around her like the biting January wind, putting her jumbled feelings into precise words. "You should've known better."

"What are you so all fired up about?" he demanded. "It was only a fight. I've been in fights before."

God, men could be so stupid!

"*Only* a fight?" She gritted her teeth to keep from screaming so she wouldn't wake her boarders. "You could've hurt Drake seriously. You could've broken his nose or his jaw. Damn you, Michael Boswell Cooper, you could've killed him! And over a saloon girl!"

Michael grew very still. "Hold it right there. Ruby

may be a saloon girl, but she's still a human being worthy of respect. Kendall tried to force his unwanted attentions on her. I'm surprised at you for defending him."

Cat's cheeks burned. "I'm not excusing his actions. But he admitted he behaved badly and said he was sorry. I'm sure he'll never do it again." She raised her brows. "The man makes one mistake and you've got to beat him senseless for it?"

"I didn't beat him senseless. And roughing up a woman is a big mistake in my book."

"You just have to take one look at Drake's jaw to see he's paid for that moment of blind stupidity. In spades."

Michael snorted in derision. "I see Kendall didn't waste any time running over here to tattle."

"I'm sure he realized he made a mistake and he didn't want me to hold it against him."

"Why would he care what you think?"

"Maybe because he values my opinion."

"No, I think there's more to it than that."

"Such as?"

"Getting even with me."

Cat's temper flared like a brush fire in August. "You're just sore because Drake told me you intended to spend the night with Ruby."

His temper matched hers. "Damn it, Willie, I said that I wasn't spending the night with Ruby. I haven't slept with her since—" He stopped.

Pain socked Cat in the heart. So he had gone upstairs with Ruby, and been her lover. She had suspected, but was never certain. He'd always refused to admit it when she teased him. Until now.

"Willie," he said softly, taking a step toward her, "don't look at me that way."

"What way?" She sucked her lower lip to keep it

from trembling. "Like I'm hurt? Disappointed? Well, I am."

When he reached for her, she stepped back. "I think you'd better find somewhere else to sleep tonight, Cooper. Maybe One-Eyed Jack's. Or Sally's."

He sighed. "I don't want to go to Jack's, and I've never slept over at Sally's. I want to stay here."

Cat marched over to the front door and stood beside it. "You beat up Drake Kendall over a saloon girl. Maybe she should be the one to tend your wounds."

His eyes turned to ice. "Maybe she should."

He stalked out without a backward glance.

Cat couldn't sleep.

She lay on her side, her head pillowed on her folded arm. She watched a long rectangle of silvery moonlight inch across the carpet. She listened to the silence. The darkness weighed her down, as heavy as her thoughts.

She flung back the covers and rose, dislodging Ulysses, who lay tightly curled at the foot of her bed. She walked over to the window and parted the curtains. She looked out at her mother's overgrown and neglected herb garden, but all she saw was Michael's battered face.

Damn him! When she tried to tell him she loved him, he dismissed her feelings as joking. But when another man insulted Ruby, Michael rushed to her defense.

Ulysses suddenly leaped up and sat balanced like an acrobat on the windowsill, his mysterious eyes staring into Cat's.

She stroked his head. "Who am I trying to fool? Michael doesn't think of me romantically, and he never will. Not when he can have his pick of women like Ruby Delight."

Or Sally.

Ulysses butted his head against Cat's hand, demanding more attention. She petted him harder.

"He thinks of me as a friend. *Friend*," she scoffed. "How I'm beginning to hate that word."

Good old Cat, as familiar and comfortable as an old shirt.

Tears stung her eyes. "Why am I wasting my time mooning over Michael Cooper? I want him, but he doesn't want me. Time to move on before I really get hurt."

She wiped away her tears with the back of her hand. "I'm going to save myself a heap of heartache while I still have a heart left to save."

She returned to bed. Judging from the dull pain in that troublesome organ, she hoped she wasn't too late.

The only welcome Michael got when he opened the door to the small barn behind the boardinghouse was a soft, sleepy whicker from Rascal.

He took the lantern off its peg and lit it, illuminating the mare staring at him over the stall door.

"No offense, honey," he murmured, looking around, "but you're not my idea of the perfect bed partner."

She snorted and turned away.

Michael eased himself down on a pile of straw, extinguished the lantern, and closed his eyes. Sleep wouldn't come. He couldn't stop thinking of Cat.

A whirlwind of emotion swept through him, bewilderment, anger, resentment that she'd defended Kendall. A man who had forced his attentions on an unwilling woman.

What had gotten into her? She had turned into a stranger almost overnight.

Michael shifted in his straw bed, trying to make

himself more comfortable. He knew the reason for Cat's anger.

He groaned. He'd give his right arm if he could take back his heedless words about him and Ruby. He hadn't intended to cause Cat such pain.

He laced his fingers behind his head and stared up at the darkness. Why had she defended Kendall, a man she barely knew, over Michael, whom she'd known all her life? Her defection stung.

He rolled over on his side and winced as his shiner ached and throbbed. Straw jabbed at his neck, making it itch.

He swore and rose. He wasn't spending another second here. Maybe he should rent an empty bed at Jack's. He discounted that at once. Cat would surely assume the worst.

He asked himself why it mattered as he fumbled his way out of the dark barn and back to the boardinghouse.

He discovered that Cat wasn't sleeping either.

"What do you want, Cooper?" she said the minute he opened her bedroom door and tiptoed inside.

He sat down on the edge of the bed and looked over at her sitting there, her knees drawn up to her chin. Even though he couldn't see her clearly in the darkness, he sensed her anger clear enough.

"I'm here because your barn is damned uncomfortable," he said.

"I've heard that Jack's beds are real comfortable, especially with a soft, willing woman in them."

"I've never known you to be so hard, Willie. Or so cold."

She rose to light the lamp on her bedside table, then put on her robe. She turned to face him, fire still smoldering in her eyes. "I've got my reasons."

He rose to stand before her. "You know I've had

my share of women. I've never lied to you about that. Ruby was one of them, but that was a long time ago, and I haven't been with her since, I swear." When Cat made no comment, he ran his hand through his hair in frustration. "I can't change the past, Willie, not even for you."

She stared down at the floor for what seemed like an eternity. Then she looked at him. "No, I guess you can't."

She reached up and turned his face to the light. "Is that shiner paining you bad?"

"Hurts like hell."

"Come out to the kitchen and I'll put something on it. Then you can sleep in the spare room."

As she walked past, he reached out, grasped her hand, and brought it to his lips. "Friends?"

Her lips curved in a faint smile. "Friends."

Denny Dunleavy heard about the fistfight the following morning at breakfast. He waited until evening to go over to One-Eyed Jack's because he knew Ruby wouldn't be up and around until dusk fell and her customers came out. As she had once told him saucily, she never saw the sun.

Michael hadn't come to town today, so Denny knew he wouldn't be at the saloon. He needed time to heal that great purple shiner, and Cat needed time to cool off.

Denny ordered one beer that he would never finish, went to sit at Michael's corner table, and waited for Ruby to make her entrance.

Watching her glide down the staircase, he could see that whatever malady had been plaguing her yesterday appeared to be gone tonight. That gladdened him. He hated to see her in pain.

First she made her rounds, chatting and joking suggestively with the men at the bar, wishing several others playing poker good luck, stopping at every table to see who needed drinks and who wanted to go upstairs.

Then she stopped at his table. She smelled of the saloon, a mixture of smoke, whiskey, and a musky, heavy perfume that wasn't altogether unpleasant.

"Buy you a drink?" he asked.

"Sure." She signaled to Jack, and sat down.

Jack brought her watered whiskey and took Denny's money.

"How are you feeling tonight?"

She gave him an arch look. "Back to my old saucy self." The laughter went out of her eyes. "I'm sorry Michael had to get hurt defending the likes of me."

Anger flared deep in Denny's breast. He hated it when she denigrated herself because of her profession. "He's not the kind of man to walk away from a fight, especially when a woman's being threatened."

She drained half her glass, obviously uncomfortable with the direction their conversation was taking. "We all like the pictures you took."

He smiled slightly. "I had excellent subjects."

Puzzlement flickered across her features. "You're an odd one, Denny Dunleavy. Most folk don't give a damn about us whores. They'd just as soon spit on us as give us the time of day."

"Most folk don't separate what you do from who you are," he said.

She raised her finely arched brows. "And you do?"

"Yes, I do. Taking pictures taught me that. The camera captures an image, and tells us something about the person or object we photograph. But it's a limited story, restricted only to what the subject wants us to see."

Denny could see his words intrigued her, even

though she resisted. In the time he'd known her, he'd come to realize that Ruby Delight didn't wish anyone to see beyond her paint and powder and short, flouncy dresses, the glittering picture she presented to the world.

Sometimes she talked of her horrible past with her abusive husband. Then she would regret the impulse and fall silent.

"Take you, for example." He watched her squirm just a little. "If you look at the picture I took of you, you'll see a woman who appears to enjoy sitting on a man's lap in her unmentionables. Maybe she does, but maybe she doesn't."

"She does," Ruby said lightly, rising. "Thanks for the drink, but I have to get back to work. Unless—?"

"No, I won't go upstairs with you. What I'd like better is to take you to the Fourth of July festivities."

"Did I hear you right?" At least she didn't laugh. "You want to take *me* to the Fourth?"

"Yes. Will you go?"

"Why not? I've always wanted to see daylight."

He smiled and watched her saunter off, her full hips swaying suggestively.

Ruby watched his reflection in the big mirror over the bar as she bantered with several of her regular customers tossing down one drink after another. Though she appeared to be listening attentively, and responding, her thoughts were on Denny Dunleavy.

She still couldn't believe he'd asked her to the Fourth. No man had ever asked her out to any public gathering. She was a whore, a woman who sold her body, not a respectable woman like Cat Wills.

Ruby glanced into the mirror and caught Denny watching her. He made her uneasy with all his messy, mystifying talk of images and separating people from what they do. But at the same time, his genuine interest touched her deeply.

One of the men at the bar leaned over and said he was ready. Ruby slipped her arm through his and headed for the stairs.

She glanced over at Denny's table, but he was gone.

Two weeks later in the middle of June, heartache was the last thing on Cat's mind as she slogged across Gideon Wright's waterlogged field, the mud squishing and sucking at her boots with each step. She glanced worriedly at the low, leaden sky, hoping they'd seen the last of the torrential rains plaguing the area for the last three days.

"You going to the Fourth of July festivities with anyone?" Gideon asked Cat as he trudged along beside her. He sniffed and wiped his red, runny nose with his shirtsleeve, leaving a dark streak.

"I'm going with Drake Kendall," she replied. He had asked her just that morning.

Drake's invitation had set her rocking back on her heels. She and Michael had always gone to the Fourth together. But he had never actually *asked* her. And they had never gone as a couple.

Cat had almost refused Drake, seeing her acceptance of his invitation as a betrayal of Michael. Then Sally Wheeler sashayed by, all sweet and frilly and demure. Cat decided it was high time she found a man for herself.

When she'd accepted Drake's invitation, his handsome face lit up with pure delight. Cat's guilt and misgivings about Michael vanished into thin air.

Now she wondered how Michael would react when she told him this afternoon.

"That's too bad." Gideon cleared his throat. "I was thinking of asking you myself."

Cat glanced at him in astonishment. Two invitations in one day. She chuckled to herself. She was becoming a regular Sally Wheeler.

Of the two men, she vastly preferred Drake. Gideon was almost as old as her father, and his breath often smelled like the floor of a stable. The randy old rooster had already buried two wives and was looking for a third to share his bed and his brood.

Cat had no desire to inherit thirteen wild, unkempt children and service their father in her spare time.

"Sorry," she said. "I'm spoken for." And she always would be as far as Gideon Wright was concerned.

They came to a cow, and the farmer slipped a halter on her so Cat could examine her for any signs of anthrax. Gideon's cattle had been vaccinated in the spring, and Cat checked them to make certain the disease didn't develop.

"You riding in the big race?" he asked.

"Sure am. And this time, I'll win."

When Cat finished, Gideon let that cow go and moved on to another. He held its head while Cat examined the animal.

How times had changed. Maddy Wills had used herbs to heal sick animals with wide and varying results, but her daughter used vaccines to prevent deadly diseases.

"Isn't Dr. Kendall supposed to be a vet?" Gideon asked.

"Yes." Cat looked up at him. "Why?"

"Jenny, my youngest, has been feeling poorly, and Dr. Kendall came out here to tend to her. While he was at it, I asked him to take a look at my herd." Gideon frowned and scratched his head. "At first, he acted real reluctant. Then he agreed. He checked a few of the cows, but he didn't check them like you're doing now."

Cat finished her examination and straightened. "I don't know what to tell you, Gideon. As far as I know, Dr. Kendall is a qualified vet."

Gideon let the cow go, and Cat stepped back while the cow mooed and ambled back to the herd.

"I haven't heard any of the other farmers complain about him," Cat said. Yet they still kept calling on Cat to doctor their animals.

Gideon ran the back of his hand across his running nose. "All I know is that I've never lost a cow, thanks to your doctoring. You may be a woman, but you're a damn good vet."

"Thanks for the vote of confidence," Cat said.

She finished examining the rest of Gideon's herd, then left to ride over to the Cooper place.

"I hope this dries out before Saturday," Michael muttered as he led the way to the barn's new addition.

In the stable yard, the horses' comings and goings had churned the wet, loose earth into a quagmire. Jace stood washing mud from Gus's legs and belly after Clementine had returned from visiting a sick neighbor. Cat heard Belle yell at the dogs to stay out of the house with their dirty paws. Cat looked down at her own boots caked with drying mud.

She glanced up at Michael. His shiner had long disappeared, and he was back to his former self. He never mentioned the fight. He was cordial to Drake. He still treated Cat like a friend.

She wondered what he would say when she told him that Drake had invited her to the Fourth. And that she had accepted.

She matched her stride to Michael's. "If it doesn't,

I may as well not enter the race at all. Rascal hates running in mud.''

"So does Rogue. He may've won last year, but in mud, he'll come in dead last.''

He opened the door for Cat to walk through, then he followed her and closed it.

She looked around at the dozen extra box stalls, some already occupied. "Nice job. You'll be able to add even more broodmares to your stock.''

"We needed the room.''

He showed Cat to a stall where a chestnut yearling filly stood with her head drooping. Michael accompanied Cat inside and patted the filly's neck to soothe her while Cat conducted her examination.

When she finished listening to the chestnut's heart with the stethoscope, Cat said, "Did you know that Denny's asked Ruby to go to the Fourth of July festivities with him?''

"Denny and Ruby?'' Michael's eyes widened in surprise. "That's news to me. Is she going with him?''

"He told me that she is.'' Cat took a deep breath. It was now or never. "And I'm going with Drake.''

"What did you say?''

She ran her hand down her patient's foreleg. "I said I'm going to the Fourth with Drake. He invited me just this morning, and I said yes.''

Silence.

Feeling suddenly awkward, she straightened and faced him. Her heart sank when she saw nothing but mild surprise on Michael's face. No disappointment. No jealousy. No regret. Nothing whatsoever to give her second thoughts about accepting Drake's invitation.

He stroked the filly's face. "You've only known Kendall for about a month.''

"That's long enough for me to know that I like him."

"Enough to go to the Fourth with him?"

"Sure. He enjoys my company, and I enjoy his. I like hearing him talk about the books he's read, and the places he's been. Paris, London. Do you know they have veterinary colleges there? My father wanted to go to one, but his family couldn't send him."

"I remember him saying that."

"And I like hearing Drake talk about Boston, and what life is like back East. It's so different from out here." She lifted the filly's hoof. "He's very smart and worldly, you know."

Michael shifted. "I don't recall you ever saying that you liked wordliness in a man."

"That's because I never met a worldly man before. There sure aren't any of them in Little Falls, are there?"

"No, there aren't."

Cat went to the filly's head and listened to her breathing. She stepped back. "She's got catarrh all right. With the weather being so cool and wet, I'm not surprised." She advised Michael to feed the filly hot mash and cover her with a warm blanket.

As Cat and Michael left the stall and he closed the door behind them, she noticed that he was unusually quiet, with a line of preoccupation between his brows. He seemed a million miles away. She waited, wondering if he was going to say anything else about her going to the holiday celebration with Drake, but he didn't.

They left the barn and walked into the muddy stable yard. Jace must have finished washing Gus, for the big Hanoverian was gone. Now Jace was struggling to lead a dancing, wild-eyed iron gray stallion that Cat had never seen before into the barn. As she and Michael stopped to watch the battle between man and beast, the horse flung back his head, screamed, and reared, flailing the air with his hooves.

"Don't just stand there," Jace hollered to Michael. "Come help me."

Michael ran to his father's aid. Cat turned and headed back to the house, intending to visit Clementine and Belle before returning to Little Falls.

She hadn't taken more than a few steps, when she heard the thunder of hoofbeats and Michael yell, "Cat! Look out!"

She turned to see that the stallion had broken free and was bearing down on her like a runaway train.

With the survival instincts of a cat being chased by a coonhound, she sprang out of the horse's way and dived for the ground, her arms outstretched to break her fall. She landed face down in the muck with a disgusting plop.

The ground shook as the stallion galloped past and veered away, mud spraying from his flying hooves.

Cat spat out gritty mud and tried to keep from retching. Before she could rise, strong hands grabbed her beneath the arms and hoisted her to her feet.

"You okay?" Michael asked, wide-eyed and white-faced.

"Damn that son of a bitch," Jace said. "Look away for one second, and he takes off. He didn't stomp on you anywhere, did he?"

"He just missed me." Cat held her trembling arms away from her sides and looked down at herself in chagrin. Wet, stinking mud and dung soaked and covered her clean shirt and trousers. She could feel the cold, wet ooze coating face, neck and bare forearms with a thick paste.

"Just look at me." She wrinkled her nose. "Just *smell* me. I can't go back to town like this."

"I'm real sorry this happened." Jace swore a blue streak. "Wait until I catch that flea-bitten bag of bones." He stormed off after his runaway horse.

Michael reached for Cat's arm, then his hand fell back to his side. "Come back to the house. You can bathe and leave your clothes to be washed. I have a shirt and trousers you can borrow."

"Belle'll kill me if I track mud into her clean house. I'll change in the men's quarters, and use the outside shower."

"Okay." Michael turned and headed for the house.

Cat wasn't surprised to find the men's quarters empty. Those who worked for Jace Cooper didn't spend their afternoons napping in the three sets of bunk beds pushed against the walls.

She quickly stripped off her wet, odious clothes, grabbed a clean towel, and went to the back door. Jace had installed a makeshift shower outside for the men.

Cat peered out the door. No one was around in the back. She slipped into the stall and closed the door. She stepped under the water collector and pulled the cord. She shivered and gasped as cold rainwater sluiced down on her, washing away the mud and muck.

A minute later, Michael rounded the back of the bunkhouse, and stopped in his tracks when he noticed Cat in the outdoor shower stall.

He knew he should leave. He knew he shouldn't watch her. But he did anyway, as she opened the stall door.

The sight of her took his breath away. She stood turned toward him, drying her face, the towel covering her eyes so she didn't noticed him watching.

She held Michael spellbound. Her lean, pale body appeared softer and more curved when not hidden by shapeless shirts and baggy trousers. Small, full breasts begged for the touch of his hands, and the large, rosy nipples his mouth.

God give him strength. He closed his eyes and breathed deeply. No use. He became painfully aroused anyway.

Michael's eyes flew open and he stepped back behind the bunkhouse so she wouldn't catch him spying.

He turned and went up to the front door.

"Willie," he called through the crack in the door, "I've brought those dry clothes."

"Thanks," she called back from inside, blissfully unaware that he'd been watching her. "Just set them down. After I dry off and dress, and I'll be out of here."

He told her he'd meet her back at the house, and left.

Later that evening after supper, Michael stood alone on the front porch in the gathering darkness, listening to the faint, occasional neigh coming from the depths of the stables as the horses settled in for the night.

He couldn't stop thinking about Cat.

When she had come back to the house after showering, wearing his shirt with the sleeves rolled up to her elbows, his fingers itched to unbutton it. Innocently remarking how Michael's trousers fit her so perfectly, Cat would have been shocked to learn that he wanted to slide those same trousers off her slender hips and down her long legs. Then he wanted to explore every inch of her.

Michael took a deep breath and ran his hand through his hair. He never should have spied on her. He felt lower than a worm.

Now she was going to the Fourth festivities with Drake Kendall.

Why would a level-headed woman like Cat want to go with someone as slick and full of himself as Drake Kendall? He could see Sally Wheeler falling for the pompous, flashy Easterner, but not Cat.

Michael watched as a shooting star streaked across the night sky and disappeared. Truth be told, he was a little miffed and more than a little hurt. He and Cat had always attended the Fourth together. They were best friends. As close as brother and sister.

Sister?

As of this afternoon, his thoughts about Cat had turned decidedly unbrotherly.

9

CAT FOUND CHAOS REIGNING IN THE BOARDING-house the morning of the Fourth.

She walked into the parlor in time to see Ulysses spring eagerly at the crow's cage, his triumphant claws connecting and holding. Edgar Allan beat his wings against the bars in terror and screeched, "Cat! Cat!"

Then Ulysses lost his tenuous grip, fell to the floor with a yowl of consternation, and landed on his feet. He looked disgusted with himself.

Cat stamped her foot and shooed him away. "You've already had your breakfast. You leave that bird alone!"

No sooner did the opportunistic feline streak off than all eight of Bounder's pups, who were now getting into more trouble than Tommy Granger and Buster Blick combined, came racing into the parlor like a stampeding herd of cattle. They almost collided with Ulysses, who arched his back and hissed before turning tail and running to hide high atop the piano.

With Ulysses no longer a threat, the pups whined and wiggled around Cat's legs. Several grabbed at her trousers with their sharp teeth and played tug-of-war. The remainder shoved and crawled over each other as they vied to be petted.

Cat knelt down and rationed out attention, trying not to miss one eager, squirming body. They leaped and nipped. "You're all getting too big and too rambunctious. Time for you and your momma to go in the barn and give us all a little peace and quiet."

When she rose and walked into the kitchen for breakfast, she found a sour-faced Ida May mopping up a puddle and muttering dire threats about a sack, a rock, and a river.

Cat stared at her, aghast. "You wouldn't!"

One of the lop-eared pups trotted over to Ida May, sat down on his haunches, cocked his head, and stared up at her out of beseeching brown eyes.

"Oh, who could resist that cute little face?" Ida May said, relenting and reaching down to pet him. She received a lick on her hand before the pup trotted off to join the others, who had raced to the other side of the kitchen and their waiting mother. "Of course I wouldn't harm the little devils. But—"

"But you've reached the end of your rope." Cat raised her hands in surrender. "Time to get them out of here before they tear the house apart."

"Unless *you* want to mop up after them," Ida May said, sticking her mop back in the bucket.

Once Cat got the dogs settled in the barn, she returned to find a calmer Ida May back at the stove, taking mouthwatering biscuits out of the oven and frying sizzling bacon and eggs in the cast-iron skillet.

Denny sat drinking coffee at the table. Cat wished him good morning, poured herself a cup, and joined him.

His Irish eyes twinkled. "Maybe this year they'll have a prize for the most unlikely couple."

"You and Ruby would win hands down," Cat said.

"Oh, I don't know about that," he retorted with a teasing smile. "I'll bet the good citizens of Little Falls think you and Kendall are more of an unlikely pair than me and Ruby."

Cat didn't return his smile. "I resent that. What's so odd about Drake asking me to go with him?"

"For one thing, everybody's used to seeing you and Michael together."

"Then maybe it's time everybody got used to seeing me with someone else."

Ever since Cat had told Michael she'd be attending the festivities with Drake, a gap as wide as a ditch had grown between them. He treated Cat with an uncharacteristic coolness and reticence. Only when Cat had returned the shirt and trousers she had borrowed from him, along with a batch of Ida May's molasses cookies as a thank-you, did Michael's icy reserve melt and disappear.

"For another," Denny went on, "Kendall is a big-city fella, and you're a country girl."

"So he's more polished and worldly. That doesn't mean we won't get along." Cat sipped her coffee. "Sometimes people who are different get along better than people who are too much alike. Look at you and Ruby."

Denny saw that he had riled her past the point of good-natured teasing, so he backed off. "Touché, Miss Wills."

"Why are you taking her anyway?"

"For the same reason you're going with Kendall. I enjoy her company. You may not think so because of her profession, but Ruby's a very interesting, complex woman."

"I don't know her that well, but if you say so. . . ."

Denny rose and walked over to the stove, where he snagged a biscuit from Ida May, receiving a tap on the back of his hand. He returned to the table and buttered the biscuit. "I discover something unexpected about Ruby every time I talk to her."

Cat rose to help herself to her own biscuit. "The only times I ever talked to any of the saloon girls were when they came to my father's office for medical care. They were always nice to me, but a lot of the townsfolk disapprove."

Denny washed down a mouthful of biscuit with a sip of coffee. "Everyone's so quick to judge."

Cat shrugged. "I've never known any of the saloon girls to come to town celebrations. They usually sleep during the day."

"Well, I invited her, and she said she wanted to go with me."

"People are always looking for something new to gossip about." Ida May set a basket of biscuits in the middle of the table. "They'll talk for a while, but then everyone will forget that Denny Dunleavy escorted Ruby Delight to the Fourth. They'll all move on to something else."

Cat gingerly plucked another steaming hot biscuit from the basket and buttered it. After word had gotten around that she and Michael wouldn't be attending the Fourth together, everyone from Heck Hechinger to Buster Blick felt compelled to comment. Sally Wheeler and several other of the town's eligible beauties expressed their astonishment to Cat's face, but they couldn't hide the expectant, predatory gleam in their eyes. Yet to Cat's knowledge, Michael hadn't asked anyone else.

"I know I'm getting damn sick of being asked why I'm not going to the Fourth with Michael," she said.

"It's not over yet," Denny said, handing Ida May his plate for bacon and eggs. "Everyone will be watching us like hawks today."

Cat rolled her eyes. "Just what I need."

After cooking all morning, Ida May finally sat down to eat. She looked at Cat. "You want me to make you a box lunch for the auction?"

"You never made me one before."

The box lunch auction, one of the highlights of the day, gave all the single gents in town the opportunity to share a meal with an eligible single lady while raising money for church and community projects.

"That's because you've always eaten a picnic lunch with the Coopers." Ida May spread her napkin across her lap. "But this year, you're going with another gentleman. I thought you'd like to give him a chance to bid on your box lunch."

"No need to have Drake bid," Cat said. "I'll just pack a picnic lunch and share it with him."

"The auction could get really interesting if Michael and Drake got into a bidding war," Denny said.

"Or maybe Michael'll win the horse race and bid the entire purse for some lucky lady," Ida May added, "just like his father did one Harvest Festival."

Everyone knew the story of how Jace Cooper wooed the wealthy, socially prominent Clementine Boswell by bidding his entire hundred-dollar purse to eliminate any competition for her box lunch. His grand gesture not only won the lady's heart and hand, but also turned Jace into a local legend.

"I remember that Harvest Festival like it was yesterday," Ida May said, her eyes glazing as she looked back across the years. "Your mother made a box lunch and decorated it with green ribbons that matched her eyes. Poor child. She went to so much trouble, and had such high expectations. But none of the men bid on it. Not one. She had such a hot temper, you see. Most men were afraid of her."

"And with good reason," Cat said. "When Mama loses her temper, you don't want to be anywhere near her."

Ida May's eyes retained their faraway look. "I remember the three loudmouthed louts who made fun of her that day. Who'd want to share a lunch with Mad Maddy, they wanted to know. Maybe she put pepper in the food. First she was crushed. Then she got angry. She took back her box lunch and walked off the fairgrounds with her head held high, like a queen."

"Leave it to Mama to show 'em," Cat said.

"What happened next?" Denny asked, though he already knew, having heard the story many times since coming to Little Falls.

"Dr. Paul had intended to bid on Maddy's box lunch all along," Ida May said, "but he got held up delivering a calf, and later, someone's baby. When he finally got back to the fairgrounds, the auction was long over. Maddy had disappeared. He found her though, and they shared her box lunch."

Ida May sopped up the last of the egg yolk on her plate with a piece of biscuit, and popped it in her mouth. Her gaze grew wistful. "It seems just like yesterday."

Cat rose and placed an arm around her friend's shoulders. "With all this talk of romance, maybe you should donate a box lunch yourself. Everyone for miles around knows what a good cook you are, and there are a lot of hungry widowers out there."

Ida May turned a flustered shade of pink. "Catherine Wills, stop your joshing this instant. No man is going to want to eat lunch with me."

Cat winked at Denny over Ida May's head. "That's what my mother thought."

A knock on the front door made Cat jump.

She looked at Ida May across the kitchen table where they had been packing three apple pies in baskets to take to the fairgrounds.

"It must be Drake," she said. Why did her throat suddenly feel so dry? Why was her heart beating faster?

"Don't just stand there." Ida May made a shooing motion with her hands. "Go let him in."

As Cat walked down the hall toward the parlor, she suddenly felt compelled to glance in a mirror. She didn't know why. She looked the same. She wore one of her father's old shirts with the sleeves rolled up, and a clean pair of trousers. Her curly hair hadn't grown down to her shoulders overnight. She did, however, tie a festive red bandanna around her neck so she'd look more dressed up.

As she entered the parlor, the crow swung on his perch. "Midnight dreary . . . midnight dreary."

"Can't you tell time? It's nine o'clock on a beautiful Wednesday morning."

She opened the front door to find Drake standing there. He truly looked like a handsome big-city fellow, with a dark blue frock coat so well tailored that it fit his broad shoulders without a trace of snugness. His matching vest and striped cravat looked more suited to the streets of Boston or St. Louis than a humble country Fourth of July celebration. But he could always remove them to run in the men's footrace or enter the greased pig chase.

"You're right on time," Cat said, opening the door.

"Good morning." Drake removed his hat and ducked his head to avoid hitting it on the door frame.

Once inside, he stood there looking Cat up and down out of narrowed, critical eyes.

"Why are you staring at me?" She resisted the urge to check if her trousers were unbuttoned. "Is something wrong?"

He smiled apologetically. "Forgive me, but I thought you'd be all dressed up."

"I always dress like this."

"Isn't today a special occasion? Shouldn't you be wearing a dress like the other ladies?"

"I never wear a dress," Cat replied in surprise. "I don't even own one." She used to wear plain calico dresses as a little girl, but had stopped when she grew older and the skirts just got in her way.

His blond brows rose. "Never?"

Cat fidgeted under his scrutiny. Her cheeks felt warm. Why did she feel so uncomfortable and embarrassed about the fact that she wasn't wearing a dress? Her parents had never made a big deal about her choice of attire. Neither had Michael.

"I'm a vet," she explained. "It's easier to ride around the county and care for animals when I dress like this." Not that she'd ever tried wearing a dress on her rounds. Come to think of it, her mother did. Yet she never encouraged her daughter to do the same.

Drake looked disappointed. "Well, if you don't own a dress, there's nothing we can do about it now. I just thought you'd look even prettier in one."

Prettier? He thought she was pretty? Cat felt her cheeks grow hot again. Now she wished she had paid more attention to her attire.

Drake smiled and kissed her hand. When he raised his head, he stared deeply into her eyes. "I would so look forward to seeing you in a dress, Catherine."

She felt gooseflesh raise in a tingling ripple on her

arms. "Then I guess I'll just have to go get me one."

She had always thought that wearing a dress would be such a bother. She still remembered the first time she had worn one, tripped over it, and fell flat on her face. But seeing the anticipation in Drake's eyes made her wonder if attempting to wear a dress might not be worth a second try.

She took a minute to retrieve her wide-brimmed felt hat, then they left.

The minute Cat and Drake stepped off the porch steps, he offered her his arm as if she were the belle of the ball. Cat slipped her hand through his arm and together they walked down the brick walk.

Much to Cat's delight, none other than Sally Wheeler herself came gliding down her own walk. She paused to stare at Drake opening the boarding-house's squeaking gate for Cat as if she were a grand lady. Sally looked as though she couldn't believe her eyes, but Cat smiled and nodded at her anyway, savoring victory. Sally nodded back, but hurried off, obviously not wanting to join them for their stroll to the fairgrounds.

Drake looked around as they walked down Rose Street, which was becoming crowded with riders on horseback, carriages, and wagons.

"What do people do at your Fourth of July celebration?"

"There's something for everyone. In the morning, there's a spelling bee for the children, and a pie contest."

"A pie contest?"

"To see who makes the tastiest pies. Ida May's won it for two years in a row."

She saw Drake fight back a smirk. "That must be quite an honor."

"It is." Cat bristled. Was he making fun of Ida May?

"Then there's a bow-and-arrow-shooting contest, a footrace for the men, and a three-legged race." She looked up at him. "You entering the men's foot race?"

"I wasn't planning to," was his dry reply.

"Oh, come on, Drake, you've got to! Your legs are so long, you're sure to win."

"I'm hardly dressed for a footrace, Catherine."

"Yeah, I guess you're not." She glanced at his spotless, perfectly tied silk cravat. "You're not exactly dressed for the greased pig chase, either."

"Dare I ask . . . what's a greased pig chase?"

Cat looked at him aghast. "You never heard of a greased pig chase?"

"I'm from Boston, remember?"

After Cat explained, Drake raised his head so that he looked down at her from an even loftier height. His lip curled. "I refuse to ruin my good clothes just to amuse a bunch of farmers."

She supposed she couldn't blame him. He wasn't used to their small-town ways. "Maybe they'd give you the honor of judging the prettiest baby or the ugliest dog."

Drake's eyes widened. His shoulders shook. His lips twitched from the effort to keep from laughing. He failed and let out a loud guffaw. "There's actually a contest to choose the *ugliest dog*?"

"Sure is. It's fun, and everybody has a good laugh."

"You could always enter your dog."

Cat crossed her arms. "Bounder is not an ugly dog."

"Sorry. I didn't mean to insult you." Drake's own laughter died and he shook his head. "You people sure scrape the bottom of the barrel when it comes to amusements. In Boston, there are so many exciting things to see and do."

"Like what?"

"The beautiful Public Gardens, where hundreds of red and yellow tulips grow in the spring. My family would all dress up in their Sunday best and go walking there after church. Then we'd all go for a ride in the swan boats."

"What are they?"

"They're boats shaped and painted to look like swans, and they take people for a ride around the huge pond. Then my father would always take my brothers and me to the theater every other week, and to Symphony."

No greased pigs. No ugliest dog. No women in trousers.

Cat fell silent. For the first time in her life, she felt ashamed of her simple country life and the amusements that she, her friends, and neighbors enjoyed.

"Then in the summer," Drake continued as they walked past the post office where Cat's mother had once worked, "we'd always go to Manchester-by-the-Sea, a pretty little seaside town north of Boston." He looked down at her. "Have you ever seen the ocean, Catherine?"

"Never." Now she wished she had visited Grandpapa Wills when he invited her to come east for the summer. She had been only thirteen at the time, too scared of leaving her family to make the long journey alone.

"The Atlantic is quite majestic. The ocean is never still, always moving, never quiet. The waves lap against the sandy shore and rattle the rocks with a soothing rhythm of their own." He tilted back his head and stared up at the cloudless blue sky. "It's the sweetest music you'll ever hear."

"Maybe I will get to hear it someday."

He looked down at her with what Cat would've sworn was promise in his eyes. "I'm sure you will."

• • •

The fields south of town that served as the fairgrounds teemed with people, but Michael, riding beside the Cooper carriage, scanned the crowd for the one man towering over everyone. Once he found Drake Kendall, surely Cat would be nearby.

He couldn't see either of them.

"Damn!" he muttered.

"Something wrong?" his mother asked, regarding him from beneath her ivory-handled sunshade.

"I was looking for Leach and his bay," he said, not meeting Clementine's too perceptive gaze. "Rumor has it he's the one to beat, and I'd like to look him over."

Jace, handling the team, made a derisive noise. "I wouldn't worry about Leach's bay. Our horses can run rings around that fleabag."

"It always pays to check out the competition," Michael said, still scanning the crowd. He turned in the saddle. "I'm going to get Rogue settled, then join the festivities."

"Be sure to have a good time," his mother said. It sounded like an order.

They drove off.

Once Michael tied Rogue in the grassy shade with the other horses entered in the race, he strolled around the fairgrounds searching for Cat.

He hadn't been the same since Cat stunned him with her announcement that she'd be attending the Fourth with Kendall. Michael knew he had no claim on her. They were just friends. She could keep company with whomever she pleased. But he couldn't help wondering why she would choose that city slicker over him.

Damn, but he missed her. He woke up this morning and realized that he wouldn't be stopping at the boardinghouse for her. They wouldn't stroll around the fairgrounds together, betting which baby would be chosen the prettiest, and having a good hoot over the ugliest dog.

At least they would be together for the big horse race. That thought brightened his mood.

Still looking for Cat, Michael endured the curious looks and pitying stares the townsfolk tried so hard to hide. He didn't need to be a mind reader to know they were all wondering why he and Cat weren't together.

He saw Sally Wheeler heading his way, so he turned and melted into the crowd before she could stake her claim. Then he looked toward the long table collecting the pies and noticed Denny in his Sunday best lugging his camera along, with a strange woman by his side.

As Michael drew closer, he realized to his astonishment that the "strange woman" was none other than Ruby Delight. Her conventional attire, a high-collared long-skirted blue dress that consigned her ample charms to the imagination, had fooled him, used as he was to her working clothes of flouncy short skirts and low necklines. Or even less. Without a trace of paint and powder, she looked as prim and proper as Sally Wheeler. Younger, too.

He joined them and wished them good morning. He said to Ruby, "How are you enjoying your first Fourth?"

Her eyes sparkled with wry amusement. "I'm not used to socializing with respectable folk. And they're not used to rubbing elbows with me."

Denny's hazel eyes darkened and he patted her hand. "You're just as good as anyone here."

"Don't tell that to the wives of some of my best customers," she replied, watching as a well-dressed man took one guilty look at Ruby and quickly ushered his wife in the opposite direction.

Denny suddenly became distracted. He said to Michael, "Would you mind keeping Ruby company while I take some photographs?"

"Not at all," Michael replied, offering Ruby his arm.

As they walked together, she said, "So, how does it feel to finally have some competition?"

"For what? The horse race? No one can beat any Cooper horse."

Ruby rolled her eyes. "Lord give me strength. Not the horse race, you handsome dolt. I'm talking about Cat and Kendall."

"So he asked her to the Fourth and she accepted. That doesn't mean she's sweet on him."

Ruby sighed. "Wake up, Cooper. Take off the blinders and really see what's going on around you. Kendall wants your woman, and—"

"Cat isn't *my woman*. We're—"

"Just friends." Ruby glared at him. "If I hear you say that one more time, I swear I'll strangle you."

Michael fell silent as Ruby's words hit home. Was he denying his true feelings by insisting he and Cat were "just friends?" Why was he so afraid to admit that he desired her?

Because deep down inside, he was afraid he wasn't good enough for her.

10

N{EAR THE AREA WHERE THE PRETTIEST BABY WAS}
about to be selected, Cat stood deep in conversation
with Drake and Dr. Kendall, who wore a bright yellow badge proclaiming him a judge. Drake lowered
his head to speak to her. She stared up at him, hanging on his every word. She laughed.

Hot, sharp talons of jealousy clawed at Michael's
gut. He wanted to sling Cat over his shoulder and
carry her off. On the heels of that impulse came deep
shame. She was a woman he respected, not a sack of
grain.

When Cat noticed him and Ruby together, her
laughter died. Michael detected a trace of disappointment deep in her eyes.

"Morning, Michael," she said coolly. "Ruby."

No sooner did they all exchange greetings than a
flustered, red-faced Dr. Kendall said he had to judge
the prettiest baby, and walked off.

Michael's esteem for the good doctor sank like a
stone. So Kendall could fornicate with Ruby upstairs

in the saloon, but not talk to her in public. He could pay to use her body, but not show her the simple courtesy of treating her with dignity in a social situation.

Drake drew Cat's arm through his possessively, stood even taller, and looked down at Michael. "So, Cooper, which events will you be entering? The pie-eating contest? Or do you own an ugly dog?"

Don't let him rile you. "Neither. Just the men's footrace and the horse race."

Ruby regarded Drake with barely concealed contempt. "Oh, I'm sure Mr. Kendall will be entering the footrace. A long-legged fellow like him will win for sure. And I'm sure he likes to win."

"I do, Miss Delight," Drake replied. "But in this case, it'd be like taking candy from the prettiest baby."

"I wouldn't be so sure of myself," Cat said. "You've never seen Michael run. He's fast."

Michael suspected Kendall itched to get back at him for the humiliating trouncing at Jack's. What better way than beating him in the footrace?

"All right, Catherine," Kendall said. "If you want me to enter the race, I will." He gave Michael a brief, assessing glance. "Get ready to eat my dust."

Michael hooked his thumbs in his belt. "Do you want mine with salt or pepper?"

Ruby burst out laughing and gave him a congratulatory pat on the arm. Kendall didn't crack a smile. Neither did Cat. What was wrong with her? She usually appreciated his dry wit.

Kendall placed a proprietary hand beneath Cat's elbow and drew her away. He regarded Michael out of cold, dark eyes that promised retribution. "See you at the starting line."

●　　●　　●

Shortly before lunch, ten men gathered at the starting line for the quarter mile footrace.

Standing at the far end so he wouldn't feel crowded by the other runners, Michael breathed deeply and ran in place to limber up. He glanced down the line at Drake Kendall. The city slicker had removed his fancy silk cravat and frock coat so they wouldn't get dirty and sweaty. Now he looked like most of the other men in their suspenders and shirtsleeves.

Michael scanned the observers standing on the sidelines. He saw his mother, Belle, and Ida May talking and waiting for the starting gun. Michael couldn't find Cat anywhere.

"If you're looking for Catherine," Kendall called across to him, "she's down at the finish line, waiting to congratulate me when I win."

"You mean to console you for losing."

Kendall bared his teeth in a menacing grimace. "Either way, she'll be in *my* arms, farm boy."

Farm boy? Michael felt his temper rise. Beating this pompous blowhard would bring him satisfaction unmatched since the night he fought him in Jack's.

Festus Dobbs, the mercantile's owner and starter for the footraces, stepped up and squinted at the runners to make sure the line remained even, with no man having an unfair advantage by getting a head start.

"Hold still, everybody," Denny called just before his flash went off in a soft *poof* and white puff of smoke.

Festus cleared his throat and called everyone to attention. The spectators fell silent. "The men's footrace is a quarter mile long in a straight line. We want a clean race. No pushing, hitting, or tripping. You do, and you're disqualified." He paused. "Any questions?"

When no one spoke, Festus raised his pistol. "On your mark."

Michael took a deep breath and let it out slowly.

"Get set."

He let visions of winning cleanse his mind.

"Go!" Festus shouted to the crack of gunfire.

Michael shot forward. He instantly became aware of the men around him. Some surged to the front. Some hung back. Michael let the others set the pace. Several would exhaust themselves too quickly and fall behind, never to regain their momentum. The experienced runners would save their strength for one final push nearer the finish line.

Footsteps thundered ahead and behind. Shouting spectators cheered them on from the sidelines.

Michael ran. His heart pumped fast. His legs pumped even faster.

The half-way mark flew by in a blur. He surged ahead as several men fell back. Michael risked a glance to his left. Kendall kept pace, though with great effort. Soft from all that city life.

Finally came the three-quarter mark. Michael made his move. He passed the second lead. Then the first. He was in the lead. He could see the finish line.

Pounding footsteps warned him of a challenger overtaking him. Out of the corner of his eye, he saw Kendall draw alongside, breathing hard and straining, his golden hair damp, his determined face shiny with sweat.

Goaded, Michael pushed himself. Harder. Harder. His leg muscles burned. He had to win. He had to. He inched past Kendall.

The crowd at the finish line went wild. Shouting. Screaming. Jumping up and down. Throwing hats high into the air, where they wheeled, stopped, and dropped back into the crowd.

With ten feet left to go, Michael heard the unmistakable sound of Cat's voice shouting, "Come on, Drake!"

Drake? She wanted *Kendall* to win?

Michael's resolve faltered. His drive sputtered and died.

Kendall surged ahead in a burst of reserve speed. He crossed the finish line ahead of Michael, his arms raised in victory.

Michael came in second, knowing that he had lost more than the race.

"I have to say one thing for Cooper," Drake said as he and Cat feasted on cold fried chicken and biscuits beneath the shade of the old sycamore tree. "He's not a sore loser."

After the race, a somber Michael had congratulated Drake and shaken his hand.

Cat sat with her back against the hard tree trunk and sipped a cold lemonade. While the single gents went to bid on the box lunches, Cat and Drake had left the fairgrounds to eat a quiet picnic lunch away from the crowds.

"I can't understand it," she said. "Michael was right out front, heading straight for that finish line, when all of a sudden, he just slowed down."

"It only seemed that way because I ran faster," Drake said.

Cat didn't want to argue, but Drake was wrong. Something made Michael lose the will to win. She had seen the light go out of his eyes.

She surreptitiously studied Drake while eating a crispy drumstick. Though he had taken off his cravat and frock coat, he still looked so much more distinguished than anyone Cat knew. With his sun-streaked golden hair and contrasting brown velvet eyes, he possessed a compelling attractiveness. Broad shoulders and a trim, solid physique accentuated his masculinity.

He caught her watching him and she could tell he knew why. He smiled the lazy, confident smile of a man who knew women found him attractive.

Cat looked away quickly. "So, what do you think of our Fourth of July now?"

He lifted one shoulder in an elegant shrug. "I haven't changed my opinion. Simple pleasures for the simple folk."

Annoyed, Cat retorted, "These simple folk are my friends."

"I really shouldn't disparage them," Drake said. "They can't be blamed for not knowing any better. I'm sure if they all lived in Boston and had the advantages that I did, they'd appreciate the finer things in life."

"The biggest city anyone around here's been to is St. Louis," Cat said.

"Even that's a hole in the wall compared to most of the places I've been."

Cat knew he had visited New York City as well as European countries she had only read about in school and seen on maps. When he spoke of London or Paris or Rome, he made them sound as familiar to Cat as nearby Centralia.

Drake fell silent, though he kept looking her up and down until Cat shifted uncomfortably. "Why are you looking at me that way?"

"I'm trying to see the real woman hiding beneath that shirt and trousers."

Cat's cheeks turned pink. "Drake Kendall! A gentleman doesn't tell a lady he's thinking about what she looks like without her clothes on."

He furrowed his brow in concentration and looked

around. "There's a lady around here? Funny, I don't see one. All I see is a tomboy dressed in an unflattering old shirt and a baggy pair of trousers."

She raised her chin. "I'd rather be a tomboy than go mincing around like Sally Wheeler."

Drake stretched himself out on the ground and rested his weight on one elbow. He looked up at Cat, his gaze dark and serious. "Why are you afraid to let everyone see how pretty you are?"

"I'm not afraid of anything." She looked away, his scrutiny making her feel uncomfortable again. "I'd rather people see how good a vet I am."

"I'd rather see how pretty you are, Catherine."

His silken voice sent shivers racing up her arms. She fidgeted, not knowing where to look, or what to say next, feeling like a butterfly pinned to a piece of pasteboard and mounted beneath a glass picture frame.

"I'll bet there's a narrow waist hiding beneath that shirt. A waist so small I could put both my hands around it and the fingers would meet."

She laughed nervously. "My waist's not *that* small."

"But ladies know what to wear to give the illusion of having a dainty waist."

Cat knew he was referring to corsets. She couldn't imagine having her innards squeezed together just to make her waist smaller. She took an involuntary breath.

He reached up to brush an errant lock of hair off his forehead. "Do you know who's an absolutely stunning woman?"

"Sally Wheeler."

"She's merely pretty. I was referring to Mrs. Cooper."

Cat stared at him in shock. She wasn't aware that Drake had ever taken special notice of Michael's mother. "Clementine? Why, she's forty if she's a day, and she's married!"

"That doesn't mean I can't admire her."

"She is beautiful," Cat conceded. "When my father first came to Little Falls, she set her cap for him. She wanted to marry him so bad, she could taste it."

"I'm surprised he didn't marry her."

"You've never met my mother."

Drake undid the top button of his shirt. "Mrs. Cooper has more than surface beauty. She knows how to dress to tantalize a man's imagination."

Cat wrinkled her nose. Tantalizing a man's imagination? "How?"

He stared at Cat's head. "She sweeps back her long black hair and arranges it in a knot. That makes her husband want to pull out the hairpins and see it flowing loose and free about her shoulders."

"Yeah, that sure sounds like something Jace would think about."

"And from what I've seen, she always wears a pretty dress or a neat shirtwaist and skirt. A man can see her dainty waist, but nothing else."

Cat nodded as comprehension dawned. "So he wonders what the skirt and long sleeves are hiding."

Drake smiled. "Exactly. It makes her mysterious. And men love mysterious women."

She reached for a dried twig and twirled it. "But what about the girls at One-Eyed Jack's? Their clothing doesn't leave anything to the imagination."

Drake's expression turned stony and censuring. "They're fallen women, not respectable ladies. They've got to show their wares right up front."

Cat sighed. She found all this talk of imagination and mystery so confusing. But there was something beguiling about it as well.

"I didn't mean to be so frank and forward," he said.

"It's just that I think you could be just as attractive to a man as Mrs. Cooper."

Could she make herself tantalizing and mysterious to such a worldly man as Drake?

The appearance of Heck Hechinger walking toward them interrupted Cat's thoughts.

"It's almost time for the horse race," the blacksmith said, his curious gaze taking in Cat and Drake's private picnic lunch. "Are you going to check out the horses before they run?"

Cat rose and dusted off the seat of her trousers. "Thanks for telling me. I didn't realize it was almost time for the race."

"Better hurry." His message delivered, Heck turned and ambled off.

Drake didn't make an attempt to rise. "What's this about your checking out the horses?"

Cat knelt down, picked up the napkins, and stuffed them back in the picnic basket. "I usually examine the horses to make sure they're well enough to run. There's a lot of prize money at stake. You'd be surprised how many people try to get away with racing a sick horse."

"Why don't you let my father examine them this time?" He patted the place next to him and bestowed the wide, white smile that always made Cat's insides melt. "Come on. Stay here and keep me company."

Cat rose and looked helplessly at Heck's retreating figure. "But I've got to get my own horse ready."

Drake's smile died. "Don't tell me you're riding in that race."

"Of course I am. That's why Michael and I race in to town. To practice."

"Are any of the other women entered?"

"Just me."

"Just you and a bunch of men."

"Just me and twenty or thirty men."

Drake rose in one graceful, fluid movement and grasped Cat by the shoulders. "Catherine, it's much too dangerous. You could get killed."

She looked at him as if he were speaking gibberish. "I was practically born on a horse, and I'm a damn fine rider. I've been riding in these races ever since I was sixteen. As you can see, I haven't gotten killed yet."

"There's always a first time. And then it's too late."

"Look, Drake, I'm touched that you're worried about me," she said, "but there's no need. I'll be fine."

A muscle clenched in his wide jaw and he released her. "Why do you have to race at all? Why can't you spend the rest of the afternoon with me?" A wry smile tugged at his mouth. "Am I so boring that you can't wait to get away?"

The hurt in his eyes surprised her. "You're not boring. I like being with you. It's just that I've always raced."

"Then do something you've never done before. Something unpredictable. Forget the race. Spend the rest of the day with me." His eyes cajoled and promised. "Who knows what we'll discover about each other."

Cat stood there wondering what she should do. Riders would be checking their horses and saddling up for the big race. She should be doing the same with Rascal. But the thought of spending the rest of the afternoon with Drake strongly tempted her.

Why not? He hadn't asked Sally Wheeler to the Fourth. He had asked Cat. Since they were spending the day together, the least she could do was yield to Drake's wishes and forgo the race.

The unexpected beckoned.

Cat smiled. "All right. I'll spend the day with you.

Just let me catch up with Heck and tell him to have your father check out the horses this time."

Drake grasped both her hands and drew them to his lips, making Cat blush.

Michael scanned the field of riders saddling their horses for the race.

"Where's Cat?" he asked his father, who was bridling the farm's new gray stallion. "I don't see her and Rascal anywhere."

Jace checked the bit. "Nobody's seen her for a while." He paused to watch Dr. Kendall examine the last horse. His eyes narrowed. "Does that fool know what he's doing? That roan should be disqualified. He'll be pulling up lame after the first quarter mile."

Michael frowned, feeling as ornery as a horse with a burr under its saddle, and not because of the roan. He didn't need reminding that Cat had gone off with Drake Kendall, leaving Michael to get pressured into bidding on Sally Wheeler's box lunch. Luckily, he lost to some stranger with deeper pockets from nearby Centralia. He wound up eating with his parents and the Ritters, who knew better than to remark on Cat's absence.

Michael swung into the saddle. "I'm going to look for her."

"The race starts in fifteen minutes," Jace warned him. "You'll be disqualified if you're not at that starting line."

"So will Cat." Michael touched his heels to Rogue's sides. "That's why I've got to find her."

He didn't find her anywhere on the fairgrounds. After circling twice, he headed for town, where everyone would be congregating shortly for the start of the race.

He stopped at the Kendalls' house first. He knocked

on the front door, and when no one answered, he called Cat's name. Still no answer. He cupped his hands around his eyes to shade out the light and peered in every one of the downstairs windows. No sign of Cat.

Relief washed over him. So Kendall hadn't lured her back to his empty house to have his way with her. Michael wouldn't put anything past that big-city skunk.

He continued on to the boardinghouse.

Empty.

To his astonishment, he found Rascal grazing unperturbed in the corral behind the barn.

"Where in the hell is she?" he muttered aloud. Cat's mare should have been saddled and heading for the starting line. "She's going to miss the race."

And ruin her reputation.

Unless he found her, and fast.

An hour later, Michael gave up and rode back to the fairgrounds.

To his astonishment, there was Cat walking with his father while Jace cooled the gray stallion. Without Drake Kendall tagging along.

Michael walked his own horse over to them. He remained in the saddle. He was so furious, he'd probably throttle her if he dismounted.

"In case you're interested," Jace said mildly, "I won."

"By how much?"

"Two lengths."

"Congratulations, Dad." Michael glared down at Cat. "Where in the hell were you?"

His father discreetly excused himself and led his first-place winner away.

Cat glared right back, her hands on her hips and

her blue eyes flashing. "I might ask you the same question, Michael Cooper. They held up the race for five minutes while everyone searched high and low for you, but you were nowhere to be found."

Michael's agitation unsettled Rogue, causing the animal to shift uneasily beneath him. He stilled the big gelding with a calming hand on his arched neck.

"I was looking all over creation for *you*, so you wouldn't be disqualified."

The fire left Cat's eyes and her hands fell to her sides. She looked decidedly sheepish. "I didn't race after all."

"I knew that the minute I stopped by the boarding-house and saw Rascal grazing in the corral." Now he dismounted and faced her, not caring who overheard. "Mind telling me why?"

"Drake asked me not to. He was worried that it was too dangerous and I'd get hurt."

Michael wanted to reach out and shake her. "You mean to tell me that you didn't race just because Drake Kendall told you not to?"

An angry line appeared between Cat's brows. "There'll be other races. Today, I wanted to spend more time with Drake."

And Michael wanted to kiss her so badly, his lips burned. Damn those unbrotherly feelings again. Always tearing him to pieces when he least expected it.

A vision of Cat standing in the outdoor shower stall with water shining her breathtaking nakedness suddenly hit him like a bolt of lightning. If any man suspected the sweet body she was hiding beneath that old shirt and trousers . . . he felt himself go hard.

"Well, I hope you enjoyed yourself," he snapped, turning away and fussing with Rogue's bridle to hide his own hurt.

"I did."

"If you'll excuse me, I promised Sally I'd spend more time with her."

"And I have to get back to Drake."

They turned and stormed off in opposite directions.

Drake stood beside Catherine and watched the fireworks light up the night sky in a brilliant spray that eclipsed the stars.

She oohed and aahed with childlike glee along with all the other bumpkins when another Roman candle exploded high overhead.

Drake mentally counted the ways he had repaid Michael Cooper today for that humiliating fistfight in the saloon. He had beat the farm boy in the footrace, and persuaded Catherine to spend the rest of the day with him rather than ride in the big horse race. That, Drake knew, had wounded Cooper deeply.

Drake smiled in satisfaction. He had just begun to sharpen his knife.

11

THE MORNING OF THE SIXTH OF JULY, CAT LEFT THE boardinghouse to mail a long-overdue letter to her mother. Most of the three pages she had spent hours composing were about Drake, and Cat's growing feelings for him.

"By the way," she had added in a hastily scribbled postscript, "I'm thinking of buying a dress to wear to church."

The minute Cat opened the post office door, she saw Sally Wheeler and Francie Dawlish huddled together at the counter.

"—and if Cat's mother was still here," Francie said indignantly, her voice rising and carrying, "she would never, ever let her daughter—" Francie took one look at Cat and stopped as abruptly as if a gushing tap had been shut off.

"Don't stop talking on my account." Cat walked up to the counter so the postmaster could weigh her letter.

Francie turned scarlet and averted her eyes, then

mumbled something under her breath, and hurried away. Sally stayed. Cat didn't have to wait long to find out what was on the little snip's mind.

"You sure created quite a stir the other day," Sally said with a cat-ate-the-cream smile.

"Did I?"

"Everybody in town is talking about how you and Drake Kendall disappeared just before the horse race."

Cat fished in her deep back pocket for change, and handed the coins to the postmaster. "You mean everybody in town has nothing better to do than talk about me?" She shook her head. "Drake's right. Little Falls is a hole in the wall."

Sally's cheeks turned as pink as her dress, but she recovered quickly. "You can't blame them. When a young unmarried woman goes off alone and unchaperoned with a bachelor, people will wonder."

"That's odd," Cat mused. "I've been alone with Michael Cooper more times than I can count. He even sleeps over at the boardinghouse when he's in town, and nobody's ever gossiped about us."

"That's different. You two are so much like brother and sister, everyone knows there's no chance of a romance between you. Now, you and Drake Kendall on the other hand . . ." She let her voice trail off suggestively.

Cat rested her hip against the counter and folded her arms. "I'm really surprised at you, Sally Wheeler. Listening to gossip and believing it. If there's one thing that Michael hates more than a woman who listens to gossip, it's a woman who spreads it."

Sally's smirk died and she turned pale. "Me? Spreading gossip? Never! I was merely informing you what everyone else in town is saying. So you'd be able to guard your reputation."

"Telling me for my own good, is that it?"

"Someone has to. Your own mother isn't here to provide you with proper guidance in matters of the heart, and as for Ida May . . ."

Cat's arms fell to her sides. "Well, I'm touched by your concern. I'll certainly be careful of my reputation in the future."

She wished the postmaster and Sally good day, and headed for the door. To her surprise, Sally followed and fell in step beside her as she left the post office and strode down the boardwalk.

"I don't care what anybody says," Sally said in a low, confiding tone. "I think it's wonderful that a man like Drake Kendall could be interested romantically in a tom—er, in a spirited young woman such as yourself."

"Just because he enjoys my company doesn't mean he's interested in me romantically," Cat said.

Sally rolled her eyes. "If you'll forgive me for saying so, Miss Catherine Wills, you haven't had a lick of experience with men. I have. And believe me when I tell you that Drake Kendall is interested in you romantically. I can see that as clearly as the nose on your face. Michael thinks of you as a friend. Drake thinks of you as more than a friend."

Much as Cat hated to admit it, Sally was right. Michael still treated her like a friend. They rode together. Teased each other. Shared the same thoughts. On the Fourth, he searched high and low for her when he thought she would miss riding in the race like one of the boys.

Drake, on the other hand, set her apart and treated her like a rare and precious jewel. He looked beyond the tomboy in trousers and a man's old shirt and saw a woman of mystery. He didn't want her to ride in the race because he feared she would come to harm.

"If I were you," Sally continued, hurrying to keep up, "I'd encourage Drake Kendall. He's quite a catch. He's handsome. Worldly. Interesting. I don't expect we'll see many more like him in Little Falls."

Cat raised her brows. "If he's such a great catch, why don't you cast your line for him?"

"Oh, I would if he gave me the least bit of encouragement. But he doesn't know I exist. All he cares about is you." Sally leaned closer, her big blue eyes widening. "Has he kissed you yet?"

Cat stopped in her tracks and glared down at the dimunitive blonde. "That's none of your business."

Sally stopped and smiled archly. "So he hasn't."

Now how could she tell that? From what Cat had heard, Sally had plenty of experience kissing men, including Michael. Cat opened her mouth to ask, then changed her mind. None of her business, though the thought niggled at her.

She resumed walking, only faster, intending to elude Sally. "My personal life is nobody's concern but mine."

Sally gathered her skirts and followed, as persistent as a flea on a dog. "If you want to snare Drake, you've got to encourage him. A man's got to know that you're as interested in him as he is in you. So you'd best get around to kissing him, and quick. There's nothing like a serious kiss to let a man know that you're interested. And to keep him interested."

Was that part of Sally's own devious plan to snare Michael?

"I wouldn't know," Cat said. The kisses Michael usually gave her definitely fell into the unserious category.

"Then don't you think it's time you found out? You're not a child anymore. Both of us are women full grown."

"Thanks for reminding me." Cat stopped in front of the mercantile. "I'll think about what you said."

"I know we haven't always been the best of friends," Sally admitted, "but I'd hate to see you miss out on a chance for happiness with a wonderful man like Drake. So, if you want to talk woman to woman, I'm right across the street. Drop in any time for some pointers."

So Sally Wheeler itched to become her confidante. That would be like keeping a pet snake in the closet.

Cat mumbled a perfunctory thanks and turned to go into the mercantile.

"Wait." When Cat turned, Sally said, "You won't tell Michael that I was listening to gossip, will you?"

"Not unless he asks."

Cat disappeared inside the store, leaving an chagrined Sally staring after her.

Later that morning, Cat rode out to the Wright farm to check on Gideon's cattle. Her conversation with Sally Wheeler kept niggling at her like a sore thumb.

Sally's ploy was as transparent as a windowpane. By pushing Cat into Drake's arms, Sally hoped to clear her own path straight to Michael. She was flattered that Sally considered her a threat, but she wasn't. And as for Michael, Cat wasn't sure he wanted Sally either.

Unbeknownst to Sally, Cat didn't need anyone to push her into Drake's arms. She was heading there quite nicely on her own.

Cat settled back in the saddle and let her thoughts drift like the white clouds high overhead. She had never thought she'd see the day when another man turned her head. Oh, she'd never stop caring for Michael. Some part of her would always love him. But Drake treated her like a woman, not a friend.

She sifted her fingers idly through Rascal's mane and recalled what Sally had said about kissing. *Serious* kissing. Cat frowned. What exactly was *serious* kissing? She was sure her sisterly pecks on Michael's cheek didn't count. Now, the way her parents always kissed—her mother's arms entwined around her father's neck, his hands resting on her waist, their bodies and mouths locked so tightly together they melted into one—when they thought no one was watching . . . that was serious kissing.

Cat pictured herself kissing Drake. Because of his great height, she'd have to stand on tiptoes or even on a box to reach his lips. The thought made her giggle.

She sobered instantly. Unlike Sally, Cat knew that it took more than serious kissing to make a full and satisfying life with a man. A couple needed love. Respect. Mutual interests. Common goals. She had learned that from her own parents' steadfast example.

But she suspected that kissing was a good way to get to know a man. And Cat decided to get to know Drake real soon.

On her way back from the Wright farm, Cat was riding past Hechinger's Livery when Heck himself hailed her. She turned Rascal and headed toward the stable.

"Something wrong?" she asked the scowling blacksmith wiping his hands against his ancient sweat-stained leather apron. "You look like you could strangle somebody."

Heck stroked Rascal's face. "It's that buckskin stallion I just bought."

"Banner?" The crazy three-year-old who wanted to do nothing more than kick down his stall, mate, and fight with other horses.

"That's the one."

Cat shook her head. "Didn't Jace warn you not to buy that horse?"

"He did, but the stallion was a bargain. I need more horses, and I couldn't buy a dog for what his owner was asking."

Cat looked over at the corral beyond, where the high-strung buckskin kept trotting in a restless circle, his black mane and tail flying like banners in the breeze. He held his head high as if searching the fence for a possible escape route.

"Maybe Michael or Jace can train him," Cat suggested.

"I asked. They're too busy with their own stock. I've tried myself, but—" He shrugged.

"So, what do you intend to do with him?"

"There's only one thing left for me to do." Heck's gaze wavered and slid away. He cleared his throat. "He needs—well, you know—an operation."

Personally, Cat thought it a shame to have to geld such a spirited stallion, taking away his fire and masculine temperament with a stroke of the scalpel. But stallions could be unmanageable and downright dangerous, and if training didn't work, their owners had no other choice.

"If you want him docile enough for livery work and don't intend to breed him, I'd say that'd certainly calm him down."

Heck looked up at her. "You got some time this afternoon?"

"Sure." She looked at Banner, still pacing around the paddock. "He's healthy? No strangles, influenza, or catarrhal fever?"

Heck shook his head solemnly. "You know my place is clean."

"You sure you want me to do it?" The blacksmith had always objected to Cat or her mother performing such procedures he deemed "too indecent for a woman" on his horses, but since there had been no other vets in the area, he had no other choice. Now he did. "Why don't you ask Dr. Kendall?"

"He said he didn't know when he'd be able to get to it. And I won't be able to stand another night of listening to that damn horse try to kick his stall down. He upsets the others."

Dr. Kendall sounded as if he were looking for an excuse not to geld Heck's horse. Odd behavior in a doctor who was also supposed to be a vet.

Cat turned Rascal and headed back to the boardinghouse.

Later, she arrived at the livery at three o'clock to find Heck, his groom, and the postmaster standing by. Once news had spread, several spectators had also gathered.

"Let's take him out to the open field," Cat said, when Heck and another man led out the buckskin, who danced in place and tried to rear. "And bring me a couple of buckets of water."

Once they assembled in the grassy, open field, the men threw the gelding onto his left side. Heck quickly hobbled the buckskin's forelegs and his left hind leg.

Cat scrubbed her hands with soap and water. "Make sure he's secure," she called to the men. "I don't want to get kicked in the head."

"We won't let that happen to you," one of the spectators called out.

Someone must have made an off-color comment, for a ripple of laughter emanated from their little group.

After drying her hands, Cat took her knife, a wooden clamp and a small tin of lard mixed with sulphate of copper from her medical bag. She rubbed the antiseptic mixture into the clamp's wooden grooves to sterilize the surface. She wrapped her instruments in a clean towel and brought them over to where Banner lay uncharacteristically quiet.

Heck secured a band around the horse's right hind leg and drew it up out of the way.

"Hold him steady," Cat warned.

She finished in five minutes.

She heard one of the spectators say, "I sure wouldn't want that woman anywhere near my privates."

"Don't worry, Horace," someone else retorted, "she wouldn't go near your privates if you paid her."

"Yeah, Horace," the postmaster added, "even Jack's girls won't take your money."

Cat stood back while Heck slowly and carefully unbuckled and removed the hobbles.

"Stand back and get out of his way," she said, taking her own advice.

The men jumped up and scattered to safety.

The buckskin lay dazed on his side for a few seconds. When he realized he was free, he grunted and rolled over onto his belly, then stood up and shook his head, blowing through his nose.

They watched and waited, but Banner stood there as docile as a lamb. Heck, holding the halter lead, gently stroked the horse's neck to soothe him.

Cat joined him and patted the gelding's neck. "He'll be all right now, won't you, fella?"

"Nice clean job, Cat," Heck said. "You're so quick with that knife, the operation's over before you know it."

"Yeah," Heck's groom chimed in. "I've seen horses bleed to death if the vet doesn't know what he's doing."

She basked in their praise. She *was* quick. She *did* know what she was doing. She wished all of the narrow-minded fools who had denied her admission to their veterinary schools could see her now.

"Thanks, fellas." Cat turned to plunge her bloody hands into a nearby bucket of water, when she noticed Drake standing among the spectators, watching her.

She smiled, pleased that he had a chance to see her at work, demonstrating her competence and knowledge.

He did not return her smile.

She turned her attention back to scrubbing her hands. Maybe watching her perform such a bloody procedure had unsettled him. After all, he was a big-city fellow unused to the grittiness of farm and country life.

Cat dried her hands, assembled her medicines, and told Heck to tell her immediately if infection set in, or the buckskin exhibited signs of excessive pain.

"Make sure you keep walking him," she said.

Then she turned and crossed the field to join Drake.

As she drew closer, she noticed that his fair skin had darkened like the sky before a summer storm, and his mouth remained set in a thin, uncompromising line. Cat had never seen warm brown eyes so cold they made her shudder.

What bee flew into his bonnet, she wondered?

She reached his side and smiled brightly. "How long have you been standing here?"

He did not smile back. "Long enough." He bit off the words, his tone as frosty as the glint in his eyes.

She chose to ignore his odd mood. "Did you see the operation?" she asked.

"Most of it."

"So, what did you think of my work?" She looked back at the buckskin and beamed with pride. "I think I did a fine job. Now that buckskin is as gentle as a lamb and anybody'll be able to ride him.''

"Catherine, I'd like to have a word with you.'' He glanced at the men talking and laughing among themselves. "In private.''

His attitude puzzled her. "Sure. The sycamore tree isn't far from here. We can talk there.''

Cat headed for the tree. Drake fell into step beside her. He made no attempt to converse, just stared straight ahead as though he and Cat were strangers.

When they reached the tree, Cat set down her bag and turned to face him. "You angry with me about something?''

A muscle jumped in his jaw. "Angry and very disappointed in you.''

"Why?'' She felt her mother's Irish temper begin to stir, but she fought to control it. "What did I do?''

"I can't believe it.'' He took off his hat and dragged his hand through his hair. "You actually castrated a horse, Catherine!''

She looked at him as if he'd gone mad. "I'm a vet. If someone wants me to geld a stallion, I operate. And I do a damn fine job, too.'' She stepped away, suddenly annoyed with him. "What's got into you, anyway? You're acting like I've committed some terrible crime.''

Drake sighed. "Forgive me, Catherine. I keep forgetting that because of your country upbringing, you lack a true lady's refined sensibilities.'' He reached out and placed his hands on her shoulders. "Do you know what I saw when I happened by the field?''

"You saw me operating on the buckskin.''

"No. I saw a woman touching and mutilating a horse's private parts while a bunch of rough men snickered and made uncouth comments in her presence.'' His hands fell to his sides. "How could you expose yourself to such lewd behavior? Couldn't you see that those men had no respect for you as a woman? I felt so embarrassed for you."

Cat's face grew hot. "I'm a vet. I was just doing my job."

Drake shook his head. "Do you know what's most upsetting to me? You don't feel what you're doing is wrong."

"But it's not wrong!" she cried, balling her hands into fists. "I'm a vet, just like your father. He's castrated his share of horses, hasn't he?"

Drake sighed. "It's no use. I can talk until I'm blue in the face, but you're not going to listen."

He turned and started walking away.

Cat stared at his retreating form. "Drake, wait!"

He stopped and turned, a question in his eyes.

Cat swallowed hard. "Please don't be angry with me."

He took a step toward her and stopped. "I don't want to be angry with you, but your behavior back there deeply offended me."

"Couldn't you overlook it?"

"I'm sorry," he said softly, "but I care about you too deeply to overlook it."

Cat felt her pulse race and her heart give a leap of joy. She grinned. "You care about me?"

He crossed the distance between them and reached out to cup her cheek in his smooth, warm palm, his touch sending a little ripple of awareness through her. He stared deeply into her eyes, as if he were trying to find her soul and memorize its contents. "I care about you very much. More than I've ever cared about another woman."

Cat grew very still. She held her breath. Was he going to give her a *serious* kiss?

Drake's hand fell away. "It's only because I care so

deeply about you that I'm holding you to such exacting standards, Catherine."

He wasn't going to kiss her after all. Damn. "I'm not perfect, Drake. I don't like being held to such impossible standards."

He smiled ruefully. "I know. You're used to doing what you please without answering to anyone. But that's only because no man has ever cherished you enough."

"Drake Kendall, you're not making a lick of sense."

"When a man cherishes a woman the way she should be, he holds her accountable. And she wants her behavior to reflect well on him. She would never dishonor herself, or him."

"And you feel I dishonored myself."

"You did."

Cat jammed her hands into her pockets and kicked at a clump of earth with her toe. "What would I have to do to live up to your standards?"

"Start acting more like a lady."

"And if I did start acting more like a lady?"

"Then I'd feel free to act more like the man who cares about you and do this." He cradled her face in his large hands, closed his eyes, and lowered his head.

She took a deep breath and rested her hands on his waist to balance herself when she stood on tiptoes to meet his mouth with her own. His lips were warm and smooth and hard and gentle as they pressed against hers. Cat felt a sweet liquid warmth suffuse her body like the rising sun inching its way across the sleeping land.

Then they parted.

Cat sighed. Her first *serious* kiss. She floated on air.

Drake held her in his arms and rested his chin on the top of her head. "That was wonderful."

Different from Michael's quick, punishing kiss after

she'd been thrown by the blood bay stallion, but then, Drake wasn't Michael.

Cat said, "Let's do it again."

And they did.

12

"HE *KISSED* HER?"

Michael stood in the middle of the parlor and stared in dumbfounded silence at Ida May, who was dusting the piano.

"Or *she* may have kissed *him*," Ida May replied, running her feather duster over the ivory keys, adding a pleasant musical tinkle to the room's lazy summer silence. "Francie Dawlish wasn't sure which."

Michael stroked Ulysses lying across the back of the sofa, causing the cat to stretch and purr contentedly. "When exactly did Francie see all this?"

"Yesterday afternoon. She told me that she was taking a shortcut to the church when she noticed Cat and Drake Kendall kissing beneath the sycamore tree."

Michael rubbed his jaw. "Cat wouldn't let just anybody take such liberties. She must feel something for Kendall."

"She must." Ida May next attacked the windowsills, her zeal causing dust motes to rise and dance in the light. "No one was more surprised than I when Francie told me."

"So Cat hasn't confided in you."

"Not about this. That girl can be as tight as a clam." Ida May next dusted the table supporting the birdcage, causing Edgar Allan to glare at her out of bright black eyes and flap his wings in vexation. "In hindsight, we all should've seen this coming."

"What do you mean?"

Ida May stopped her housework and looked at him. "First, they went to the Fourth together. Secondly, Cat didn't ride in the race. You know she never misses a horse race. But she missed this one, and simply because Drake Kendall asked her to."

Michael felt a sinking feeling deep in his gut. "You don't think she's falling for this smooth-talking city slicker, do you?"

"Cat's always had a mind of her own, just like her mother. She must like Kendall a lot if she let him talk her out of racing."

Not a good sign.

"And if she let him kiss her," Ida May added.

Not a good sign at all.

Ida May shooed the cat off the sofa and diligently brushed his place with her feather duster. "That Drake Kendall is the kind of man who can sweep a woman right off her feet and take her back to Boston with him."

Michael's eyes narrowed. "You don't think she's fixing to *marry* him, do you?"

Ida May stopped dusting long enough to sneeze. "Cat didn't say anything about him courting her, so maybe not." She sneezed again and reached into her apron pocket for a lace-trimmed handkerchief to blow her nose. "But you never can tell. Suitors haven't exactly been lining up outside the boardinghouse door, when along comes this handsome, charming big-city fellow who starts paying Cat a lot of attention. Showing her what she's been missing. Could turn a girl's head."

Michael walked over to the front door, hooked his thumbs in his belt, and looked out over the yard to Rose Street. He could see Sally sitting on her porch swing, pretending to read a book. He knew that the minute he walked out the door, she would come racing across the street like Maddy Wills's old coonhound on the scent. Today he was in no mood for Sally's silly games.

He turned back to Ida May. "Where is Cat now?"

"She said she was going to visit several of the farms, and then she was heading to your place, to see your mother."

Michael raised his brows. "My mother? Why?"

Ida May set down her feather duster and pried open a tin of beeswax furniture polish. "She said she needed to ask your mother's advice."

"About what?"

"She rushed out the door before I could ask."

Now, what kind of advice could Cat possibly want from his mother?

Ida May rubbed a bit of cloth against the beeswax. "Sometimes a young woman has delicate questions that only her mother can answer. Since Cat's mother is too far away for a chat, maybe she's turning to yours." She regarded Michael out of the corner of her eye. "Considering what's been happening around here lately with this Kendall fellow, I would suspect that Cat needs some advice about men."

Michael made a production of retrieving his hat from the coatrack, not wanting Ida May to see his distress. He thanked her and strode out the door.

Ida May watched him descend the porch steps

slowly, as if he'd just been told his best friend died. She looked over at Edgar Allan pecking at some corn-bread crumbs in his feeder. "That boy'd better start fighting for her, or he's going to lose her for sure."

For once, the crow remained silent.

He was losing her.

Michael sat back in the saddle as his horse settled into a smooth, slow canter. He momentarily regretted being so curt with Sally when she came running across the street, but all he could think about was Cat.

He was losing her.

And he had no one to blame but himself.

Who always insisted that he and Cat were too much like brother and sister to become romantically in-volved? Michael mentally kicked himself. Every time Cat suggested that they might make a good team, who always refused to take her seriously? He kicked himself again, harder. Who kept telling himself that Cat couldn't possibly be interested in him?

"Blind as well as stupid, Cooper," he muttered.

Now she'd finally given up banging her head against the fence post and turned to another man.

Not that Michael could blame her. On the surface, Kendall had so much more to offer a woman. He could turn on the charm. He'd seen the world. He surely knew powerful, influential people in Boston, and could open doors for her, possibly even get her into veterinary school.

Cat had always measured a person's worth by what they were like inside, their integrity and character. But what had Ida May said a short while ago?

Suitors haven't exactly been lining up outside the board-inghouse door, when along comes this handsome, charming big-city fellow who starts paying Cat a lot of attention.

Showing her what she's been missing. Could turn a girl's head.

Either that, or she was falling in love with Drake Kendall.

Cat and another man. Kissing. Marrying. Loving.

Michael suddenly shivered as though someone were walking over his grave. Above him swept the sky, vast and blue and empty to the edge of infinity, without a scudding white cloud or a spiraling hawk to fill it. Not a rider or a carriage raised white dust in the road ahead. Not a cow regarded him in curiosity as she grazed in neighboring fields. Even the clopping of Rogue's hooves and the soft creak of saddle leather offered no solace.

Michael was alone in an empty land.

This, he knew with a sinking heart, would be how he would feel forever if he lost Cat. Alone. Empty. Always searching the horizon for any sign of her.

Too late, taunted the rhythm of his horse's hoof-beats.

Too late.

When Michael returned home, he went straight to the stables. He searched both barns, but his father wasn't in either of them.

In the tackroom he found Curly hanging up a harness.

"You seen my old man anywhere?" he asked.

Curly opened a tin of saddle soap. "One of the fillies got curious and went wandering. Jace went out to bring her back."

"Which direction was he heading?"

"West. Toward the river."

Michael thanked him, got back on Rogue, and rode out to find his father.

An hour later, Michael saw Jace riding across a

field, the runaway filly haltered and on a lead, trotting docilely behind Jace's horse.

For once, Michael forced himself to ignore their familial connection, and look at his father impartially, as a stranger would. He already knew him as the loving parent who had taught him how to ride and hunt and shoot, hollered the roof down when he got into mischief, praised him to the skies when he excelled. Now he wanted to know Jace Cooper the *man*.

A virile man attractive to women.

He watched Jace approach and studied him. If anything, his father was handsomer now than he had been as a young man, if Michael took his mother's word. Jace's tall, rugged physique hadn't gone to fat, though his dark, almost black hair was now threaded with silver. His blue eyes still lit up appreciatively at the sight of a pretty woman, and his quick, lopsided grin had been known to melt more than a heart or two. Still did, according to his wife.

But Jace Cooper's appeal had more than mere surface handsomeness. The man *knew* women. That's what Michael wanted and needed, his father's knowledge. His secrets.

"So you found her," Michael said, drawing his own horse alongside his father's.

Jace glanced back at the filly. "Headstrong little thing. Gave me quite a chase, but she's glad I caught her. Ain't that just like a woman."

He stared straight ahead. "So, son, what's on your mind?"

Michael shook his head. He never could put one over on his old man. "Cat."

"Now, there's a woman who can tie a man into knots."

Michael certainly knew that feeling.

"She's got a lot of her mother in her," Jace said.

"She's a little slower to anger than Maddy, but she's still got a temper. I wish she were a little more feminine, like your mother, but that's just my taste."

"I like Cat's honesty," Michael said, "and the way you can always tell what she's thinking just by looking into her eyes."

"Sometimes it's best not to know what a woman's thinking, son. Saves a man a lot of sleepless nights. But you'll learn that when you're older." Jace gave an admiring whistle. "Cat's a damn fine vet, though. Just as good as her father."

"I'm worried about her. She's falling for Drake Kendall."

Jace nodded. "That was obvious on the Fourth."

"So what can I do about it?"

"What do you *want* to do about it?" His father swore and turned in the saddle. "Son, sometimes you sorely try my patience. Didn't I teach you anything? First you have to decide what you want. Then you have to figure out a way to get it."

And suddenly he knew as sure as his name was Michael Cooper. "I want her."

"So you do love her?"

Ruby was right. He did love Cat. "I've always loved her, but I couldn't believe that she loved me. Now she's fallen for Kendall, and I'm too late."

Jace swore and shook his head. "It's never too late until she's got a wedding ring on her finger."

Michael waited. When his father just sat there in silence, Michael prodded him with, "Well, Dad? What do I do next?"

"Depends on the woman." Jace glanced back at the filly, who cocked her ears to catch his voice. "Take your mother. When we were first getting acquainted, she loathed me. Couldn't stand the sight of me." He grinned. "Hard to believe, I know, but she did. She thought I was too rough for a refined lady such as herself.

"But I wore her down with my charm. Showed her I was capable of a grand, romantic gesture."

Michael knew the story of how his father, at a Harvest Festival horse race, rode up to Clementine Boswell in front of the whole town and asked her for a token to carry in the race, just like a knight of the Round Table before a tournament.

Then when he won the race and used his prize money to buy Clementine's box lunch, she realized the true depth of Jace Cooper's love for her.

Michael shook his head. "Cat isn't Mama."

"No, she isn't." Jace rubbed his jaw. "She's more direct. She'd want a man to come right out and tell her he loves her. And mean it."

That's what Michael would do.

Cat opened the Cooper's kitchen door without knocking and peered in. "Anybody home?"

"Just me," Clementine's sunny voice replied.

Cat stepped inside to find Clementine standing at the kitchen table, surrounded by large jars of carefully labeled preserves, several fragrant, crusty loaves of freshly baked bread, and a large basket lined with a red-and-white checkered cloth.

"You're packing a basket," Cat said, removing her hat, "and I'm interrupting."

"It'll keep." Clementine smiled. "I was just about to fix myself a cup of tea. Would you care to join me?"

"Don't mind if I do." A cup of tea might bolster her courage to ask an important favor of Michael's mother. "Are you sure I'm not keeping you from something?"

"Not at all." Clementine retrieved the teapot and filled the kettle. "Trula Olsen has been feeling poorly for several days. Even though Dr. Kendall said she'll be up and around soon, I know she hasn't been up to baking."

Cat hung her hat on the peg near the door and seated herself at the table. "So you're packing a basket for her family."

"Yes. But as I said, it'll keep."

Cat surreptitiously studied Clementine as she glided around the kitchen. Drake was right. She exuded womanliness and mystery.

"I've noticed you like to put your hair in that knot at the back of your head," Cat said. "Doesn't it take long?"

"After all these years, it's like second nature to me," Clementine replied, lighting the stove. "Actually, this chignon is quite easy to do once I'm dressed."

"Doesn't it ever come loose from its pins and get in your eyes?"

"No, I use lots of hairpins. Sometimes, when I drive Gus too fast—don't you dare tell my husband that I drive fast!—a few pins will come loose, but usually, my hair stays in place." Clementine rinsed out the teapot. "Now, your mother's hair certainly had a mind of its own. All she ever did was pull those springy auburn curls out of the way and tie them back with a ribbon."

"I always wondered why Mama didn't just cut her hair short like mine and be done with it."

Clementine got this set, wary look on her face that told Cat she was choosing her words carefully. "I suspect your mother just liked to keep her hair long and was willing to tolerate the inconvenience."

"I suppose." Cat tousled her own hair. "Maybe I should let my hair grow."

If Cat's announcement startled Clementine, she concealed it admirably. She continued measuring teaspoons of tea into the warmed pot. "If you didn't like the way it looked long, you could always cut it short again."

Cat brightened. "I could do that." She shifted in her chair, suddenly feeling uncomfortable. "Mrs. Cooper, do you mind if I ask you a personal question?"

She smiled. "I don't mind your asking me anything, but if it's too personal, I may choose not answer it."

"Fair enough." Cat took a deep breath. "Don't you ever get tired of wearing skirts and dresses all the time?"

"I can't say that I do," she replied without hesitation, adding boiling water to the teapot. "I've never worn anything else."

"But don't you find that they get all tangled up in your legs while you're trying to do your work?"

Clementine frowned thoughtfully as she opened a tin, removed several of Belle's shortbread cookies, and arranged them on a plate. "I guess I'm used to them," she said, bringing the plate to the table and sitting down across from Cat.

"Wouldn't you find trousers more comfortable, and practical?" Cat asked, helping herself to a cookie.

"I'm sure I would," she said, "but as a woman, I prefer to wear skirts and dresses. They make me feel more feminine."

Clementine's message was as clear as a brand on a steer's hide: Intriguing, mysterious women wore dresses.

"I'm not criticizing you for wearing trousers," Clementine added hastily. "You're a vet. You work as hard as any man, and you need to be comfortable."

But Cat's mother was a vet, and she always wore dresses. And long hair. So why hadn't Maddy insisted her daughter do the same?

"Cat," Clementine asked softly, "what is this all

about? Why are you asking me all these questions about long hair and dresses? You've never been interested in clothes before.''

Cat leaned back in her chair, crossed her arms, and let out a dismal sigh. "I'm twenty-one, and I've decided that's too old to be a tomboy anymore. It's high time I started acting and dressing like a woman.''

Clementine stared at her out of wide, astonished eyes. "Why, Cat, that's—well, I never. Heavens, I'm quite at a loss for words.'' Her hands trembled slightly as she poured tea. "If you don't mind my asking, what brought about such a—such a change?''

Cat lifted one shoulder. "I just decided, that's all.''

"Drake Kendall couldn't have had something to do with your decision, could he?''

"Well, now that you mention it, he did have something to do with it.''

"I see.'' Clementine hesitated. "Are you courting?''

Cat's face grew hot. "No—at least, not yet. I like him a lot, though.'' She recalled the sycamore tree and the sweetness of Drake's kiss. Nothing brotherly about that kiss. "And I can tell that he likes me. But I want to take things slow.''

"That's wise. You wouldn't want to rush into anything.'' Clementine sipped her tea. "I must confess that Jace and I were hoping you and Michael would make a match of it someday.''

Cat had been hoping, too. But Michael didn't want her.

Cat looked down at the small yellow flowers ringing her teacup. "I did, too, when I was younger. But now that I'm all grown, my feelings have changed.'' She met Clementine's gaze. "Drake's the man I want now.''

Clementine rose, went over to Cat and gave her a hug. "Then we hope you get exactly what you want.''

"Michael's your son, but I was hoping you wouldn't hold my choice against me," Cat said, her eyes misting with tears. "You and Jace've been as good to me as my own parents."

While they drank tea and ate shortbread, Cat told Clementine all about her recent conversation with Drake. "He's right. I act too much like a man and not enough like a woman."

Clementine's eyes shone with compassion as she placed her hand on Cat's. "But if Drake really cares for you, he won't give a fig whether you're dressed in trousers or a skirt. He's going to admire you for the person you are inside."

"He does already," Cat insisted, suddenly resenting Clementine's implied criticism of Drake with a ferocity that surprised her. "I'm the one who decided I want to change. No one influenced me."

She took a deep breath to calm herself down, and knotted her fingers together so tightly her knuckles turned white. "And, if it's not too much trouble, I'd like you to help me."

"Me?" Clementine's delicate hand flew to her chest. "How can I help you?"

Cat sucked on her lower lip. "I've saved up some money and I want to buy new clothes—dresses, skirts, and such—but I don't know where to start. Should I go to a dressmaker, or order them ready-made? I don't know what size to buy, or what kind of cloth to make them in, or what colors."

Tears of frustration stung her eyes. "I'd ask my mother, but she's not here. And Ida May isn't knowledgeable about what ladies wear these days, so I don't dare ask her. So, will you help me? Please?"

Clementine's eyes shone with the enthusiasm of a general marshaling his troops. "I'd be delighted to help. I never had a daughter to dress, so this will be a pleasure for me, too."

Cat drummed her fingers against the tabletop, and took a deep breath to quell her nervousness. "So, where do we start?"

Michael climbed the porch steps just as Cat came backing through the front door.

"Thanks again," she said to someone inside before turning abruptly and almost bumping into him. She jumped back, her eyes widening. "Michael . . . you startled me."

He grasped her arms to steady her. "Sorry. I thought you heard me coming."

His mother appeared in the doorway. She was wearing what Jace called her "petticoat smile," the one that warned all men she had women's business on her mind and would brook no masculine interference.

Damned if Cat wasn't wearing the same kind of smile. Were women born with it, or did someone pass them out in a secret feminine ceremony? Michael's hands fell away from Cat's arms.

"Glad I could help," his mother said to Cat.

Help with what? He sensed a female conspiracy.

Cat headed for the porch steps. "Well, I've got to get back to town." She bade them both good-bye and trotted down the steps. The two dogs came running over to escort her to her horse.

Michael watched her mount Rascal, wave, and ride down the drive. When she rounded the bend and finally disappeared from view, he turned to find his mother still standing in the doorway, watching him.

"Why are you looking at me that way?" He tried to keep the testiness out of his voice and failed.

"I'm trying to decide whether to tell you what plans Cat and I have been hatching."

Michael smiled dryly. "I could tell the two of you were up to no good."

His mother did not return his smile. Not a good sign.

She retreated to the parlor. Michael followed.

His mother turned. "I'm pleased Cat's decided she's too old to be a tomboy."

Michael frowned. "What do you mean?"

"You didn't know? She's decided it's high time she started acting and dressing more like a woman. And all because of Drake Kendall."

Michael's heart stopped. "Kendall."

"Yes." His mother fussed about the parlor, straightening the antimacassar on the back of the sofa. "Our charming newcomer has turned Cat's head. Since he doesn't like the way Cat's been dressing and acting, she's decided to change."

"Why would she want to change?" Michael scoffed. "She's fine just the way she is."

"Drake thinks there's room for improvement." His mother stopped fussing. "She's obviously attracted to him and wants to change to please him. We women tend to do that. And she asked for my help. We spent the last hour making lists of the new clothes she'll need."

Why did his mother sound as if she approved of Kendall?

"What kind of clothes?"

"Clothes like I wear. Skirts. Dresses. Women's clothes."

Michael felt as though the ground had just fallen from beneath his feet. First Cat had gone with Kendall to the Fourth. Then she kissed him. Now she planned to change herself into whatever he wanted.

So much for his father's sage advice.

His mother plumped a pillow. "I just finished taking Cat's measurements before you arrived. I promised to send her order to my dressmaker in St. Louis by the next post. If I tell Hetty to rush, Cat's new clothes should arrive in two weeks." She looked pensive. "Cat in a dress. I'll bet none of us will recognize her. She'll be a new woman."

"There's nothing wrong with the old one," he said between clenched teeth.

Too agitated to sit, Michael paced the room. "Kendall's not the right man for Cat. He's too slick, and he's got a mean streak." As he had found out that night in One-Eyed Jack's. "Now he wants to change her, and she's going along like a lamb to the slaughter."

"A woman in love—"

"Love?" he snapped. "Cat doesn't love him."

"Well, she didn't actually say she *loves* him, but I recognize all the signs. It's as if she doesn't have a mind of her own. She becomes possessed."

"What's he going to want her to do next, give up being a vet?"

"Oh, I doubt that Cat would give up being a vet even to please Drake Kendall. But then again . . ."

Michael stopped. He had to think.

His mother smiled. "Perhaps Cat will content herself living in Boston and being a banker's wife."

Now he recalled someone saying that Kendall had been a banker in Boston. If that was the case . . .

"I'm sure Maddy and Paul would love that," his mother went on. "Boston is not all that far away from New York. They could visit often."

He frowned at his mother, but refrained from commenting.

His mind collected one thought, then another, and

another. He mentally laid them all out like a hand of cards and read them. Suddenly an intriguing question hit him in the face.

"I wonder why Kendall left his job to come to Little Falls?" he said.

"Belle heard Dr. Kendall say that Drake wasn't satisfied with banking and thought there were more opportunities for an ambitious young man out West."

"So he just left a promising position, pulled up stakes, and came out here."

"That would appear to be the case."

Michael frowned. "Since Kendall has the experience, why hasn't he tried to get a job with Grandpa's bank while he's staying here?"

Clementine blinked owlishly. "Why, I don't know."

Michael walked over to a window and looked out over the front lawn at the dogs racing and nipping playfully at each other. He looked back at his mother. "Doesn't that strike you as odd?"

"Now that you mention it, he hasn't sought any kind of gainful employment since coming to town. He lives with his father."

Michael fell silent and watched the gamboling dogs, collecting his thoughts again. "When you think about it, Mother, there's a lot about Drake Kendall that doesn't add up."

"Perhaps I could write to your grandfather and ask him to make discreet inquiries. Surely he knows other bankers in Boston."

Michael shook his head. "No, I'm going to write to Cat's mother instead. Cat's grandfather knows the Kendalls quite well. I'll ask Mrs. Wills to find out everything she can about Drake. I have a feeling that Kendall isn't all he's cracked up to be, and I intend to prove it."

"I hope you're right." Clementine sighed. "Cat

needs someone to talk some sense into her."

Michael stared at her, bewildered by his mother's abrupt shift from championing Kendall to questioning Cat's good sense.

"I'm close to her," he said, "and if I can't talk any sense into that thick skull, no one can."

"But you're like family. Young women never listen to family when it comes to matters of the heart." Her blue eyes sparkled. "Look at me. Jace Cooper was the last man your grandfather wanted me to marry. But did I listen to him? Of course not."

"Good thing you didn't," Michael said. "You and father were meant for each other."

"Just as you and Cat are meant for each other," she said quietly, and solemnly.

Understanding came to him in a flash. He arched one brow and smiled. "So, you're not on Kendall's side after all. You're just pretending in order to get me to open my eyes."

She smiled. "I always knew your father and I didn't raise a fool."

Michael hoped he didn't look as miserable as he felt. "I guess it's high time I stopped lying to myself, isn't it?"

"Yes, son. You know you love Cat just as much as your father loves me."

He did.

His mother folded her arms. "If you don't fight for her, you'll lose her."

"Then it's about time I gave Drake Kendall a run for his money."

His heart was at stake.

13

After returning from the Coopers', Cat stood in the boardinghouse parlor and regarded the animals with rising concern. "What's wrong? You're all acting like there's a big old thunderstorm headed this way."

Edgar Allan hopped around his cage and shrieked, "Midnight dreary . . . weak and weary . . . nevermore! Nevermore!" while a whimpering, whining Bounder paced back and forth, back and forth between Cat and the front door. Even Ulysses, who wouldn't bat an eye if the house were falling down around him, stood balanced on the sharp edge of the piano bench and flicked his long plumed tail.

Knowing the animals had a good reason for their uneasiness, she opened the door for Bounder and went out on the porch to take a look for herself. Blue sky hovered clear and cloudless, bright sun shone. No thunder. No lightning. No rising wind.

Just Michael striding up the brick walk.

A Michael she had never seen.

He walked with the light, determined grace of a cat

stalking supper. As he drew closer and closer, the very air about him gathered and thickened, crackled and sizzled, a warning that lightning was about to strike after all.

Cat watched him with fascination. The man approaching her was Michael, her friend, not a stranger.

Bounder trotted up to him, her tail wagging in welcome. He stopped to pat her head absently and call her a good girl. Then his hand dropped and he looked at Cat.

His blue eyes blazed with a white-hot heat and the intensity of something that Cat instinctively recognized as desire. Desire directed at her.

She started, both shocked and surprised at the force of it. Never in her life had she been the object of such raw, blatant masculine *wanting*, especially coming from such an unlikely source as Michael. The powerful emotion crashed into her like a runaway train. Her heart soared skyward. A shiver of anticipation skittered along her arms. She felt edgy. Wary. Confused.

He stopped at the foot of the porch steps and looked at her. The glittering intensity still heated his eyes. His mouth remained in a resolute, unsmiling slash.

She wrestled her emotions under control and returned his stare with what she hoped was nonchalance. "Ida May said you came by this morning, and here you are again. Must be important for you to make two trips in one day."

"It is." His words were clipped, his tone strained. "May I come in?"

"Of course."

"Are Denny and Ida May home?"

"No one was here when I rode in. They must've gone out."

Inside the parlor, Ulysses had disappeared and a quiet, subdued crow calmly swung on his perch.

Cat watched Michael hang up his hat. "So, what's so important that you had to make a second trip in to town?"

He turned and walked up to her, his eyes narrowed beneath his dark brows. He stood so close she could see the white rays surrounding each pupil, smell his unique scent of clean, work-warmed skin and saddle leather. "Is Kendall courting you?"

So Clementine had told him about the new clothes, and why Cat wanted them.

She raised her chin a defiant notch. "Not officially. But I'm sure he'll declare his intentions soon."

"So you *are* sweet on him."

"Sure am." She remembered Drake's kiss and grinned foolishly from ear to ear. "And I know he feels the same about me."

Michael stepped back and stared at her, a dumbfounded expression on his face. Then the anger sparked again. "Dammit, Willie, are you out of your mind? I thought you had more sense than to fall for a brassy city slicker like Drake Kendall."

She planted her hands on her hips and glared back at him. "Michael Cooper, you've been picking on Drake like a buzzard on a carcass ever since he got here, and I'm getting sick and tired of it. I don't know why you don't like him, but I do. A lot. He's a fine, decent—"

"Fine and decent?" Michael's roar caused the crow to squawk and beat his wings against the cage. "Have you forgotten that this fine and decent man tried to force himself on Ruby? Have you forgotten that he tried to beat me senseless?"

"How many times do I have to tell you that he apologized for that!" she roared back so loudly they could have heard her outside. "And he hasn't done it again."

Michael opened his mouth to say something, but Cat held up a warning hand to silence him. "You've always been a good friend ever since I can remember. It'd really mean a lot to me if you let bygones be bygones and try to get to know Drake better. For my sake."

"I can't do that," he said.

"Why not?"

"Because he's not the right man for you." His eyes blazed with hunger. "I am."

He reached for her, pulling her against him before Cat could resist. She barely had time to register the sensation of his solid, muscular body molding itself to her own as if it belonged there when he kissed her.

Her eyes widened in surprise and she whimpered in protest, intending to pull out of his embrace, but his mouth on hers soon banished all rational thought. After the initial, claiming pressure, his demanding kiss softened, becoming sweet and gentling. Cat savored the liquid lassitude creeping through her limbs like warm, melting honey until she floated. Her arms slid around his waist of their own volition, pulling him closer and anchoring her to the ground.

Michael smiled in triumph before his lips parted beneath her own. She responded in kind willingly. Without warning, his tongue plundered the innocence of her mouth.

Cat stiffened and gasped at the bold, shocking intimacy, her protest escaping as nothing more than a soft moan. Her body arched and tightened in response. A warm knot of unfamiliar, searing pleasure tightened deep within her.

Oh, God, she thought. *What is happening to me?*

Unexpected heat roared through her like a flame

stirred by a gust from the blacksmith's bellows. She wanted *more*. She wanted him to kiss her silly. She wanted him to unbutton her shirt and touch her bare breasts. She wanted—

Drake.

With superhuman effort, she pulled away, breaking the spell Michael had cast over her.

Why am I kissing him when I really want Drake?

"Why'd you do that?" she demanded, breathing hard, her sharp voice filled with reproach.

Michael looked as stunned as she felt. He cleared his throat. "I couldn't help myself."

As if that excused him.

She touched her tender, swollen lips. "Who in the hell do you think you are, to kiss me without asking?"

Michael's eyes narrowed. "I didn't think you'd mind. You certainly didn't the first time."

Cat's cheeks turned hot at the memory of lying against Michael's body, her head against his shoulder, his mouth inches from hers.

"I'd just been thrown from a horse and got the wind knocked out of me," she retorted. "I didn't know what I was doing."

"I don't mind you lying to me, Cat, but don't lie to yourself. You kissed me back."

"This wasn't exactly a brotherly peck, Cooper," she muttered. Against her will, she still felt its aftershocks all the way down to her toes.

"I'm not feeling at all brotherly right now," he admitted, watching her with all the steel-eyed patience of a stalking wolf. "I haven't felt that way about you for some time."

"Then why in God's name didn't you ever *tell* me?" Before she met Drake.

Michael smiled his engaging, lopsided grin that had

left a twisted trail of broken hearts across three counties. "Better late than never."

He reached for her again, but Cat stepped back. "Oh, no, you don't!"

He stopped in bewilderment. "What's the matter? Don't try to tell me that you don't like my kisses, because I know better."

She liked them, all right. Too much.

"You mustn't kiss me. I love Drake."

He looked appalled. "You're joking."

"When I first told you I loved you, you accused me of joking. Now I'm telling you that I'm falling in love with someone else, and you insist I'm joking." She thrust out her stubborn chin. "Well, Cooper, I wasn't joking then, and I'm not joking now."

Hurt filled Michael's beautiful eyes. "Come on, Cat. You've punished me enough."

She threw up her hands in exasperation. "I'm not saying this to hurt you, or to get back at you. Get it through your thick skull that I am falling in love with Drake. Hopefully, he'll ask me to marry him and build a life together."

Michael raked his fingers through his hair. "You can't be serious." Desperation and urgency made his voice sound thready. "In the shed, when we found Bounder's pups, you said you loved me and wanted to marry me."

"I've changed my mind."

"I love you, Cat. I want you. I can't put it any plainer than that."

"Why are you telling me this now? Because another man's shown an interest in me?"

"That's insulting and beneath you. I don't want you just because another man does. My feelings run much deeper than a childish case of sour grapes."

She fought back self-righteous tears. "You know,

you've treated me pretty shabbily, Cooper. You've taken me for granted. You've stomped on my feelings.''

She ignored his stricken look. "I wanted you to be my lover.'' Her voice shook. "Just once I wanted you to look at me the way my father looks at my mother, or Jace looks at Clementine. Like you adored me. Like I'm the only woman in the whole world. But you never did.

"And you know what? I'm damned tired of it. At least Drake treats me like I'm special. He doesn't see me as good old Cat, always around, as comfortable as an old shirt.''

"Taken you for granted? Stomped on your feelings? Cat, I—'' Michael ran a hand over his face. "I'd rather cut off an arm than hurt you. You know that.''

"I used to think so. Now I'm not so sure.''

"I'm sorry for being so thoughtless.'' He walked toward her, but stopped when he saw her stiffen and pull away. "It's funny. Everybody else could see I was falling for you. Everybody except me.''

"Who's everybody?''

"Ruby—''

"Oh, isn't that just dandy. You've been discussing me with your—your mistress.''

"She's never been my mistress,'' he said quietly. "She provided pleasure, bought and paid for, and when that ended, friendship.''

"So you say.''

He ignored her jibe. "My parents could see that I was falling for you, but I kept denying it, insisting that I loved you as a friend, nothing more.''

"Well, congratulations, Cooper. You told me that so often, I finally believed it. And now I've found someone else.''

"You can't mean that,'' he said softly. He moved

closer, but made no attempt to touch her. "I love you, Catherine Wills."

"It's too little, too late. My feelings have changed. I never thought they would, but they have. I want Drake, and I know he wants me."

Michael's eyes flashed sapphire sparks. "Why? Because he can mold you into something you're not?"

Cat glared at him. "What are you talking about? Drake isn't trying to change me."

"Oh, isn't he? Then why did you just talk to my mother about buying all these frilly new clothes?"

"That was my idea," she snapped. "I thought it was high time I started dressing like a woman instead of a man. Drake had nothing to do with it."

"A likely story. What's he going to do next? Make you give up being a vet?"

That was the last straw. Cat marched up to Michael and stood toe to toe. "You're jealous because Drake sees something in me that you don't," she said, poking him in the chest for emphasis. "He's just trying to open my mind, to show me that there's a big, wide world outside Little Falls."

A dark flush crept up Michael's face. "You know me better than that. I've always wanted what's best for you."

She stepped back, and folded her arms to put a barrier between them. "I used to think that you were what's best for me, but now I know differently."

"I am what's best for you, Cat. Not Kendall. You're just too hurt and angry with me at the moment to see straight."

"Haven't you been listening to a word I've said?" she cried. "I don't want you anymore."

He studied her for what seemed like hours. She could almost hear the wheels turning in his mind as he considered their conversation. "I know you. You'll change your mind about Kendall."

"No, I won't."

"We'll see."

What did he mean by that? "I'm tired of battering my head against a brick wall. I think you'd better leave."

Cat saw the pain written on his shocked face, but she hardened herself against it. She mustn't let him sneak around the defenses she had put up to guard her heart, a heart that now belonged to Drake.

Michael took a deep, shuddering breath. "Am I still welcome to sleep in the spare room when I'm in town?"

"I don't think that would be such a good idea. If I let you stay here now that Drake and I will be courting, it wouldn't be proper."

"Since when did you ever care what other people think?" he scoffed. "When last I checked, this was *your* boardinghouse. You can let the rooms to whomever you please."

"And I choose not to let you stay here. It would hurt Drake too much to know that we were sleeping under the same roof."

His expression became shuttered. "Fine. I'll be at Jack's. I have some hard thinking to do."

He turned and grabbed his hat on the way out, then stopped expectantly in the doorway.

Call him back, a little voice urged. *There's still time.*

Then she thought of Drake.

She said nothing. Michael's shoulders tensed, then slumped. He closed the door behind him. Gradually his slow, heavy footsteps faded and died away, leaving Cat in the silence she craved.

She sank down on the sofa, propped her elbows against her knees, and cradled her spinning head in her trembling hands. Sadness seeped so deep inside, she could feel it numbing her soul. Then pain like a thousand jabbing white-hot needles made her want to scream.

Why hadn't she realized that the hurt of wanting Michael would be nothing compared to the agony of not wanting him?

She hugged herself and moaned, letting the tears stream down her face, hoping they would wash away the pain. They didn't.

Catherine Augusta Wills, you are one prize fool, she thought. *You've waited all your life for Michael to admit that he loves you, and when he finally does, you tell him that you love another man.*

"Weak and weary," Edgar Allan said, swinging on his perch.

Cat stared balefully at the crow, envisioning him baked in a pie. "Has anyone ever told you that you have a big mouth?"

This time, he wisely kept it shut.

She had to get away. She rose and dried her eyes, then marched out the door. The sight of Rascal and Rogue tied to the hitching post, side by side like the matched pair she and Michael had once been, brought a lump to her throat and fresh tears to her eyes.

She untied her mare, swung into the saddle, and rode off, not down Main Street where everyone could see her, but around the house and through the back-yard.

She leaned forward and touched her heels to her horse's sides, urging her to run faster, faster, as if she could outrun the pain. And for a while, she did. With the wind blowing against Cat's face and sifting through her hair like a lover's fingers, with the countryside sliding by in a blur, she forced all thoughts of Michael Cooper from her mind.

Eventually they caught up with her.

Hearing Rascal's labored breathing, Cat patted her on the lathered neck and slowed her to a walk.

"No use killing us both," she muttered.

Michael had finally said the words she had waited her whole life to hear: *I love you, Catherine Wills.* She still had time to tell him that she had made a mistake, that she really wasn't falling in love with Drake. She still had time to tell him that she loved him still, and no other man could ever take his place in her heart.

But she'd be lying.

She envisioned Drake, so tall and handsome, his golden hair bright with sunlight, his dark eyes sparkling with warmth and interest whenever he looked at her. She hadn't known him for very long, but there were some people you meet for the first time and know them for a lifetime. When she was with him, she felt as though she were embarking on an exciting adventure like the characters in those dime novels Teddy and Buster were always reading in secret behind the mercantile.

Cat patted Rascal's neck. "Michael's wrong about Drake. He doesn't want to change me into something I'm not. He wants to bring out what's already there."

She thought of Drake's kiss beneath the sycamore tree. A gentlemanly kiss that asked permission, rather than demanded and took, unlike Michael's raw, uninhibited kiss in the parlor. Drake would be a tender lover, sweet and gentle.

And Michael?

Cat recalled the feel of his hard body against hers and shivered violently, her reaction causing her sensitive horse to shy. She calmed the restive mare with a few soothing words.

"There's more to life than sweet kisses," she muttered. "There's adventure. The unknown. Growing."

What was one of her father's favorite sayings? "You can't discover new lands if you never risk leaving the shore."

She had to take the risk and leave her safe shore behind.

Michael was the shore, and Drake new lands to discover.

She turned her horse and headed back to town.

Michael slid his glass across the bar's polished surface and told Jack to refill it.

"A little early for you to be drinking, isn't it?"

He turned to find Ruby standing at his elbow. Amusement danced in her brown eyes. "Sometimes a man needs a drink no matter what the time."

Jack returned his glass. Michael downed the whiskey in one swig, savoring the searing heat traveling down his gullet, making his eyes water and clearing his nose. But it didn't burn away the memory of Cat's tormented face, the sweet taste of her mouth, the bittersweet regret in her eyes.

He slid the glass back to Jack.

Ruby raised her brows. "How many's that?"

"None of your business."

She didn't take offense at his curtness, just placed her foot on the brass rail and leaned against the bar. "Usually it's woman trouble that makes a man drink too much, too fast."

Jack handed him his glass and muttered something to Ruby about not discouraging a paying customer.

Michael only took a sip. "Too much? I haven't even gotten started."

"Must be *bad* woman trouble."

"Ruby . . ."

"I know, I know. None of my business." She studied him in silence out of speculative, narrowed eyes.

"You look like a man who's had something taken from him and plans to get it back."

He stared into the depths of the amber liquid in his glass. "Let's just say that if Drake Kendall were to come in here right now," he growled, "only one of us would be walking out."

Ruby regarded him with astonishment and laughed uneasily. "I've never seen you like this. What in blazes has come over you?"

"Not a damn thing. I'm the same as I ever was. Good old Michael Cooper."

"Not from where I'm standing." She looked over her shoulder. "See that big old mirror? Take a look, honey, and tell me what you see."

He didn't recognize himself in the crazed glass. His eyes, as cold as a winter sky and as hard as blue steel, turned his expression dark and menacing. Wild. Dangerous. Predatory. He looked away in disgust.

"Judging from that fire in your eyes," she drawled, "I'd say the good citizens of Little Falls had better lock up their daughters tonight."

"Just one."

"Calm down, Cooper. The state you're in, you'd only scare her."

If he was drunker, he'd be sorely tempted to go upstairs with Ruby. But not even an hour or two lost in mindless pleasure with a skillful, willing woman could erase Cat from his mind, or take away his desolation.

He dug into his pocket and dropped a handful of coins on the bar. He turned to leave.

"Want some free advice from an expert?"

He stopped, turned, and looked back at her, still leaning so nonchalantly against the bar. "Sure."

"Stop being so damned noble. Don't play fair. Fight dirty."

Good advice. He was fresh out of nobility. And damned tired of playing fair.

But he didn't know how to deal any other way.

Rascal warned Cat that they weren't alone.

She brushed the mare's neck with long, sweeping strokes, only stopping when Rascal raised her head and nickered softly in welcome, her ears at attention.

Cat turned to see Michael striding toward her. She stopped brushing and watched him warily, not knowing what to expect. She felt as though she were doing a balancing act on a circus high wire. One false step and she'd fall.

He did look mighty fine, with his dark hair and chiseled features. She could still recall the feel of his hard body pasted against hers, the warmth and sweet wetness of his mouth. He had wanted her.

Drake. Keep thinking of Drake. He's the one you want.

She took a deep breath and forced the distracting thoughts from her mind.

Michael walked up to Rascal and extended his hand so she could nuzzle his palm.

Cat wrinkled her nose. "You been drinking?"

He looked at her hard, but for once his pale blue eyes remained shuttered and didn't reveal his thoughts and feelings. "Yeah." He reached out to cup her cheek in his palm. "I'm sorry for the way I treated you. If Drake's the man for you, I won't try to come between you."

His hand fell away, taking the warmth with it.

She pulled black horse hairs from the brush bristles to look busy and hide her awkwardness. "Glad you've come to your senses, Cooper."

He fished in his back pocket. "I got this for you." He handed her a small box.

She blushed. "Gee, what'd you go and do that for?"

"To make my apology official."

She opened the box. Inside lay a small, intricately carved cameo brooch set in gold. "Oh, Michael, it's beautiful." And must have cost him a pretty penny. "You shouldn't have."

He smiled. "I thought it would go with all those fancy new clothes you're getting."

In all the years she'd known him, he'd never given her something as frivolous or personal as jewelry. His birthday and Christmas gifts had always been practical: Rascal, her medical bag, veterinary instruments. One year, he even built her the nearby barn that now housed Rascal, and Bounder's pups. The closest he had ever come to something personal was the pair of butter-soft leather boots she wore to this day.

Maybe he was starting to see her in a different light.

But it was too late.

Cat grabbed Michael's hand, placed the box in his palm, and curled his fingers around it. "I can't accept it."

He looked crestfallen. "Why not?"

"Drake would want to know where I got it, and I'd have to tell him."

"It's just a gift from an old, close friend."

"A woman shouldn't accept jewelry from a man not her intended. People saw me wearing this, they'd make assumptions. I'd hurt Drake."

He held out the box. "He doesn't have to know it's from me. You could tell him that your parents sent it. Or Miz Sims left it to you."

"But *I'd* know where it came from. Besides, a woman shouldn't keep secrets from the man she loves."

"What's the harm in taking it?" His eyes were soft with persuasion. "Something to remember me by when you embark on your new life."

A new life without him in it.

Surely no one would condemn her for accepting such an innocent gift from a long-time friend.

She stared at the proffered box and debated what to do. Finally she sighed and took it. "To remember you by." She thanked him again and hugged him.

When they parted, he kissed her on the forehead and told her he'd be back for supper.

Walking away, Michael smiled to himself. She had accepted his gift with less resistence than he expected. He had won one battle, and he planned to win the war.

14

Two weeks later, Cat received a surprise at the post office when she went to pick up her mail.

"Any packages arrive for Mrs. Cooper from St. Louis?" she asked the postmaster.

He bent down behind the counter to retrieve four large rectangular boxes and one smaller oval one, which he stacked on the counter.

"These just came in for her," he said. "The stage almost couldn't hold them all."

Cat's new clothes.

"I'll take them," she said. "I'm riding out there this morning."

Her fingers itched to cut the twine and tear off the wrapping paper as if they were Christmas presents.

The postmaster squinted at one of the address labels. "Looks like she bought out Henrietta's. Her dressmaker, you know."

"I know." Cat pushed the oval box over to one side of the pile, then hoisted the boxes into her arms. She headed for the door before the postmaster could comment further.

He rounded the counter and hurried over to hold the door open. "Hope Mrs. Cooper likes her new dresses."

"I'm sure she will."

Hurrying down the boardwalk, balancing the boxes in front of her, Cat became the object of blatantly curious stares. By noon, everyone in Little Falls would think that Clementine Cooper had received a shipment of clothes from her dressmaker.

That's exactly what we want everyone to think, she thought. *No one will learn the truth until I'm good and ready to show them the new me.*

Approaching an alley, she noticed Buster Blick leaning against a building and testing his new slingshot. Ever since he had acquired his new toy, every woman's bonnet and every horse's rump became a potential target.

Cat glared at him as she passed. "I'm warning you," she growled. "Don't even think of using it on me. It'll be the first and last time."

"We'll see about that," he sneered. His mischievous eyes widened in curiosity. "What's in the boxes?"

My future. "Clothes for Mrs. Cooper."

She walked faster, watching Buster out of the corner of her eye. She tensed, expecting a stone to hit her in the back at any moment. Luckily for Buster, he resisted temptation and wandered off in search of another victim.

Cat breathed a sigh of relief.

Her euphoria plummeted, however, when she noticed Tessie Dobbs heading straight toward her. Cat turned sharply to the right and stepped off the boardwalk, intending to elude Tessie by crossing the street.

Her ploy failed. Tessie caught up, fell into step beside her, and peered at the oval box. "Why, Catherine Wills!" Her long nose positively twitched. "If I'm not mistaken, you're carrying a hatbox."

As the wife of the mercantile's owner, Tessie could tell what was in a box, a bag, or a barrel just by looking at the size and shape of the packaging.

"I wouldn't know," Cat replied, stopping so a carriage could speed past. "I'm just picking these up for Clementine Cooper."

"Those look like dress boxes to me," Tessie said. "Mrs. Cooper must've ordered new clothes from her fancy dressmaker in St. Louis."

"She must've." If Tessie only knew . . .

When they reached the other side of the street, Cat wished Tessie a good morning, left her standing in front of the mercantile, and continued on her way.

She decided not to return to the boardinghouse, where she'd face a barrage of questions from Ida May and Denny. She wanted Clementine to be with her when she first opened the boxes.

She decided to escape the prying eyes and questioning glances of Little Falls by renting Heck's buggy and driving her precious parcels out to the Cooper farm.

The two dogs came barreling off the porch to greet her the minute she reached the halfway point along the long drive. Their excited yips and barks pierced the air, announcing her arrival as they raced to see who would reach her first. Both did, in a tie.

As she drove up to the house, her escorts now trotting sedately and silently on either side of the buggy, Cat scanned the stable yard for any sign of Michael. She frowned. Even though he had claimed he wouldn't try to come between Drake and her, his behavior of the last two weeks made her suspect his motives.

He was always relentlessly *there*. He came into town more times in the last two weeks than he had in the past two months, and of course, he stayed at the boardinghouse. Cat would come to breakfast and usually find him sitting at the kitchen table, his dark hair damp from washing and freshly combed, his strong jaw clean-shaven. She couldn't deny that seeing him didn't cause her to think unseemly thoughts. But she always looked away quickly and thought of Drake.

When she came home from having supper at the Kendalls' one evening, Michael was lounging on the porch swing as if he lived there, his long legs stretched out and resting on the rail, his hands behind his head. He had been waiting for her, though he denied it later, when she confronted him.

Yet he always behaved like a perfect gentleman. He never tried to draw her into his arms, never tried to kiss her again.

Cat pulled up her horse in front of the hitching post and stepped out of the buggy. Well, Michael Cooper could show up at the boardinghouse as often as he pleased, but she still wouldn't swoon in his arms.

She tied her horse, collected her parcels, and headed for the house, the dogs following. The front door opened, and Clementine hurried out to meet her. She shooed away the dogs and took several boxes.

Her blue eyes sparkled with infectious excitement. "Are these what I think they are?"

"My new clothes," Cat replied. They walked back to the house. "They just came in. Good idea of yours, having them addressed to you. Now no one in town suspects what I've planned."

"I'm glad the plan threw the gossips off the scent." She looked at Cat. "Nervous?"

"A little," she confessed. "I haven't worn a skirt since I was ten years old."

"Don't worry. It'll all come back to you."

They entered the house.

Cat looked around for any sign of Michael. To her relief, he didn't suddenly appear in the parlor doorway. "Where's Belle?"

"Working in her garden," Clementine replied. "Let's go upstairs to my bedroom and see what delights Hetty has created for you."

Once in Clementine's bedroom, they set the parcels on the bed. Clementine handed Cat a pair of shears like a nurse handing the doctor a surgical instrument. Cat snipped the packing twine on the first box, ripped off the brown paper, and lifted the lid.

She reverentially parted the tissue paper to reveal two shirtwaists. She lifted them out of the box and brought them to her face, breathing in the particular fresh scent of new clothes. Then she held them up, wondering in dismay how she would ever be able to tolerate the long, tight sleeves and the high collar after the freedom of her father's loose old shirts.

Clementine examined one with the critical eye of a lady of fashion. "Aren't they smart? Notice the fine tucks on this one, and that pretty ivory lace on the other? They're wrinkled after their long journey, but a good hot iron will take care of that." She spread them on the bed. "What's next?"

Inside the second box, Cat found two identical plain serge skirts, one a dark blue and the other a dark brown. She shook out the dark blue one.

"Hetty made this too small." She caught her lower lip between her teeth to keep from crying. "The waist will never fit me."

"Don't worry," Clementine said gently. "Once you're laced into a corset, it will fit you perfectly."

"Oh." She had forgotten that she would now have to wear a corset. Cat spread the skirt on the bed. "But this is so straight, how will I ever ride astride?"

Clementine parted another layer of tissue paper to reveal a third skirt, this one made of plain black serge. She held it up and spread the fabric. "Look at this."

Cat smiled in delight. "It's full like a skirt, but it's cut in two up the middle, like trousers."

"I had Hetty make you a split skirt," Clementine said. "You'll be able to ride astride as you normally do, but when you're walking, it'll look like you're wearing a skirt."

"That's more like it." Cat unwrapped the third box and gasped in wide-eyed astonishment when she saw the contents. "Oh, my God! This dress looks like it came straight out of Sally Wheeler's closet."

Clementine stiffened. "I certainly know better than to dress you like that tasteless creature."

"I didn't mean to insult you, Mrs. Cooper. I just meant that it's frilly, like Sally's dresses."

"I know exactly what you mean, and no offense taken." The fine lines at the corners of her eyes deepened with amusement. "Skirts and shirtwaists are all well and good for wearing every day, but every woman needs at least one dress." She reached for the hatbox. "And a matching bonnet."

Actually, the dress wasn't as frilly as Sally's, and was a beautiful blue to match Cat's eyes. She liked the overskirt, and the pointed waist, which Clementine assured her would elongate her torso and make her look even taller. The bodice's lapels were trimmed with several rows of plain ribbon.

The fourth box contained the dreaded corset, several lace-trimmed camisoles, and clocked stockings.

"Shall we have a fitting?" Clementine asked.

Cat's stomach fluttered with a hundred butterflies

beating their wings in unison. "I guess it's now or never."

Cat stared at the stranger in the mirror. She couldn't tear her eyes away from the vision in a blue dress.

The dress's formfitting bodice made Cat's bosom look as voluptuous as Ruby Delight's, and her waist so narrow it could be spanned by a man's hands. Of course, being laced into the damned corset, she couldn't manage a deep breath, but that was unavoidable.

"Now put on the bonnet," Clementine said.

Once Cat tied the long, wide grosgrain ribbons beneath her chin, the straw bonnet framed her face and made her eyes appear as wide as saucers.

She squealed in delight. "Ooh, I can't believe I look so—so—"

"*Beautiful.*"

Cat blushed. "Do you think so?"

"Don't take my word for it. Wait until Drake Kendall sees you in your new clothes. He'll be speechless."

She hoped he'd think her as womanly and mysterious as Clementine.

As Cat turned away from the mirror, she remembered Clementine's admonition to "glide, not stride" when she walked. She mustn't go stomping around as if she were stepping on ants.

She took smaller, dainty steps and glided across the room to the bed, relishing the soft, feminine rustle of her long skirt.

"I think I heard a door slam," Clementine said. "Belle must be back from her gardening. Why don't you go downstairs and show off?"

Cat grinned. "She's not going to believe her eyes."

When she walked—*glided*—into the kitchen, she

found not Belle, but Michael rummaging around in one of the cupboards, his back toward her.

She froze. He mustn't see her like this. She wasn't ready. She quickly turned, ready to flee back upstairs to the safety of Clementine's bedroom.

"Ma'am?"

Michael's voice stopped her in her tracks. *Ma'am?* Hadn't he recognized her?

"Do you know where my mother's gone?" he asked in the reserved, polite voice he used with strangers. "One of the men cut himself, and I can't find any bandages."

Cat slowly turned.

Michael's eyes widened as he looked her up and down. His jaw dropped. Surprise stunned him speechless.

He cleared his throat. "I didn't recognize you in that dress."

He didn't like it. She could tell. Her confidence cracked and shattered. "I look stupid in it, don't I. Like a little girl playing dress-up in her mama's clothes." Tears of humiliation stung her eyes. "That's what you're thinking, isn't it. Don't lie to me."

She turned to go. Suddenly his hands on her shoulders stopped her. He gently turned her to face him, but she was so mired in self-doubt that she kept her eyes averted.

"Cat, look at me."

When she didn't, he curved his index finger beneath her chin and gently lifted it, forcing her to drag her gaze up from the floor to meet his.

"Don't presume to tell me what I'm thinking," he said softly. "You don't look stupid, or like a little girl playing dress-up. I think you look beautiful." He looked at her lips as if they were delectable sweet cherries, and his eyes darkened with desire. "Beautiful enough to kiss."

She stepped back out of reach before he could carry out his threat. "Behave yourself, Cooper. The only man I'll be kissing from now on is Drake."

A slow, lazy smile spread across his face and he raised his hands. "Don't worry. You're safe with me."

Why did she doubt his sincerity? Could be that wicked gleam that suddenly sprang to his eyes.

He stepped back, hooked his thumbs in his belt, and studied her. Then he let out a low, admiring whistle that made Cat blush. "That dress sure doesn't look like it came from the mercantile."

"It's from Henrietta's in St. Louis."

"She's dressed my mother for years, and my father's never complained." Now his gaze lingered at her waist. He shook his head. "In all the years I've known you, Willie, I've never seen this side of you."

She beamed with pleasure. "Amazing what the right clothes can do, isn't it?"

"Truly amazing."

"I have others upstairs." She told them what they were.

His scrutinizing look lingered for a second too long on her bosom before traveling up to her face. He sat back on the edge of the table and crossed his arms. "Why the sudden urge to wear dresses?"

She raised her chin. "I just thought it was high time I started dressing like a lady."

He didn't believe her. She could see the skepticism clouding his expression. But he didn't contradict her.

"You look like you could dethrone Sally Wheeler as the Princess of Little Falls," he said with a teasing grin. "You'll have so many beaux coming to call, you'll have to build a bigger front porch to hold them all."

Cat almost swatted him, then remembered she wasn't dressed for it. "Don't you try to butter me up with your smooth talk, Michael Cooper. I've known you too long to believe a word of it."

Still, she liked being on the receiving end of such sweet compliments.

"I don't know what came over me." He grinned a wider smile that showed gleaming white teeth. "Seeing you in that dress must've turned my tongue to honey."

Cat rolled her eyes. "Now you sound like your father."

"Who do you think gave me lessons?" Michael stepped away from the table. "So, when are you going to make your debut as a lady?"

Her straw bonnet made her scalp itch, so she untied the ribbons and took it off. She scratched her head. "I was thinking of wearing this dress to church."

Michael fanned his face with his hand and stared at the ceiling. "Catherine Augusta Wills," he began, imitating Belle's drawl in a prissy, high-pitched voice, "the Reverend Dawlish takes one look at you, missy, and he'll deliver one hellfire and brimstone sermon about Eve tempting Adam."

This time, she did swat him before they both burst out laughing.

Michael stood and waved good-bye to Cat. He waited until the buggy disappeared from sight in a cloud of dust before he started walking aimlessly to clear his head.

He felt dazed. Stunned. He couldn't think straight.

His initial reaction to seeing Cat in a dress had been astonishment, like seeing Ruby dressed so respectably at the Fourth of July celebration. Once the first shock had receded, he realized that the dress made Cat look even more beautiful and—he mentally groped for the right word—*womanly*.

Now, walking past the stables, he couldn't get her out of his mind. Having once seen her naked, he knew she possessed a woman's curvaceous body, but it was different seeing her in a dress. More exciting. The formfitting attire revealed much more than her loose-fitting shirts and baggy men's trousers, yet still managed to tease suggestively.

He had wanted to slide his hands around that narrow, corseted waist and pull her into his arms for a hot, openmouthed kiss that would brand her as his forever. But that would have scared her off. He had to handle her gently, as he would a skittish filly.

He had noticed how she ran her hand lovingly over her skirt, smoothing the fabric as if she were petting an animal. She straightened her cuffs. Then she stole a peek at herself when she passed by a reflective surface.

He had never seen this side of her before and found her feminine fussings oddly endearing. The gestures made the strong, capable Cat seem softer and gentler. They also made him feel more masculine by contrast, and brought out his protective instincts.

The ferocity of his own reaction stopped him in his tracks. His vehemence went deeper than mere concern for a friend's welfare. He wanted her. Period.

He stopped at a corral fence and watched several grazing mares and the gray stallion in the field beyond. These mares weren't in season, so the stallion didn't try to cover them, but he still asserted his masculine dominance by nipping at their hindquarters and necks to herd them to the other side of the field.

One mare flattened her ears back and kicked at him, refusing to submit to his will. She'd run off, but he'd patiently steer her back to the herd. Finally he wore her down, and with a flick of her long tail, she joined the others.

Michael smacked the top rail of the fence with his hand. He wanted Cat as much as the gray stallion wanted that mare. Even though Cat insisted that she had fallen in love with Drake, Michael wouldn't give up fighting for her unless she became Mrs. Drake Kendall.

The faint music of church bells ringing in the distance forced Cat to hurry.

"Oh, my!" She stifled a little squeal of delight as she looked at herself in the mirror. "I'm a *woman!*"

A knock sounded on her bedroom door. Ida May called out, "You'd better hurry, or we'll be late for the service." Ida May hated to be late for church.

When Cat had returned home from the Coopers' with her new clothes, she had shown them to her boarders and made them swear not to tell anyone her plans. Denny had seemed surprised, but Ida May uttered a terse "About time" before busying herself making pies.

Cat almost told Drake, then decided against it. She wanted him to be surprised along with everyone else. Once she appeared in her feminine finery in front of the entire town, Drake would realize the seriousness of her need to please him.

Now Cat put on her straw bonnet and tied the ribbons under her chin, making sure some of her own natural curls peeked out. Then she ran a nervous hand down the front of her dress to quell her quaking insides. The ensemble needed something.

Then she remembered the cameo brooch Michael had given her. She took it out of her bureau drawer and pinned it at the base of the dress's high collar.

Now she had a bridge from the past connecting her to the present.

She strode out of the bedroom. After a few steps, she reminded herself, *Glide, don't stride,* and slowed down to a sedate walk. She just wished her knees would stop knocking.

She paused in the parlor doorway to gauge everyone's reaction. When Cat appeared, Bounder yipped, tucked her tail between her legs and scooted behind the sofa. Ulysses arched his back and hissed. Edgar Allan Crow just stared at her in stupified silence.

Cat glared at her menagerie. "So this is the thanks I get for giving you a home."

"Don't pay them any mind," Denny said, his hazel eyes sparkling appreciatively. "You're going to have to let me photograph you, you know."

Ida May's eyes filled with tears. "Oh, Catherine Augusta," she said, her voice trembling, "I wish Miz Sims was alive to see this day. And I wish your mama was here, too."

Cat crossed the room to give Ida May a hug. "I'm sure Miz Sims is looking down at us from heaven, and someday my mother will see me in my new clothes."

Ida May took a deep breath and dabbed at her eyes with a handkerchief. She squinted at Cat's brooch. "Where'd you get the cameo? I've never seen you wear it before."

"It was a gift from a friend," Cat replied.

If Ida May suspected the identity of the friend, she didn't say. "Let's be on our way. We mustn't keep the good Lord waiting."

Cat hoped they would be late. She had to face everyone sooner or later, but she could do without running a gauntlet of enervating stares and whispers before she arrived at the church.

Cat squared her shoulders and led the way. She knew that when she stepped through the front door, there would be no turning back.

Heck Hechinger saw her first.

He was just crossing Rose Street and happened to glance Cat's way. He must not have noticed her, for he kept walking. Suddenly he stopped dead in the middle of the street and spun around. He stared at Cat as if he had just seen a ghost.

Uncertainty and astonishment flitted across his features. Then he looked her up and down as she and the boarders drew closer. "Cat. What happened to your clothes?"

"Nothing," she replied. "I'm wearing them."

"But you—that's a *dress*." He made it sound as if she had just robbed the bank.

She smiled. "I always did think you were as sharp as a tack, Heck Hechinger."

"I think she sure looks pretty," Ida May piped up as Heck fell in step with them.

"So do I," Denny added.

"As pretty as her mama," Heck said gravely, unable to tear his eyes away.

Cat's confidence soared as she thanked him for the compliment. But Heck was only one in a church full of townsfolk.

15

THE MINUTE CAT WALKED THROUGH THE CHURCH door and saw pew after pew filled with townspeople she had known all her life, her feet turned to stone. She froze. Her heart slammed against her ribs. Her mouth went dry.

For the first time in many a year, she wouldn't be standing in the rear of the church with Heck, waiting for the service to end. The thought left her faint and trembling. She grabbed Ida May's hand and whispered, "I can't."

And then she saw the back of Drake's golden head shining like a beacon from one of the front pews.

I can't disappoint him.

Confidence banished her nervousness. She smiled at Ida May, mouthed, "I'm fine now," and placed her hand beneath the older woman's elbow, and together they proceeded down the aisle. *Glide, don't stride,* she mentally reminded herself over and over as she took smaller steps.

The whispers and gasps of astonishment started the

minute Cat passed several of the rear pews.

"Who's that?" someone asked.

"Well, I'll be . . . it's Cat."

"Cat Wills? In a *dress*?"

"About time."

She stared straight ahead and resisted the urge to turn and shoot off a scathing retort, focusing on Drake for courage. Out of the corner of her eye, she saw heads turn and necks crane for a better look at the amazing sight of tomboyish Cat Wills in a dress.

The whispers grew into buzzing, like the dull drone of bees on a hot summer day. Cat felt the weight of all those gazes riveted on her, looking her up and down, staring and speculating. She felt her cheeks grow pink under their scrutiny.

Now members of the congregation seated in the front pews began turning in their seats to see the cause of all that whispering. More faces gawked at Cat in disbelief.

If anyone laughs, she thought, *so help me, I'll—*

Suddenly Drake turned, obviously just as curious as everyone else about the commotion. His dark eyes widened in surprise as he stared at Cat's transformation. Then he broke into a delighted grin and nudged his father sitting beside him to turn and take a look.

Drake approved.

Cat smiled back, and let out the breath she had been holding. Her relief almost caused her to overlook the Coopers and the Ritters filling one whole pew, but she'd have to be blind to miss their smiles of encouragement and regard, especially Michael's when his gaze lowered to her brooch.

Finally their little procession came to an empty pew right in front of the Coopers and across from the Kendalls. Ida May filed in first, followed by Cat, then Denny.

Cat risked several glances at Drake, who silently mouthed, "You look stunning."

Stunning. No one had ever called her that before. Her spirits soared.

The buzzing dwindled and died into hushed, respectful silence the minute the Reverend Alexander "Buddy" Dawlish appeared and took his place in the pulpit. He was just opening his mouth to greet his congregation when his gaze fell on Cat. He blinked. His lips moved, but words failed him.

To Cat's relief, he made no comment about her sudden promotion from the back of the church to a front pew, but began the service as if seeing Cat Wills in a dress was an everyday occurrence.

And contrary to Michael's teasing prediction, the minister's sermon had nothing to do with Eve's temptation of Adam.

When the long service finally ended and everyone started filing out of the church, Cat couldn't wait to talk to Drake, who had kept casting surreptitious glances at her throughout the service. Cat had certainly felt the weight of Michael's gaze on her.

The minute Cat stepped out of her pew, Drake appeared at her side. He smiled down at her from his great height, but Cat thought she detected a certain coolness in his demeanor.

"Why didn't you tell me?" he said.

He sounded so hurt, she hesitated, suddenly unsure of herself. "I wanted to surprise you." She moistened her lips. "You're not angry with me for not telling you sooner, are you?"

"Of course not." His smile deepened and he

squeezed her hand. "I couldn't have asked for a better surprise."

They walked down the aisle together, the last to leave the church.

Once outside, everyone wanted to tell Cat what they thought of her new look. She already felt like a bride in a receiving line.

Tessie Dobbs's homely face wore a look of reproach. "Well, you certainly fooled me, Catherine Wills. And all that time I thought those parcels were for Mrs. Cooper." She gave Cat's ensemble a quick scrutiny, followed by a disdainful sniff. "Of course, you could've bought something just as pretty for less money at the mercantile."

"I'm sure I could've," Cat replied, "but that would've spoiled my surprise."

Sally Wheeler edged through the crowd. "Cat Wills, is that really you?" Her pretty face turned sullen with blatant envy. "I just couldn't believe my eyes when I saw you walking down that aisle." She leaned closer. "Quite frankly, I'll bet Michael prefers you in trousers."

Cat smiled. "I have it on the best authority that he doesn't."

Dr. Kendall nodded benignly at her elbow. "You look very feminine, my dear. You outshine many a Boston lady."

Belle came up and gave Cat a teary-eyed hug. "Clementine told me you were a vision, and she's right."

Michael followed and kissed her on the cheek, ignoring a glowering Drake. "I guess I was wrong about the sermon, Willie."

"Why do you call her that?" Drake snapped. "She's not a man." He smirked. "Or haven't you noticed yet?"

Michael resisted the other man's barb and looked at Cat's brooch. "Oh, I've noticed."

Jace clapped one warning hand on his son's shoulder. "Well, get a load of you, Miss Catherine Augusta Wills. If I wasn't already married, I'd be knocking down your door."

She smiled back. "If you were twenty years younger, I'd let you in."

Drake looked truly appalled. *"Catherine!"*

Jace flung back his head and roared. When he stopped whooping, he clapped Drake on the arm. "Just having a little fun with her, son. That's our way. We don't mean anything by it."

Then the Cooper men said their good-byes and left to join the rest of their party heading back to the farm.

After just about everyone made some comment about Cat's new clothes and drifted off, Drake placed his hand on her arm. "Would you care to join Father and me for Sunday dinner?"

"We'd be honored to have you," the doctor added.

"I'd like that," Cat said. "Just let me tell Ida May not to set another place at the table."

Later, in the Kendalls' cool parlor waiting for the housekeeper to put dinner on the table, Cat sat on the edge of the settee like a very proper lady. The corset encased her in a suit of armor and forced her to sit up ramrod straight, as she had in church. She kept her legs together demurely and her feet flat on the floor, though after five exhausting minutes of such stiffness, she wished she could lean back, cross her legs, and lounge as casually as the men across from her in their comfortable chairs.

As she used to.

Dr. Kendall smiled. "Forgive an old man for staring, my dear, but I find the change in you astonishing. May I ask what brought it about?"

"I'm responsible, Father," Drake said, looking at Cat with a triumphant gleam in his eye.

The doctor raised his brows. "Really?"

Before Cat could comment, Drake said, "Yes. From the first moment I met Catherine, I recognized a rare beauty hidden beneath those horrid men's clothes. I convinced her that by giving up her tomboyish ways, she would enhance her own womanliness."

"My son is a true connoisseur of female beauty," Dr. Kendall informed Cat.

She opened her mouth to comment, when Drake cut in yet again. "All she had to do was let it blossom." He smiled. "And she has."

Annoyed that they were discussing her as if she weren't in the room, Cat said, "I thought it was high time I started dressing like a lady."

"I trust this is a permanent change," the doctor said. "You intend to wear dresses and skirts from now on, don't you?"

"I put all my trousers and shirts away in a trunk in the attic, and hung my new clothes in the armoire."

Already she missed the blessed freedom of her father's old shirts, the room to move her arms around. She'd never needed a corset, either. She reminded herself not to dwell on what she had been, but on the woman she intended to be.

Dr. Kendall ran a hand over his shiny bald dome. "Women weren't meant to act and dress like men, my dear. Quite frankly, I'm surprised your parents allowed you to dress that way for so many years."

Cat stiffened. "I'm a vet, Dr. Kendall. I spend most of my day slogging around dusty, muddy barnyards and doctoring animals. Some of them can get real ornery, so I have to be able to get out of their way, fast. If I wore a skirt, I wouldn't be able to do that. That's why I've always worn trousers.

"My mother also thought they were more decent for riding. When a woman wearing a skirt rides astride, she shows a lot more leg than if she's wearing trousers."

Dr. Kendall's face turned as pink as the crown of his head. "I didn't mean to criticize your parents, my dear. I realize that I'm expressing how people view such things in Boston."

"No offense taken. I realize Boston isn't Little Falls."

The doctor drummed his fingertips against the arm of his chair. "Since you've turned in your trousers for skirts, does that mean you're going to give up your veterinarian duties as well?"

Cat raised her brows in surprise. "Of course not."

Drake's face fell. "But you just said that wearing skirts would hamper you and even place you in danger."

"Clementine Cooper had her dressmaker make me a split skirt," she said. "The skirt part's divided, so it looks like a skirt, but gives you the freedom of trousers." She smiled. "It's quite comfortable, and I think it'll do quite nicely when I make my rounds."

More comfortable than this dress and corset.

"Call me old-fashioned, my dear," Dr. Kendall said, "but I don't think being a veterinarian is any sort of occupation for a lady."

Cat tried to hide her annoyance behind a teasing smile. "Why, Dr. Kendall, if I didn't know you better, I'd swear you were trying to talk me out of being a vet so you could eliminate the competition."

Both Drake and his father laughed.

Drake shook his head. "Catherine, where do you get these outlandish ideas?"

The housekeeper appeared in the doorway to announce that their Sunday dinner awaited.

• • •

The setting sun washed the horizon in broad strokes of brilliant orange and red.

Drake strolled out onto the veranda to join his father, who was sitting like an Oriental potentate in a huge white wicker chair, and puffing on a thick cigar.

"I'm warning you right now, Drake," he growled, his bristly brows coming together in an intimidating frown, "if Catherine winds up like one of your Irish girls, you'll answer to me. I'll not have her ruined and saddled with an illegitimate child, do you hear me?"

Drake leaned against the railing and curled his lip into a sneer. "No matter how little you think of me, I don't intend to seduce her."

His father gave a snort of disdain. "If you did, Michael Cooper would kill you."

"That farm boy . . . I'm shaking in my shoes."

"You should," his father snapped. "Are you so quick to forget what that *farm boy* did to you in the saloon?"

Drake clenched his teeth. He could still feel Cooper's fist slamming into his jaw. A lucky punch, nothing more. He shook his head. "You're always so quick to believe the worst of me, aren't you? Just because I've made a few mistakes."

"Everyone makes mistakes. The trick is to learn from them. You never do."

Drake rose and towered over his father eying him balefully from the depths of his chair. "I've done what you've wanted, and this is the thanks I get. Another lecture."

"What are you talking about?"

"I'm talking about Catherine. As you saw, she's stopped dressing like a man. I've cured her of her tomboyish ways just to please you." He crossed his arms. "I thought you'd be happy."

"She may be dressing like a lady, but she's not giving up being a vet."

"She will." Drake returned to his place on the porch rail. "And when I accomplish that, I expect you to do something for me in return."

"I might have known you'd want something."

"I want you to order those two brothers of mine to find me another position back in Boston."

"They can't work miracles. Bankers don't take kindly to embezzlers."

"They don't have to find me another position in banking. I'm a talented, enterprising fellow. I can work at something else."

His father studied him out of narrowed eyes as he blew another cloud of gray smoke into the listless summer air. "What makes you think they'll listen to me?"

"You still own the house they're all living in. Threaten to sell it, or better yet, turn it over to me. That'll bring them in line."

His father took another leisurely drag. "What are you up to, Drake?"

Drake looked down the street in the direction of the boardinghouse. "I'm going to give you your heart's desire. I'm going to reform and settle down. I've decided to marry Catherine after all. She's much prettier than my brothers' wives, and with a little tutoring, she'll never embarrass me socially."

And if she bored him in the boudoir, he could always take a mistress.

"Does she love you?" his father asked.

"I daresay she wouldn't be so willing to change for me if she didn't." He raised an inquiring brow at his father. "Do we have a deal?"

"You get Catherine to marry you, and I'll see to it that your brothers welcome you with open arms."

• • •

Though Horatio Kendall had never dared admit his lack of experience to the anxious young farmer standing at his side, he had only actually delivered three foals, and they were normal births. But he had read textbooks and those veterinary journals Catherine had given him, and he felt confident that he could deliver Seth Stevens's foal successfully.

They stood outside the box stall at five o'clock in the morning and regarded Flying Cloud, a chestnut mare lying on her side in a bed of clean, fragrant straw.

Stevens grasped the stall door with rough, red hands the size of small hams. His florid face looked unnaturally pale in the lamplight. "Something's wrong with her, Kendall. That's why I sent my boy for you."

"How long has she been in labor?"

Stevens stood almost as tall as Drake, but was twice as broad, with a full, bushy brown beard and a fearsome demeanor that made most men give him a wide berth. He turned paste white. "She's been like this for an hour."

A normal delivery took five or ten minutes. The foal's forelegs should have emerged first, followed by its head and the rest of its body. From Stevens's description, Kendall knew something was wrong.

The mare groaned and grunted in pain.

"She's been breeding for a full twelve months," Stevens said. "That means it's likely this foal will be a colt, right?"

Kendall knew that although the gestation period for the horse was eleven months, the longer the pregnancy extended into a twelfth month, the greater the probability of male offspring.

"She should have a colt," he agreed.

Stevens opened the stall door and talked quietly to the mare, his voice soft and gentle for such a big, rough man. He knelt down and stroked her sweating neck.

He looked up at Kendall, his eyes red rimmed and desperate. "Flying Cloud isn't just a horse, Dr. Kendall. She's my family's future."

Kendall knew that Stevens had a lot riding on Flying Cloud and the precious colt she carried. Stevens had had to borrow money from the bank to buy the mare, more money than he could afford. Then he paid even more to breed her to Jace Cooper's champion stallion, North Wind. He was betting that Flying Cloud would produce a champion colt that he'd be able to sell for a nice tidy profit.

When Kendall had arrived in Little Falls, Stevens was one of the first to go to him instead of Catherine Wills. The farmer himself was a newcomer to the area, having bought his spread two years ago. He had always used the services of Dr. Paul Wills rather than his wife or daughter. Now he preferred Kendall to the tomboyish Cat. As any self-respecting man should.

"Don't worry, Stevens. I understand how important this horse is to you." Important enough to rouse him out of bed in the darkest night. He stepped into the straw-carpeted stall. "Now, if you'll leave and let me tend to her . . ." He was no fool. He didn't want any witnesses in case anything did go wrong.

The farmer lumbered off. He stopped and turned, his massive bulk filling the doorway. "You need anything, you let me know."

"I'll need a bucket of clean, warm water and some lard to oil my arm," he said, taking off his coat. "So I can examine her womb." One of the more disgusting procedures, but it couldn't be avoided.

Stevens nodded. "I'm sure the wife has some in the kitchen."

He left, and returned a few minutes later with a full bucket of water and a tin of lard.

After Stevens left again, Kendall suppressed a yawn and urged himself to stay awake. He chloroformed the mare to ease the frequent, violent contractions that would hamper the internal examination. Those contractions could squeeze a man's arm into numbness.

Once inside the womb, his searching fingers first encountered the outline of the foal's hindquarters, its tail in the center, and the sharp points of the hocks just beneath.

Sweat broke out on his forehead, and he swore under his breath.

A breech birth.

Sweat rolled down his face, and he huffed and puffed with exertion. He had to move the foal's hind legs into the birth canal.

Suddenly a powerful contraction squeezed his arm so hard Kendall thought he'd faint from the pressure. When it passed, he felt his way beyond the foal's right hock, grabbed the leg, and pulled.

The leg moved only so far with an odd sluggishness, then caught on some part of its mother's body and stopped.

Kendall swore again and withdrew his arm. After carefully and thoroughly washing off the lard and unrolling his shirtsleeves, he called to Stevens and told him to send his son for Cat Wills.

Cat came rushing into the stall an hour later. Good thing she had already risen, washed, dressed, and eaten her breakfast when the Stevens boy came pounding on her door.

Although Seth Stevens had never once requested

her services to care for his livestock and had been quite vocal in his disapproval of women doing anything except cooking and cleaning, Cat's first concern was saving his prize mare and her foal.

She set down her bag, and after giving Dr. Kendall a perfunctory greeting, she looked over the mare. Flying Cloud barely made a sound, her eyes dull and staring, her breathing shallow and ragged.

"How long has she been in labor?" she asked Kendall.

His gaze slid away and he busied himself arranging instruments in his medical bag. "A little over two hours. I sent Stevens's boy for you as soon as I saw the mare was in trouble."

Cat removed a smock with the sleeves cut out at the shoulders for freedom of movement, and disappeared into the next stall to change. She told Kendall to keep talking. While she removed her shirtwaist and put on the smock, Kendall told her the foal was a hind presentation with the legs bent at the hock.

"A breech," Cat said, oiling her arm to protect it from infection and ease of mobility. "It's a shame, but I may have to sacrifice the foal to save the mother."

Kendall turned around and stared at her bare arms. His ears and the top of his head turned a faint pink. "Too bad. Stevens is certain Flying Cloud here is carrying a colt. He has high hopes for it."

"Sometimes Mother Nature overrules our highest hopes." Cat finished greasing her arm. "Did you try to bring its feet into the birth canal?"

He shook his head. "I didn't even touch her. I assumed you've done more of these breech births than I have, so I thought I'd give you the honor."

Cat, her arm already inside the mare and too busy attempting to pass a rope around the foal's limbs at the hock, didn't stop to wonder why Kendall hadn't even tried, and why he had summoned her in the first place if Stevens preferred his services.

Once she secured the rope, she pushed the hindquarters backward and upward, and brought the feet into the birth canal, taking care to shield the foal's sharp hooves with the palm of her hand so they didn't tear the womb as she brought them over the rim of its mother's pelvis.

"Got him!" She felt a rush of euphoria as she pulled with all her might and extracted the foal.

A chestnut colt lay motionless in the straw.

Her soaring spirits plummeted, replaced by a sickness in her stomach.

Kendall peered over her shoulder. "It's dead." He checked the mare's heart, and fixed an accusing stare on Cat. "So's Flying Cloud."

Cat rose, numb with disbelief. "She *can't* be. The procedure was going so well."

Kendall examined the mare and shook his head. "Looks to me like she died of internal bleeding."

"I protected the hooves with the palm of my hand, just like my father taught me," Cat said. "One of them couldn't have lacerated the womb."

Kendall's eyes darkened and chilled with censure. His lips pursed in a thin, disapproving line. "Well, Catherine, from where I stand, that's exactly what occurred."

Cat washed the lard from her arm. "This shouldn't have happened."

Indignation radiated from Kendall in palpable waves. "You obviously did *something* wrong."

"If you'll excuse me . . ." She went into the neighboring stall to take off her smock, and put her shirtwaist back on. Once she'd changed, she came out and faced him.

"How's my colt?" came a hopeful voice from the doorway.

Cat looked at Seth Stevens. Best to tell him quickly. "I'm sorry. They're both gone."

The farmer stared at her, his stolid face devoid of all emotion. "What did you say?"

Kendall said, "Flying Cloud is dead. So is her colt."

Suddenly Stevens's face turned a dark, furious red as he realized the full enormity of the situation. "She had a colt?"

Kendall nodded.

Stevens flung open the stall door with a crash and strode in. He stopped and stared down at the wreckage of his high hopes and dreams. Then he looked from Kendall to Cat with murder in his eyes. "Which one of you did this? Who killed my horses?"

"The colt was in a breech position," Cat said, meeting his hot, enraged gaze squarely. "Something went wrong when I attempted to move him into position."

"So you did this." Stevens turned so red he looked on the verge of exploding. His eyes went wild, and his nostrils flared. His hands balled into huge fists at his sides.

Cat took an involuntary step back, suddenly afraid for her life. She felt as though she were in a pen with an enraged bull snorting, pawing the earth, and about to charge.

Sensing danger as well, Kendall stepped between them. "Stevens, don't."

"Look what you've done!" he roared, glaring at Cat, his voice echoing in the cavernous barn. "You killed my horses. Nobody should've let a damn woman touch them in the first place. Women don't know beans about anything."

"I tried my best, Mr. Stevens."

"Yeah, well your best wasn't good enough, was it?

And now what am I supposed to do with two dead horses?" His voice rose like a howling winter wind. "Where am I going to get the money to pay back the bank? Maybe I'll lose this farm because of you. My family'll be destitute. Christ, a wife and three kids to feed."

Cat felt sick inside. "I'm truly sorry. I know it can't bring your horses back, but—"

"Get out!" he bellowed, the cords standing out in his thick neck. "Get out of my sight before I kill you with my bare hands."

Cat grabbed her medical bag and hurried out of the stall, giving the half-crazed farmer a wide berth.

After Cat was out of earshot, Horatio Kendall placed a reassuring hand on Seth Stevens's shoulder. "Don't worry. I'll see to it that she never, ever does this to anyone else."

Stevens gave him a look. "That's small consolation to me."

16

❤

"It wasn't your fault," Michael said to a dejected Cat sitting across from him at the Cooper kitchen table. "Birthing's always chancy. Any vet can lose a mare, a foal, or both."

Half an hour ago, she had ridden in from the Stevens farm, and told him in a quivering voice about the horses' deaths. The last time Michael had seen her this distraught was when her parents told her they were moving back East.

The fact that she had sought comfort with him and not Drake Kendall spoke volumes, whether Cat realized it.

Now Cat propped her elbows on the table and held her head in her hands. She looked deathly pale, her brow furrowed with worry. Her expressive blue eyes held a haunted quality that worried Michael.

"I can't understand it," she said, over and over. "I've delivered breech foals before. I did everything right this time, and they both still died."

"How long was the mare in labor before Kendall sent for you?" he asked.

"He sent for me as soon as he saw she was in trouble. Of course, it took me an hour to ride over there because the Stevens farm is so far away from town."

Michael shook his head. "You know as well as I do that when there's a difficult birth and a mare experiences violent and prolonged contractions like that, the foal usually doesn't survive."

Cat placed her palms against her cheeks and sighed. "But even if the foal died, Flying Cloud should've survived. I thought I made sure the foal's hooves didn't lacerate the womb. Obviously I didn't, because she died of internal bleeding."

Michael pulled her right hand away from her face and held it tightly. "It's not your fault, Willie."

Her eyes filled with tears, and she clasped his hand. "But it *is*!" She sniffed. "Seth Stevens was depending on me to deliver that colt, and I failed him."

"Now, hold on just one minute. Didn't you tell me that Stevens always had your father doctor his livestock because he didn't trust you or your mother?"

"He always made it very clear that he didn't trust women vets. That's why he sent for Dr. Kendall."

Michael released her hand and folded his arms on the table. "Then it was Kendall's responsibility, not yours." Before Cat could comment, he added, "Why didn't he try to turn the foal himself? Why did he wait for you?"

Cat explained that Kendall didn't have as much experience delivering a breech foal as she did, so he sent for her.

Michael leaned back in his chair and gave her a skeptical look. "Now, let me get this straight. Dr. Horatio Kendall, who with his city-slicker son, believes that women have no business being veterinarians, sent for you to deliver a breech foal because he didn't have the experience."

"He only wanted what was best for the mare and her foal, so he overcame his professional prejudices."

Michael shook his head. "If he doesn't have as much experience as you, then he should stick to doctoring people and leave the animals to you. I know I wouldn't want him delivering any Cooper foals."

"Even though you don't like Dr. Kendall," she said stiffly, "it doesn't change the fact that I'm still to blame."

Cat pushed her chair away from the table and rose to pace the kitchen, twisting her fingers together. "Maybe all those veterinary schools were right not to admit me. Maybe I'm not a good vet at all."

He rose to his feet and grasped her shoulders, forcing her to face him. "That's nonsense, and you know it. So you lost two horses. How many animals have you saved over the years? Don't they count?"

"No one remembers the animals you saved," she retorted. "At times like this, they only remember the ones you lost."

Michael's hands fell to his sides. He didn't know what to say because he knew she spoke the truth.

"Stevens's hopes were riding on that mare and her colt," Cat said, the haunted look seeping into her eyes once again. "I destroyed that poor man's dreams, and maybe his whole family."

Michael didn't know Seth Stevens very well, but he didn't like him. The man always used some tale of struggle and woe to try to shave a few pennies off the asking price of everything from nails at the mercantile to North Wind's stud fee. Jace had tolerated Stevens's hard-luck story for only fifteen minutes before he lost patience and told the man either he paid the fee like everyone else, or took his mare to another breeder.

Stevens had relented, but never stopped complaining.

"Don't feel too sorry for him," Michael told Cat. "My father explained the risks of horse breeding to him before he bought that mare. We know Flying Cloud's breeder, and he told us the mare was priced way beyond Stevens's means, but he scraped up the money to buy her anyway."

Cat's gaze sank to the floor. "That makes me feel even more guilty."

He didn't care that she had told him she loved Drake Kendall; he pulled her into his arms anyway, and held her tight. "It kills me to see you torturing yourself this way, Willie. Please stop."

She gave him a quick hug and drew away. "Thanks for the shoulder to cry on, but I've got to get back to town and explain matters to Drake."

Michael walked her out to where Rascal stood tied to the hitching post, and watched her mount. He noticed she was wearing her new split skirt and a shirtwaist instead of her father's old shirt and trousers. When she had said she would dress as a lady from now on, she meant it.

He handed her the reins. "Don't worry. This will all blow over."

His words didn't reassure her. She smiled a brief, preoccupied smile, said good-bye, and rode away, with the two dogs racing after her.

When Cat disappeared from sight, he turned and headed for the stables, his thoughts in turmoil. For this to happen to Cat just wasn't fair. The injustice of it made his blood boil. Worse than her being blamed for incompetence was the fact that she was beginning to doubt her own abilities.

He stopped at the corral where several breeding mares grazed listlessly in the shade, their long tails switching at their flanks. He replayed the scenario in his mind.

Several matters still puzzled him. Why had Kendall sent for Cat if he considered her skills to be inferior to his own? Why hadn't he attempted to deliver the foal himself? Michael didn't believe Cat's reason that Dr. Kendall felt that in this instance her experience with breech births surpassed his.

Michael knew Cat was a good vet, and highly skilled. From the time she could walk, she had accompanied her father on his rounds to the neighboring farms. Paul Wills patiently explained every nuance of caring for animals, and let his daughter try herself. Cat looked forward to her work with an enthusiasm and fearlessness that surprised even her mother. She read veterinary journals as avidly as Buster Blick read dime novels.

Cat could turn a breech foal in her sleep. That's why Michael had a hard time believing she had been so careless or so rattled as to allow a colt's hoof to lacerate its mother's womb.

What could have possibly gone wrong?

Several possibilities kept niggling at the back of his mind, all having to do with Dr. Kendall. What if he *had* tried to deliver the foal himself and failed? What if he pinned the blame on Cat?

You're grasping at straws, he thought. *You want Kendall to be at fault because you don't like his son.*

Still, every hunch was worth pursuing. Cat's hard-earned reputation was at stake.

He turned and headed back to the house. He had to find a way to prove his suspicions.

When Cat arrived back in town, she found Drake waiting for her on the boardinghouse porch.

She tied her horse to the hitching post and walked

up the brick walk, feeling more dejected with every step. As she approached the porch, she hoped Drake would walk down the steps to enfold her in his arms and reassure her that she wasn't a failure.

He didn't. He waited until she reached the foot of the steps before he said, "My father told me about the horses."

Fresh tears filled her eyes. "I can't understand what happened. I've never lost a foal before."

He took her hand and held it to his chest, his brown eyes soft with sympathy, yet stern. "I'm so sorry, Catherine. I know this must've been a very painful lesson for you."

She frowned in puzzlement. "Lesson?"

"Yes, lesson." He led her inside. Except for the crow sitting quietly on his perch, neither the animals nor the boarders occupied the parlor. Drake indicated that Cat should sit on the settee, and he sat down in the chair across from her.

"You won't want to hear this," he said firmly, "but I know you value honesty." He leaned forward. "Catherine, a woman like you belongs at home, caring for those who love her, not subjecting herself to such rough, degrading work."

She clenched her hands into fists in her lap. "But how can easing an animal's suffering be degrading?"

"My father told me the extreme measures you had to take to try to save this horse." He wrinkled his nose. "You had to spread lard all over your arm and stick it into a *horse*, Catherine."

"There's no other way to do it."

"Then a man should do it, not a woman."

She tensed. "Your father was there, and he didn't try to stop me."

"He didn't want to lose the colt, and though he

disapproved, he thought you could save it. Obviously he was wrong."

Cat rose and turned away from him. Edgar Allan Crow cocked his head to the side and regarded her out of bright black eyes. "Nevermore," he said.

How appropriate, she thought. *I may never practice veterinary medicine again.*

"I'm not telling you this to be hurtful," Drake said. "But the farmers around here trust you to keep their livestock healthy. Take this Stevens fellow. My father told me he spent more than he could afford to buy that mare. Now, because of you, he's in danger of losing everything he's worked for. He's got a wife and children who depend on him for support. You may be responsible for taking that means away from him."

Guilt weighed her down like a ton of bricks. The blame for losing the horses was hers and hers alone.

Drake rose to stand behind her. He rested his hands lightly on her shoulders. "I hope you'll consider giving this up, Catherine."

She turned to face him. "But I'm a good vet." Why did her protest sound so weak and hollow, even to her own ears?

"Until today. And what about tomorrow? What if you lose someone else's calf, or another horse?"

She sighed, crossed her arms, and hung her head.

"You're also a woman," he said, his breath soft on the back of her neck. "Did you ever stop to consider that perhaps your lack of male physical strength caused you to lose those horses?"

She turned and looked at him. "It's never hindered me before."

Drake raised his brows. "Wasn't your father always with you? Or the farmer, to assist?"

Cat sighed, closed her eyes, and rubbed her forehead to ease a headache beginning to form, draining her. "Yes. But your father was with me today, and I still lost those horses."

Drake looked as though he were about to say something, then changed his mind. He slipped his hands into his pockets, and walked over to the window, where he stared into space.

"Have I ever told you about my stepmother?" he asked.

Cat gave him an exasperated look. "What does your stepmother have to do with my predicament?"

"Quite a lot, actually. She was a nurse, you see."

"A nurse? You never told me."

"She worked at St. Luke's Hospital, where my father was on staff. After my mother died, Father married Belinda. He thought their marriage would run smoothly since they shared the same profession." Drake smiled wryly and shook his head. "He made the biggest mistake of his life."

"If your father is married, why isn't his wife here with him in Little Falls?"

"They aren't married anymore. Belinda divorced him."

Cat's eyes widened in astonishment. Once married, people stayed married until one of them died. Divorce was unthinkable.

Drake looked at her. "I can see that you're shocked and appalled. I can assure you that everyone in our family and circle of friends reacted the same. The divorce caused a scandal and ruined my father's chances to be promoted to head of surgery at the hospital." He shook his head. "And all because of Belinda's selfishness and ambition.

"We all begged her to reconsider for the good of our family, but she refused. She had to follow her own path, she said. Even if it meant destroying my father in the process."

"I'm sorry," she said, placing a hand on his arm. "That must've been terrible for you."

"It was, especially since my own mother was a paragon of feminine virtues. She dedicated her life to my father and her three sons. When she died, she left such a void in our lives."

He cupped her cheek in his palm and looked deeply into her eyes. "I refuse to have half a life with another Belinda, Catherine."

Then he brushed her lips with his own, said goodbye, and left.

Cat stood at the window, watching Drake stride down the brick walk. She had never felt so torn, so indecisive and unsure of herself. Her confidence lay shattered at her feet.

Perhaps Drake was right. Perhaps she wasn't cut out to be a vet.

She heard the click of nails on bare floor, then felt a cold, wet nose press into her palm. She looked down to see Bounder staring up at her out of concerned brown eyes.

Cat petted her, then sat down on the settee. Bounder sat at her feet and rested her head on Cat's knees. A minute later, Ulysses came trotting into the parlor from his explorations, and leaped onto the back of the settee, where he sat curled against Cat's shoulder.

"Weak and weary," said Edgar Allan Crow.

Later that evening after supper, Cat left an indignant Ida May sputtering about damn-fool men who thought they knew everything, and went out onto the porch to watch the sun set. No sooner did she settle herself on the swing than Denny appeared in the doorway.

"Mind if I join you?" he asked. "I've got something to show you."

She could tell they were new photographs. She shooed Ulysses off the swing, ignoring the indignant flick of his bushy tail and his low meow of protest. "Have a seat."

She knew it was Denny's turn to try to impart some wisdom designed to cheer her. Ida May had spent most of dinner telling Cat another oft-repeated story about how Maddy grew to doubt her healing skills in the face of Dr. Paul's modern veterinary techniques.

"But when Zeke became deathly ill, they worked together to cure that coonhound," was the moral of Ida May's tale, "and she realized her skills were as valid as Dr. Paul's."

Unfortunately, Dr. Kendall had no intention of working with Cat again. And as for realizing the value of her skills, Dr. Kendall would need to see the sun rise in the west first.

She looked up at Denny. "I know Ida May meant well, but I'm not my mother, and my situation is different."

Denny's hazel eyes shone with sympathy. "Ida May means well. She just doesn't know how else to make you feel better." He sat next to her. "I, on the other hand, do."

He handed Cat several photographs mounted on pasteboard. She saw a stranger looking out at her, a pretty young woman in a shirtwaist sitting primly in the parlor with her hands folded demurely in her lap. Denny had taken the photographs of Cat in her new clothes shortly after they arrived.

"For a minute, I didn't recognize myself," she said.

"Oh, they're you. Just a different you from"—he withdrew an older photograph of Cat dressed in her shirt and trousers and standing beside Rascal—"this one."

Cat held the photographs side by side and looked from one to the other. Although she may have been dressed differently, the same attributes illuminated her eyes. Confidence. Courage. Optimism.

She felt her spirits sink even lower. She doubted she would see these same virtues now if she looked at herself in a mirror. She wordlessly handed the photographs back to Denny.

He looked at her, the setting sun turning his auburn curls to fire. "What I'm trying to show you, in my clumsy Irish way, is that you're both women. One is Cat, the veterinarian. The other is Catherine, the woman. You shouldn't have to deny one or the other."

Denny quietly rose and left her alone with the photographs and her thoughts.

Cat crossed her arms and stared at a horse and rider ambling down Rose Street, the soft clopping of hooves barely disturbing the peacefulness of the warm summer evening. She knew which woman Drake preferred. Catherine, not Cat. And she knew why. To him, a woman who sought fulfillment outside a normal woman's sphere of home and family invited disaster.

She sighed, rose, and leaned against the porch rail, watching the lights go on in the houses along Rose Street. She wondered if any of her neighbors had heard of her blunder, and what they were saying to each other across the supper table.

By tomorrow morning, everyone in Little Falls would know that Cat Wills was a failure.

Michael gave Seth Stevens a couple of days to cool off, then he rode out to see him in the hopes of learning what had really happened to Flying Cloud and her colt.

Two years ago Stevens had bought the old Lockwood farm, a small spread the locals dubbed the "Knock-wood" farm because ill luck had plagued most of its owners ever since Johnny Lockwood and his wife had been murdered by the infamous outlaw Rawley gang after the Civil War. Now Seth Stevens had joined the ranks of the unlucky.

Riding into the yard, Michael noticed how the farm had changed over the years since his youth. A previous owner had torn down the original ramshackle two-room cabin and put up a rambling, two-story farmhouse. The original barn had been struck by lightning and burned to the ground several years ago in another owner's spate of bad luck, but its larger replacement had so far escaped that fate.

The sound of a hammer pounding in the distance caught Michael's attention. He turned in the direction of the banging and saw someone who must have been Stevens putting up a section of fence. Michael touched his heels to Rogue's side and rode over.

The farmer stopped hammering when he heard the approaching hoofbeats and looked up. From the sour expression on his stolid face, Stevens did not look pleased to see Michael.

He halted his horse, dismounted, and walked over. He gave him a curt nod. "Morning, Stevens."

"Cooper." He kept on hammering. "What brings you out this way?"

"I heard about Flying Cloud and her colt." He shook his head. "Rotten luck."

Stevens fleshy face turned red behind his beard. "Rotten luck? Incompetence, more like it. If that stupid Wills bitch knew what she was doing, my horses would still be alive."

Michael's temper sparked at the insult to Cat, but he managed to control himself. He couldn't afford to antagonize Stevens just yet.

"But you're good friends with her, aren't you," the farmer said, testing the solidity of his fence post. "She doctors your horses all the time."

Forgive me, Cat, he thought. "She *did*. I don't know for how long, after what happened to you."

Stevens scowled. "You got a reason for coming here, Cooper? I've got work to do, though who knows for how long if I lose this place."

Michael reached into his pockets and removed a small pouch. "My father feels bad that you lost Flying Cloud and her colt, so he wants to refund North Wind's stud fee."

Stevens's anger dissipated like smoke in the wind. "Why, that's mighty generous of him." He reached for the money and pocketed it quickly. "I'm much obliged."

Michael offered silent thanks to his father for coming up with the idea of refunding the stud fee. "You can catch more flies with money than vinegar," Jace had said, grinning.

"Mind telling me what happened that day?" Michael asked.

Stevens set another fence post into the ground. "What's to tell? Dr. Kendall let a woman try to deliver my colt, she didn't know what she was doing, and she killed it."

"I know that. I'd appreciate it if you'd give me more details." Seeing Stevens's blank look, Michael elaborated. "Where were you when all this was going on? Did you leave them alone in the barn?"

Stevens hammered at the post. "When Dr. Kendall got here, I showed him to Flying Cloud's stall. He told me to bring him a bucket of water and some lard. Then I left him alone.''

"He asked you to bring him some lard?" When Stevens nodded, Michael said, "He must've suspected it was going to be a difficult birth."

Stevens shrugged.

"How long was he alone before he sent for Cat?"

"I don't remember. I lost track of time." Stevens's expression darkened. "But she was in there a long time. When I looked in on them, she told me my horses were dead."

"Did Dr. Kendall try to save your colt?"

"No, and I don't understand why he didn't. That's why I called him, to deliver my colt. But what does he do? Turns it over to the Wills woman."

"So if Cat hadn't been there, your horses would've died anyway, because Dr. Kendall didn't even try to deliver the colt himself."

When Stevens realized he'd been led into a trap, he turned a dark, furious red. "I don't know why he didn't try to do it himself," he sputtered. "If he had, I know he would've saved my colt."

Michael took off his hat and wiped his brow on his shirtsleeve. "Sounds to me like Dr. Kendall was just as much to blame for losing your horses. He's the one who turned over the delivery to a woman."

"He thought he was doing the right thing," Stevens growled. "Can't fault a man for that." He started hammering again. "Now, if you're through, I've got work to do."

Michael mounted his horse, wished Stevens good morning, and rode off.

He shook his head at the injustice of it. After what Stevens just told him, it was apparent that Kendall wasn't entirely blameless. He had turned the delivery over to Cat, and when disaster resulted, he backed out of the line of fire and pushed her to the fore.

Michael touched his heels to Rogue's sides and urged the gelding into a slow canter. He couldn't put his finger on it, but something wasn't right. The pieces of the puzzle weren't fitting. Cat insisted she hadn't made any mistakes, yet both the colt and his dam died.

What had gone wrong?

Michael swore in frustration. He would learn the truth if it took forever.

17

CAT HALTED RASCAL BESIDE A NARROW, ROCKY stream and dismounted. While the mare lowered her head to drink her fill on this hot August afternoon, Cat dipped her handkerchief in the cold water, wrung it out, and wiped her tear-stained cheeks.

She patted Rascal's neck. "Now I know what a leper feels like."

She had just spent all morning and the better part of the afternoon making her usual rounds, riding from farm to farm to see if anyone required her veterinary services.

No one did.

Where the people Cat had known all her life used to smile and welcome her warmly into their homes with offers of lemonade and a slice of apple pie, now these same people stood outside their doors and regarded her with about as much welcoming warmth as if she were a stranger selling snake oil.

My animals are fine, they all insisted, so we don't need your services today. *Or ever.* But many looked over Cat's shoulder at something in the distance, or down at the ground when they spoke to her. Those who held Cat's gaze couldn't conceal the doubt and accusation in their eyes.

In the three weeks that had passed since the catastrophe, every farmer within a thirty-mile radius of Little Falls had heard about the bungled delivery. They all blamed her. They didn't trust her now.

The most painful defection occurred just yesterday when Cat happened to be riding past the livery and saw Dr. Kendall examining one of Heck's horses. Cat felt as though Heck had stabbed her in the heart. If her family's longtime friend no longer trusted her, no one else would.

Her reputation lay in pieces like broken pottery. Cat wondered if she'd ever be able to put them back together.

She knew Michael had spoken to Seth Stevens about that terrible day, trying to find some evidence that would absolve Cat of the horses' deaths. But so far his investigation proved fruitless.

Drake, on the other hand, persistently urged her to accept the inevitable even as he comforted her.

She put her damp handkerchief into her medical bag and mounted Rascal. She had one more stop to make, Gideon Wright's spread. Considering that Gideon had once questioned Dr. Kendall's doctoring of his herd, Cat was confident that this time she would receive a warm welcome.

Cat noticed Dr. Kendall's buggy the minute she rode into Gideon's yard.

She didn't give it a second thought. No doubt one of the thirteen Wright children had some childhood illness immune to tried-and-true home remedies, and Gideon had no recourse but to call in the doctor.

She dismounted, tied her horse to the hitching post, and went in search of Gideon.

Passing by the open barn door, she heard faint, muffled voices. She went inside, hesitating so her eyes could adjust to the sudden plunge from bright daylight into dusty darkness. She headed toward the voices, her footsteps muffled by the straw strewn about the floor.

At the other end of the barn stood Gideon and Dr. Kendall discussing one of the plow horses heavy with foal.

Dr. Kendall ran his hand down the mare's swollen abdomen. "She should be dropping the foal any day now. Make sure you send for me if it's not a normal delivery."

"I want you here beforehand," Gideon insisted, "even if you have to stay here all night. The last foal Winnie had was a breech, so I don't want to take any chances."

A foal that Cat's father had successfully delivered, with Cat in attendance, but Gideon didn't mention that.

She turned and quietly left the barn before either of the men noticed her.

How easy it is to ruin a reputation, Drake thought as he finished brushing his hair.

A backhanded compliment here, a bit of sly innuendo there. Sometimes a pursing of the lips and a sad shake of the head planted a seed of doubt. Often a prolonged silence accomplished the same objective. There were so many ready to believe the worst of someone.

He inspected himself in the mirror and adjusted his cravat. The campaign to discredit Cat was a masterpiece of ingenuity and subtlety. For the past three weeks, he and his father had been sowing the seeds of her professional destruction, and she didn't even suspect them.

He slipped on his coat. Ever since their campaign started, demand for his father's veterinary skills had tripled even as Cat's dwindled down to almost nothing. Drake smiled as he left his bedroom and headed downstairs. Poor, doomed Cat. Only those tiresome Coopers remained steadfast and loyal.

Drake stepped onto the porch and looked down the dusty, unpaved main street, with its monotonous storefronts, some of which hadn't been painted since the Civil War. He might as well take one last look at this dreary hole in the wall these bumpkins called home, and make one last visit to One-Eyed Jack's. In a week or two, his father would be buying him a one-way ticket back to Boston.

And he planned to take Cat with him.

When Cat returned to the boardinghouse, she found Ida May standing at the kitchen counter, dicing turnips for supper. "Any luck?"

Cat sat down at the table with a weary sigh and rubbed the back of her neck stiff with tension. "None of the farmers will let me touch their animals."

"I can't understand it," Ida May sputtered. "You've been doctoring animals all your life. I've never known anyone to complain. And just because one colt dies, they're acting like you've got the plague."

"But now there are two vets in town," Cat explained. "If they don't think a woman's competent, they can go to a man. And a lot of them have been doing exactly that."

Ida May threw a pinch of salt into a pot of boiling water. "I asked the quilting circle if they'd heard any rumors. They were reluctant to speak up, but Tessie

Dobbs told me that she'd overheard one of the farmers' wives in the mercantile saying something about how you recently lost one of Jace Cooper's prize colts, but he hushed it up because you were a friend."

Cat jumped to her feet. "That's a lie! I've never lost a Cooper horse. Never. And if I had, that'd be the last time Jace would let me anywhere near them, friend or no friend."

Ida May made a calming motion with her hands. "I know, and their ears are still ringing from the tongue-lashing I gave them. But that's how rumors get started. Something happens to the Stevens's colt, and before you know it, you're to blame if a horse sneezes."

Cat folded her arms and took a deep breath to keep fresh tears of frustration from falling. "Ida May, what am I going to *do*? If this keeps up, I'm not going to practice veterinary medicine at all. I won't be able to make a living."

A masculine voice from the doorway said, "You could come to Boston with me."

Cat looked up to see Drake standing there, his sensual mouth quirked in amusement. Had she heard him correctly? Did he just ask her to marry him? She would never go to Boston or anywhere else with a man not her husband.

"Why don't you two take a walk?" Ida May said, adding her turnips to the boiling water.

The minute they were outside and out of earshot, Cat looked up at him, suddenly hesitant and unsure. "What did you mean about my going to Boston with you?"

"Isn't it obvious?" He stopped and faced her squarely. "I want you to marry me, Catherine. I want you to come back to Boston with me as my wife."

His wife.

Drake Kendall was asking her to marry him.

Cat remembered asking her mother how she had felt when the man she loved asked her to marry him. Maddy replied that she felt dazed, numb, and astonished. And happier than she'd ever been in her life.

Why wasn't Cat feeling any of these emotions? She knew the answer.

Drake's never said he loves me.

She stared down at the ground. "Boston is so far away."

"It's far away from Little Falls, but not so far from New York City. You could visit your parents whenever you pleased."

She looked up at him. "Would I be able to be a vet?"

Impatience flashed briefly across his features, then died. "We've had this conversation before, Catherine. You know how I feel about that."

All too well. "I'm a simple country girl, Drake. I don't think I'd fit in with all your big-city friends."

"Nonsense. You've already stopped being a tomboy. My brothers' wives would teach you how to behave properly in society."

Suddenly the prospect of leaving behind all she held dear and traveling to an unknown, unfamiliar city felt as constrictive as her corset.

Tell me you love me. Say it. Please.

Drake took her hand. "You'd be my *wife*, Catherine. We'd be together. Surely that would more than compensate for everything you had to leave behind."

Would it?

She withdrew her hand. "It's a big step for me, Drake. I'll need time to think about it."

He kissed her on the forehead. "Don't take too long, dear Catherine. I'm not a patient man."

Then he said good-bye and left her standing alone

at the edge of her mother's overgrown herb garden, wondering why a man would even offer marriage to a woman who had to *think* about it.

Michael stood downwind of Gideon Wright and flipped a shiny twenty-dollar gold piece into the air.

"If you send for me when your mare foals," he said, snatching the coin out of the air as it descended, "I'll make it worth your while."

Gideon eyed the coin as it spun end over end into the air again, glinting and catching the light. "Maybe this time she'll have a normal delivery."

"Maybe. Maybe not. But if she doesn't, I want to be here to make sure Kendall doesn't lose it, like he did the Stevens colt."

Gideon grunted and wiped his nose on his sleeve. "Everybody's saying Cat lost that colt."

"I know she didn't."

"I can't take that chance. I'm not a rich man."

Michael held out the coin. "You willing to help me prove she didn't?"

"Sure. I like Cat. Always have." Gideon took the coin and pocketed it. "No skin off my nose." He glanced at his barn. "I noticed the mare's udder's swollen and it's been oozing."

"A whitish liquid that wets her legs?"

Gideon nodded.

"It'll be tonight," Michael said.

That evening at seven o'clock, Gideon sent one of his sons to fetch Michael.

When he arrived half an hour later and came striding into Wright's barn, Dr. Kendall stared at him in shocked surprise. Then the doctor turned an indignant shade of red.

"What in the hell are you doing here?" he sputtered, glaring at Michael out of furious brown eyes.

"I'm here to see that you don't lose another foal, and blame it on Cat," Michael said.

Kendall turned on Wright standing nearby. "What's the meaning of this, Wright? I thought you trusted me."

Wright looked him in the eye. "Why you getting so hot under the collar? What difference does it make who's here to see you do your job?"

"Unless you've got something to hide," Michael added.

"This is an insult to my professionalism," Kendall said. He picked up his medical bag. "I've half a mind to leave right now."

"You do, and everybody in town will hear about it," Michael said. "They'll all wonder why you left."

Kendall set down his bag. "Stay if you want. I have nothing to hide."

Michael smiled. "We'll see."

They took turns watching and waiting. Wright took Michael into the house for coffee, while Kendall stayed in the barn, reading a medical journal by lantern light. Then Michael stood watch while Kendall went into the house.

Around midnight, Michael heard the mare stir uneasily in her stall.

"What's the matter, Winnie?" He leaned against the stall door and murmured soothingly. "Is it your time?"

She gave him an anxious look and blew softly through her nostrils, whisking her long tail in a gesture reminiscent of Ulysses indicating his supreme displeasure. Then the mare dropped to her knees, and with a low moan, lay down.

Michael watched and waited. After two or three contractions, the mare's waters would burst, followed by the appearance of the foal's forefeet for a normal delivery.

The waters burst.

He waited. The foal's feet appeared. Five minutes passed. Ten. No rest of the foal.

Don't panic, Michael thought. *Give her a few more minutes.*

Several minutes later, he ran to the house to get Dr. Kendall, and tell him that it looked like another breech birth.

To Kendall's credit, he displayed no lack of confidence. After ordering Wright to bring more warm water and some lard, he ran out of the house with Michael as if they were going to a fire.

Once back at the mare's stall, Kendall rolled up his shirtsleeves past his elbows.

Michael leaned against a stall and crossed his arms. "Isn't it about time you sent for Cat?"

The doctor plunged his hands into a nearby bucket of water and began scrubbing them furiously with a cake of soap. "Why should I do that? I can handle this."

"I thought you sent for her to deliver the Stevens colt because she had more experience with a breech."

Caught in a lie, Kendall turned so red Michael could almost see the steam coming out of the man's ears. "I don't have time for this, Cooper. Just shut up and let me do my job."

Michael fell silent. He didn't want Wright to lose his plow horse and her foal because Michael had rattled the doctor into making a mistake. Yet he couldn't help but wonder, if Kendall did indeed have experience delivering a breech, why he had not tried to deliver the Stevens colt himself, and instead sent for Cat.

Kendall administered chloroform to the mare. When Wright appeared with the lard, the doctor oiled his arm and began examining the mare. Several minutes later, he removed his arm and stood looking at Wright gravely.

"The foal is malformed," he said. "It has no head."

The blood drained from Wright's face, and his jaw slackened. "N-no head?"

Kendall nodded curtly. "Unfortunately, animals are sometimes born without heads or other limbs. Your foal is dead, of course. If you want me to save its mother, I'll have to amputate its forelegs. There's no other way," he added defensively.

Michael uncrossed his arms and stepped forward. "Why are you so sure the foal has no head? Maybe it's positioned to the side, or on the foal's back, and you didn't feel it."

"I gave this horse a thorough examination," Kendall said in cold, clipped tones. "I didn't feel the head on the foal's side, or on its back." He looked at Wright. "You have to make a choice. Are you going to take my professional advice and let me do my job, or do you want to lose both your mare and her foal?"

Wright looked helplessly at Michael. "I—"

"Don't agree to anything," Michael said, striding down the row of stalls, "until I get back."

He found Cat where he prayed she would be, waiting with her horse behind one of Wright's outbuildings.

"Finally!" she muttered, stepping away from the building's wall and out of the shadows.

"You got my note," he said. When Gideon had sent for Michael, he wrote Cat a note telling her to come to the Wright farm and to wait for him behind this outbuilding until he came for her. Then he paid Wright's son to ride into town and deliver his instructions to Cat.

"I got your note, and as you can see, I'm here. I'm

also tired, stiff, and irritable, so you had better have a damn good reason for all this secrecy, Cooper."

"The best reason in the world." He grinned. "You're about to be vindicated."

"Vindicated?" The bright silvery light from the full moon illuminated her eager expression. "What do you mean?"

"Grab your medical bag and come with me."

If Cat lived to be a hundred, she'd never forget the expression on Dr. Kendall's face when he saw her come running into the barn.

"What's *she* doing here?" he demanded.

"I'm here to try to save Gideon's horses," she replied, going into an empty stall to take off her shirtwaist and put on her smock.

Once ready, she oiled her arm and examined the mare. She frowned in dismay. "The head is turned upward across the foal's back."

Gideon glared at Kendall. "What kind of vet are you? You said the foal didn't have a head."

"I stand by my diagnosis," Kendall insisted with a huff. "The foal has no head."

"It only seems that way," Cat said. "You have to feel carefully, but it's there."

Gideon leaned forward, his expression hopeful. "Can you save them?"

"I'll do my best," Cat replied. And this time, her best had to be good enough. "Michael, hand me that rope."

She proceeded to tie the foal's forelegs, and told Michael to hold them off to the side while she tried to turn the foal in its mother's womb. Using her experienced sense of touch, she slowly turned the foal's body until the head came within reach near the entrance of the pelvis. She felt around for the foal's nose.

When she found it, she seized it and brought the foal's head into the birth passage.

"I've got it!" She grasped the foal's forelegs and eased him out into the world. She smiled up at Gideon. "It's a colt, and he's alive."

The farmer scowled at Kendall. "No thanks to you."

Cat cut the umbilical cord and cleaned up and dried off the colt, who lay blinking at his strange new world out of soft brown eyes. He gave a weak little whinny and struggled to stand on his long, spindly legs. He teetered, then fell back down into the straw.

Cat rose and said to Gideon, "Keep an eye on the mare. She should be awaking from the chloroform any minute, and she'll be disoriented. You don't want her to accidentally step on her new baby. Not after all she's been through."

She washed off the lard, then went into the other stall to remove her stained smock and put on her shirtwaist. When she emerged, she saw Dr. Kendall reaching for his medical bag and turning to leave.

Michael placed a restraining hand on his shoulder. "Where do you think you're going?"

Kendall turned, his face twisted with resentment. "There's nothing more for me to do here, so I'll be heading back to town."

Cat stepped forward. "I want to hear the truth about what happened with the Stevens colt. You owe me that much."

Kendall regarded her with frank dislike. "My dear, I don't owe you anything."

Cat's temper ignited like a match to paper. She was tired and cranky. She wanted answers. "You lied about what happened that night. I want to know why."

"I don't know what you're talking about," Kendall said.

"You'd better come clean," Michael said at Cat's side. "After what we all just witnessed here tonight, it's obvious that you know very little about doctoring animals."

"I'll vouch for that," Gideon piped up from the depths of the stall.

The enraged doctor glared at them. "I have been practicing medicine for over thirty years, and you have the gall to question *my* competence?"

"Yes," Cat said.

"I know exactly what happened," Michael said. "Stevens told me that when you arrived to deliver his colt, you asked him to bring you water and lard. Now, why would you want those items if you weren't planning to examine the mare yourself?"

"I was about to send for Cat, and I knew she'd need them," Kendall said.

"So you say." Michael shook his head. "But I'll bet you examined that mare yourself. When you tried to bring the hooves into the birth canal, you didn't protect them with your hand. They tore the mother's womb, causing internal bleeding. Then you waited, hoping the colt would be born. When nothing happened, you finally sent for Cat. By the time she arrived, it was too late to save the mare or her foal. But you had a convenient scapegoat, didn't you, Kendall?"

Cat felt as though someone had lit a lamp in the darkness. "That's the only explanation that makes sense."

He glared at Michael. "You'd say anything to prove Catherine's innocence."

Michael resisted the urge to grab the doctor by the collar and shake him. "If you're not going to tell the truth, I will, and let the people of Little Falls make up their own mind. They may not be worldly, but they recognize a liar when they see one. You'll be lucky to have a practice left once folks learn the truth."

Dr. Kendall sighed, a long, drawn-out hiss of surrender that caused his shoulders to sag. "You're right. I did examine the mare myself. The colt got stuck somehow and I waited too long to send for Catherine. When they both died, I blamed her."

Michael's face darkened ominously. "Why, you cowardly, lying son of a bitch, ruining a woman's hard-earned reputation just to save your own miserable hide."

"At the time, I didn't see any harm in it," Kendall said. "She's a woman. She'll marry someday, and her husband will support her. But I have my own livelihood to consider."

Revulsion rose in Cat's throat like bile. "I thought you liked me, but all this time, you've been working behind my back, haven't you. Starting rumors and spreading lies. Ruining my reputation as a vet. Undermining my confidence in my abilities." She glared at him. "Dr. Kendall, you are beneath contempt."

Kendall's cheeks turned as pink as if Cat had just slapped him hard. "I never wanted to assume any veterinarian duties, but they went with the job." He raised his chin defiantly. "I was trained to care for sick people, not animals, and I'm damn good at it. Just ask anyone who's come to me for treatment since I arrived."

His admission deflated Cat's anger. She knew that when her own father first came to Little Falls, he preferred doctoring animals to people, and tended to treat his human patients gruffly and with little forbearance. He wanted the opportunity to practice veterinary medicine, so he did both.

But he had never tried to ruin anyone's reputation.

"You may be an excellent physician when it comes to people," Cat said, "but animals deserve the same high level of medical care. And you haven't provided it."

Kendall hung his head, his lips tightly pursed. "I've made a place for myself here in Little Falls. I consider it my home. But once people find out what I've done, I'll be ruined."

"You've broken a sacred trust with the farmers around here, Dr. Kendall," Cat said. "You have to pay a price."

"You'll be lucky if you're not tarred and feathered," Michael muttered.

Kendall looked at Cat. "I'm truly sorry for all the vile things I've said about you, and I humbly ask your forgiveness."

Cat hesitated. Could she forgive him? Could she live with herself if she didn't?

"I have a proposition for you," she said. Her forgiveness had a high price. "First you have to agree to clear my name by owning up to the mistakes you made with the Stevens horses. And then you have to promise to stick to doctoring people and leave the animals to me."

"You're staying in Little Falls?" Kendall asked.

She knew he sounded surprised because he assumed she would be marrying Drake and moving to Boston. She gave him a sharp warning look. "Yes, I'm staying in Little Falls." She raised her brows. "Will you agree to my terms?"

He nodded in defeat.

Satisfied, she wished everyone good night, and she and Michael left.

Once outside, she sighed in relief. "That was a close call. Thanks, Cooper."

"Damsels in distress are my specialty." The bright moonlight illuminated some of his features as clearly as if it were noon, and plunged others into shadow. "It's late, and you're not riding back to town alone. My place is closer. You'll spend the night."

What had gotten into him? Cat sensed an edginess beneath his quiet calm, a thread of tension winding itself around her as tightly as a wire.

"But no one's home," she said. "Your parents are still in St. Louis visiting your sick grandmother."

He cradled her face tenderly between his hands and kissed her, a long, slow, heavy kiss that made Cat's knees wobble and her toes curl. When they parted, he whispered, "That's the idea."

"You're plotting something," she said. Hard to remain suspicious with the delicious taste of his lips still on her own.

His eyes danced with devilment. "I just want to be alone with you. All alone."

She had to tell him. "Drake's asked me to marry him."

He smiled slowly. "But you're not going to."

She wanted him to kiss her again, harder. "You're awfully sure of yourself."

He lowered his head and looked deeply into her eyes. "That's because I know you don't love him. You love me."

"I do. I've loved you from the time I could walk. And I'm going to love you forever."

"Good, then you'll come home with me."

18

AFTER BATHING IN THE WATER CLOSET'S TUB THAT Jace had installed especially for Clementine, Cat went to Michael's room to find something to wear. As she set her lamp down on the nightstand, she noticed Denny's photograph of Rascal and her propped up against the clock.

She smiled. So Michael kept a picture of her next to his bed.

She rummaged through his chest of drawers until she found clothes. She pulled on a pair of Michael's trousers and slipped into one of his shirts before going downstairs. The shirt smelled faintly of laundry soap and sunshine. The trousers fit her the way he did.

She caught him just coming through the kitchen door from outside. While she was bathing, he had been out in the stables, bedding down their horses for the night, seeing to their welfare before his own.

He looked tired. He looked wonderful.

His hot blue gaze roved over her from head to toe. Now he looked wide awake.

"I hope you don't mind my borrowing your clothes again," she said, rolling up the long shirtsleeves, her voice soft and husky with a late-night hush.

"They never looked that good on me." He took off his hat and hung it up. "What's wrong with the clothes you were wearing?"

"They don't suit me anymore."

"I thought they looked pretty on you, too."

"Then I'll keep them for special occasions."

"You know how late it is?" he said, running a hand through his midnight dark hair. "Almost two-thirty in the morning."

She looked out the kitchen window at the inky blackness beyond. "It can't be."

He took a lamp and went into the parlor. Cat followed. When Michael sat on the settee and patted the place beside him, she stood there without budging, her arms crossed.

"What's wrong?" he said softly.

"I want to know how you really feel about me." When he looked puzzled, she added, "Compared to your other women."

He rose and placed his hands on her shoulders. "There *are* no other women, Willie."

"What about Ruby?"

Michael looked so pleased Cat wanted to swat him. "Ah. You're jealous."

She did try to swat him, but he caught her wrist, and brought her palm to his lips. "Damn right," she said, finding it impossible to stay angry whenever he kissed any part of her.

Suddenly his teasing grin vanished. "Ruby was a long time ago. Paid-for pleasure is a lot different than what I feel for you."

"You fought Drake over her."

"I would've done the same for any woman being bullied by any man, not just Kendall. You know that."

Deep in her heart she did. That's why she loved him.

He kept holding her hand. "There hasn't been any other woman in a long time. And there never will be. I love you and need you too much to ever risk it."

He sat down on the settee and drew Cat down beside him, wrapped his arms around her and held her close. He felt so strong and solid against her, his cheek pressed against hers.

"Tell me something, Cooper. Why'd it take you so long to come to your senses?" She turned so she could see his face. "You know I've always loved you. Lord, I've told you often enough."

"I never quite believed it," he replied. "We were always so close, I thought you wanted me out of habit. Once you became a woman and met someone else, I was sure you'd realize you didn't love me after all."

"And then Drake Kendall came to town and proved you right," she said. "I fell for him, hook, line, and sinker."

He stroked her cheek with his thumb. "I realized that on the Fourth. During the men's footrace, I was just about to cross the finish line when I heard you cheering for Kendall instead of me."

"So that's why you lost." His admission touched her so deeply she thought she'd shatter.

"If I couldn't win for you, what was the point?"

And she lost her heart to him all over again.

"Then I wandered off with Drake and made you miss the horse race." Cat winced. "I have a lot to answer for."

"We've both been a pair of prize fools."

She nestled against him, savoring the warmth and closeness. "Drake wanted to marry me, but he never once said he loved me." She shuddered. "How could I ever think I was in love with him?"

"You didn't think I loved you, and along came this handsome, big-city fellow with his smooth-talking ways, and he charmed the pants off you."

"That he did, right out of my trousers and into a skirt."

Michael nuzzled her ear. "Those weren't the pants I was referring to, my love."

Cat blushed, and sought to divert him. "Drake may be handsome and charming, but inside, he's a cold, selfish man," she said. "And speaking of close calls, thanks again for clearing my name tonight."

"I knew you weren't to blame, so the doctor had to be lying."

"That's why you set this trap for him at Gideon's."

"Clever of me, don't you think?"

"Don't break your arm patting yourself on the back. We were both lucky old Winnie had a breech." Cat shook her head. "I thought Dr. Kendall was a kind man, with my best interests at heart, but he turned out to be a lying, cowardly snake in the grass. To think he could've been my father-in-law."

Michael hugged her tighter. "Jace will make a much better father-in-law."

She turned in his arms and smiled in delight. "You asking me to marry you, Cooper?"

He released her and rose from the settee, only to kneel on one knee at her feet. He took her hand, his expression suddenly serious. "Catherine Augusta Wills, will you do me the honor of giving me your hand in marriage?"

Now she felt dazed, numb, and astonished. Just as her mother said she would. "I'd be honored to marry you, Michael Boswell Cooper." She brought his hand to her cheek.

He rose, drawing her to her feet. Cat ran her hands up his hard chest and rested them on his shoulders. She looked into his eyes, and knew that he wanted her as much as she wanted him. Her heart beat faster. She smiled and stood on tiptoes so she could reach his mouth.

His arms slid around her waist, and he drew her against him. Cat marveled at their perfect fit, hip to hip, her breasts crushed against his unyielding chest. She locked her arms around his neck and closed her eyes for his kiss.

Unlike the first time Michael had really kissed her, this time all barriers between them had fallen. His lips were a warm, tender pledge, both claiming and affirming.

Cat sighed. A delicious warmth spread through her body like ice cream melting in the hot summer sun. Michael's hard, strong body heated her own flesh. His kisses tasted as potent as whiskey. The familiar masculine scent of straw, leather, and fresh air filled her nostrils and went straight to her head. The only sound she heard in the dark, hushed house was the beating of her own heart.

The kiss lasted forever. When they finally parted, both panting, Cat rested her forehead against Michael's chest and closed her eyes.

"Is the room really spinning, or is it just me?" she whispered.

She could hear the smile in his voice when he replied, "It is spinning, and I hope it never stops."

Suddenly a lifetime of wanting him emboldened her. Cat reached up and threaded her fingers through his hair, pulling his head down so she could reach his lips. She kissed him hard, brazenly plunging her tongue into his mouth, catching him by surprise. She drew away and playfully nipped at his chin before trailing kisses down his neck.

"Cat—?"

Her head fell back and she looked at him. "What time will Belle be here to fix you breakfast?"

"Early. *Real* early."

She knew what she wanted. She started unbuttoning her shirt. "Then we don't have much time." Just the thought of making love to him made her want to sprout wings and soar like an eagle, riding the wind so high above the clouds "Take me upstairs?"

He grew very still. "Are you sure?"

She kissed the tip of his nose. "As sure as I am of anything."

"There may be consequences."

"My father's not here to shoot you."

"No, but my father is."

"I want you, Michael Cooper." She almost stamped her foot like Sally Wheeler. "I've waited too long as it is to wait another minute." She took a deep breath. "And if I should conceive your child tonight, I know it'd be a girl. Someday she'll be one of the first women to graduate from a vet school, and—"

He stopped her nervous chatter with another decisive kiss. He released her hands, but only so he could pass his own down her shirtfront, stopping to touch her breast.

A jolt of unexpected, unfamiliar pleasure rocked her. She moaned against his mouth. His thumb teased her nipple, and she thought she would die.

They parted reluctantly. Michael looked so deeply into her eyes that they became one. He unbuttoned the second button of her shirt, then the third, and the fourth. He stopped halfway down. Then he pushed the soft material off her shoulders and down her arms to the elbows, baring her breasts.

She blushed, for no man had ever seen her half-undressed, but didn't try to cover herself. That would only end what she so desperately wanted to continue.

"Beautiful," he whispered, before lowering his dark head to take one rosy peak into his mouth.

Cat felt a tug of pleasure deep inside. She grabbed his shoulders to steady herself, flung back her head and groaned mindlessly. "Don't stop."

He didn't.

Finally, when his ardent caresses turned Cat's knees to water and they buckled beneath her, Michael swept her into his arms and effortlessly carried her upstairs to his bedroom.

He noticed she had left a lamp burning by his bed-side. Her willful premeditation tickled him.

When he set her on her feet, she said, "Where'd you get the photograph? I don't remember giving you one."

"I asked Denny to make me a copy. Do you mind?"

"As long as it's not the one of Ruby in her unmentionables."

He took her face in his hands and kissed her again. "Let's not discuss Ruby tonight, or ever again."

She grinned as she started to unbutton his shirt. "Agreed."

He stood still and watched her undress him, her expression a mixture of curiosity and pure lust. Once his shirt was discarded, she memorized his body with her fingertips, up his arms, across his shoulders and chest, down to the waistband of his pants.

He couldn't keep his eyes off her small, full breasts, peeking out from her half-buttoned shirt every time she moved. God, she was making him hard.

She struggled with the first button. "Your pants are tight."

He suppressed a smile. "There's a reason for that." He unbuttoned his pants himself, slid them down his hips, and showed her.

Her cheeks turned a fiery red at the size of him, but she didn't look away. "Oh. *That* reason."

She made him laugh. She surprised him. She had loved him forever. Where else could he find such a perfect woman?

"Undress for me," he whispered.

She stepped back, her glittering gaze holding him prisoner. To his surprise, she didn't start with her shirt, as he expected. Her trembling fingers unbuttoned her trousers—*his* trousers—first. When Cat wriggled out of them, Michael's pulse raced in anticipation, but to his frustration, the long tails of the shirt concealed her modestly, save for her long, shapely legs that went on for miles.

She was catching on quickly, this game of arousal.

"The shirt," he whispered thickly.

She sucked her plump lower lip between her teeth and slowly unbuttoned the remaining buttons. Then she turned, and shrugged off his shirt.

Michael drank his fill of both her back and her tight, curved backside before he decided he had been denied long enough, and turned her to face him.

Finally she stood gloriously naked before him, and his heart overflowed. "You are so beautiful."

Her eyes, large and luminous, roved over him. "So are you, Michael Cooper."

She turned and pulled back the covers, then slid into the bed. His bed. Their bed. She held out her arms to him in mute invitation and trust, and he climbed in beside her.

He propped himself up on one elbow and stared

down at her. He realized that even though they had
known each other all their lives, in the bedroom they
were strangers.

"Don't be afraid to tell me what you like," he whispered, tracing the delicate curve of her jaw with his
fingertips. "And what you don't."

"Don't worry. I'm going to like everything." She
sighed, and touched his smooth, erect flesh. "Too
much."

Her words and touch enflamed him, but he forced
himself to go slowly. For all of Cat's bold words and
bravado, she was still innocent, though he suspected
a lifetime of riding astride would make her first time
easier.

So he loved her with his lips and tongue and hands,
savoring every one of her soft moans and sighs, her
sharp intake of breath when he delighted her unex-
pectedly. He explored every peak and valley of her
as if he were mapping an undiscovered country.

And she was right. She did like everything.

"Don't stop," she'd whisper. "Please. More. Lower.
Dear God, yes. Right there."

And he obliged, until they were both delirious with
passion.

When she was ready, he positioned himself above
her and possessed her as tenderly as his waning self-
control would allow. She gasped at the unfamiliarity
of him, but he stilled until her body grew accustomed
to his size.

Then he rocked against her, watching her passion
rise higher and higher, until he felt her own release
and she screamed his name.

All self-control vanished. He abandoned himself to
his own feverish pleasure, and when he exploded, he
gave himself to her forever.

•   •   •

When Cat next opened her eyes, she found Michael's bedroom bathed in morning light. A cool summer breeze blew in, billowing out the curtains.

She smiled lazily to herself when she realized that she was lying naked in her lover's bed. Her lover. She sighed and stretched. Her accomplished, inventive, exciting lover. She blushed when she recalled specifics of their wild night.

She looked over at Michael, lying on his back just inches away, one arm flung above his head in repose, his dark hair adorably tousled. She rested her head in her hand and just stared at him.

He must have sensed her looking, for he opened his eyes and grinned. "Good morning."

She kissed him lightly on the cheek. "Good morning, yourself."

"How do you feel?"

"A little sore."

He raised one brow. "Second thoughts?"

"Never. I was just thinking how your visit to that St. Louis whorehouse sure paid off."

"I learn quickly." He reached over and caressed her breasts. "So do you." She arched her back in mute invitation.

He flicked his tongue over one straining nipple. "This isn't the first time I've seen you naked, you know."

Cat was too distracted to do more than groan. Finally she murmured, "I remember. You were pretending to be a doctor, and I was your patient."

"Not that time." He didn't stop his relentless assault. "I mean the day you fell in the mud, I saw you washing yourself outside the bunkhouse. Naked as the day you were born."

That brought her to her senses. Her eyes flew open, wide with indignation. "You *spied* on me?"

He gave an unrepentant nod. "I'm a skunk."

She ran her hand down his torso. "A rat."

"A rogue," he agreed.

Her hand disappeared beneath the sheet. "An outlaw."

He gasped and all talking ceased.

Later, Cat heard the dogs barking, but they always barked at every little thing. She heard a door slam somewhere downstairs, but even if it was Belle coming to fix Michael's breakfast, they had plenty of time to rise and think of an excuse for Cat's presence.

Then she heard a familiar voice call up from the foot of the stairs, "Catherine Augusta Wills, I know you're in this house somewhere."

She sat bolt upright in bed. *"Mama?"*

"Mrs. Wills?" Michael turned white and uttered a string of oaths that would have done his father proud. He jumped out of bed as if the mattress had suddenly turned into a bed of hot coals. "If she finds me in bed with her daughter . . ."

Cat ran to the open bedroom door. "I'll be right down."

"My goose is cooked." Michael slipped on his pants and tugged on his boots. "My father won't have to shoot me." He jammed his hands into his shirtsleeves. "Your mother will."

"No, she won't." Cat put on her pants. "As long as you make an honest woman of me." Her shirt came next. She grinned and swatted Michael's backside. "Ready to face the firing squad?"

"Very funny, Willie. You'll notice I'm not laughing."

"Oh, poor Cooper."

She strode out of the bedroom with Michael hot on her heels. What in blazes was her mother doing here in Little Falls? She was supposed to be in New York City.

Cat ran down the stairs and into the parlor, where her mother, Madeline Sullivan Wills, stood waiting. She looked elegant and quite citified in a bottle green ensemble complete with a stylish bonnet set rakishly atop her upswept auburn curls. She also looked as though she were fighting to keep her famous Irish temper from boiling over.

But she smiled warmly when she saw her only child, and opened her arms. Cat ran to her mother and hugged her with all her might.

"Oh, Mama, it's so good to see you. I've missed you and Papa so much."

"And I've missed you, baby," Maddy said through her tears.

When they finally parted, Maddy held Cat at arm's length. "Let me look at you."

As usual, Maddy's sharp green eyes missed nothing. First she studied Cat, then her gaze cooled with suspicion as it sought out Michael lingering in the background.

"Good morning, Mrs. Wills," he said, sounding as guilty as a little boy caught with his hand in the cookie jar. "I'm surprised to see you here."

"About as surprised to see me as the time I caught you playing doctor and patient with my daughter," was Maddy's dry reply.

Michael turned red.

"What are you doing here, Mama?" Cat asked. "Why didn't you tell me you were coming? Is Papa here, too?"

"No, your father couldn't come with me, so I came alone. Actually, I'm here because of a letter Michael wrote to me."

Cat gave him a puzzled look over her shoulder. "A letter?"

"Why don't we all sit down," Maddy said. "I have much to tell you."

When they were all seated, Maddy smoothed her skirt, and looked at Michael. "I'm assuming you haven't told Cat about the letter."

"No, I haven't." He looked over at Cat. "I wrote to your mother about Drake Kendall. I told her how you were attracted to him, but that we didn't know anything about him, except for the fact that he's Dr. Horatio Kendall's son, and he's from Boston."

"Michael was very suspicious, and after reading his letter, so were your father and I," Maddy said. "Since your grandfather Wills knows Kendall quite well and recommended him to take over your father's practice here, I asked him about the Kendalls' background."

Her green eyes hardened. "We learned that Drake Kendall was dismissed from the Paul Revere Bank for embezzlement."

Cat's jaw dropped. "He *stole* money?"

Michael snorted. "Why didn't they arrest him and throw him in jail?"

Maddy smiled dryly. "His two brothers, who are highly placed in the same bank, worked a deal whereby no charges would be brought against their brother if he returned the money. But Drake was dismissed, and his brothers refused to find him another position. That's why he came out here to Little Falls."

Cat locked gazes with Michael. "He never told me."

"Oh, my dear," Maddy said, "there is so much more that he hasn't told you." As Cat and Michael listened attentively, she added, "Drake Kendall seduced two young Irish parlormaids on two separate occasions, and got them both with child."

Cat rocked back in her seat. "He didn't tell me that, either."

Maddy patted her hand. "He wouldn't, because he never acknowledged them. And Dr. Kendall paid the women quite handsomely never to darken his doorstep again."

Outrage, hot and fierce, swept through Cat like brushfire. Two innocent maids abandoned, their children branded as illegitimate. "That snake! That contemptible, loathsome—I can't believe I thought I loved him."

"I was worried about you," Maddy said. "I couldn't understand how my sensible, level-headed daughter could be involved with such a vile man, so I had to come out here to try to talk some sense into you." She looked at Michael. "I can see that's no longer necessary."

He rose, drew Cat to her feet, and faced Maddy. "No, it isn't, Mrs. Wills. I've asked Cat to marry me, and she's accepted my proposal."

"At last." Maddy rose to embrace them both. Her eyes shone with more tears. "You've made your parents very happy."

As soon as Cat and Michael reached the outskirts of town, she turned in the saddle, and said, "Want to race?"

His eyes devoured her. "I'd rather make love to you again. And again."

She smiled seductively. "Whoever wins gets whatever he—or she—wants."

She spurred Rascal on before Michael had time to reply, but she soon heard the drumming of Rogue's hoofbeats behind her.

By the time they reached Main Street, Cat raced ahead by several lengths. She purposely slowed down when they approached the Kendall house.

"You go on ahead," she told Michael when his horse drew abreast of hers. "I have to take care of some unpleasant business."

He glanced at his grandparents' former house. "You sure you want to do this yourself?"

When she nodded, he rode off.

The housekeeper showed her into the parlor. Cat didn't have to wait long before Drake walked in.

He stopped when he saw her attire and raised one disapproving brow. "I thought I made it clear that I will not tolerate my wife parading about like a man."

"But I'm not going to be your wife, so I can dress as I please," Cat replied. "I'll be marrying Michael Cooper."

Drake stared at her in stunned silence for all of a minute, then recovered his composure with remarkable rapidity. "The childhood sweethearts are going to marry . . . how heartwarming." His lip curled. "You'll come crawling back to me when you get sick of smelling manure on his boots."

How had she ever thought she loved this man?

"Well, at least he gets manure on his boots from an honest day's work. He doesn't steal money that doesn't belong to him."

Her barb wiped the sneer off his face. "What's that supposed to mean?"

"The game's over, Drake. I know you were dismissed from the Paul Revere Bank for embezzlement."

All color leached from his face. "It's a lie. They framed me. They—"

"When were you planning to tell me? After we were married? Or when you told me about the two Irish maids you seduced, and the children you refuse to acknowledge?"

His expression remained a mask of affronted innocence. "Who in the world has been telling you these lies about me?"

"You're pathetic," Cat snapped. "You're not even man enough to own up to your responsibilities." She turned on her heel and strode out of the parlor with not so much as a backward glance.

When the door slammed behind her, Drake muttered, "Bitch."

"On the contrary," came his father's voice from the door joining the parlor with his study. "Catherine is a highly principled young lady. It's too bad you weren't worthy of her."

"No loss," Drake said. "She would've bored me within a month."

"She would've been the making of you." Dr. Kendall walked over to the window and stared out at a passing horseman. "So, what are your plans now?"

Drake gave him a puzzled look. "I'm going back to Boston. You said you'd fix everything with my brothers."

"On the condition that you married and settled down," he said. "I see no sign of that happening now."

"Then I'll stay here with you."

"Little Falls is a hole in the wall, as you're so fond of saying. When word gets out about the real reason you left Boston, no one will have anything to do with you."

His father shook his head sadly. "Your dearly departed mother and I are to blame. You were the baby, and we spoiled you. No matter how reprehensible your behavior, we always made excuses for you." He sighed. "You're a grown man approaching thirty, son. I can't make excuses for you anymore. You're going to have to fix your own problems from now on."

Drake felt the floor giving way beneath his feet. "You're turning me out?"

"I have no other choice. I like this little hole in the wall, and want to spend the rest of my life here, if they'll let me. I've already made one mistake trying to ruin Catherine's reputation, but she's forgiven me, and I hope the rest of the townspeople will, too." He sighed. "You've become a millstone around my neck, son."

"So that's all I am to you, a millstone." His own father was turning his back on him. Betraying him. "Fine. I'll pack my bags and be out of your life by tomorrow evening."

When he reached the door, he stopped and turned for one last parting shot. "Don't ever call me your son again."

He saw his father flinch, then open his mouth. But he ultimately said nothing and just kept staring out the window.

"Drake Kendall's left town," Ida May announced at the supper table the following evening.

Cat exchanged looks with Michael. "Where did you hear that?"

"From the quilting circle," she replied. "Where else?"

"Is he going back to Boston to make amends to those women he wronged?" Maddy asked. She had taken down her hair and wore the wild auburn mane tied back with a narrow ribbon.

Ida May passed her the dish of roast potatoes. "Francie Dawlish heard he's headed for California."

"Good riddance," Michael said.

Denny cleared his throat. "Kendall's not the only one who'll be heading for California." When he had everyone's attention, he said, "As much as I love it here in Little Falls, it's time for me to move on."

Exclamations of protest and dismay rippled around the table.

Denny's hazel eyes sparkled. "And Ruby has agreed to come with me. I asked her to marry me," he added hastily, "but she said she won't until I'm really sure that I want her."

Cat smiled. "You'll just have to wear her down."

"I intend to," he replied.

Later that night, after everyone else had retired for the evening, Cat and Michael sat close together on the porch swing, listening to the crickets and looking at the stars.

"Fancy that," Cat said, petting Ulysses curled on her lap. "Denny and Ruby going off together."

"You still jealous?"

"No, I'm happy for her. Ida May always said that Denny can draw sweetness out of a pickle, and he'll bring out the best in Ruby. They'll have a good life together."

"You'll have to give them one of Bounder's pups to remember us by."

"Four down, and four to go." She snuggled closer to Michael. "I hope Denny and Ruby are as happy as we are."

He smiled in the warm velvet darkness. "No one can possibly be as happy as we are."

"So when are we going to tie the knot?" Cat looked across the street at the Wheeler house. "Sally wants to know, so she can wear black to our wedding."

Michael rolled his eyes. "Willie . . ."

"What about in October? The week before Harvest Festival."

"I like that idea. We can both ride in the race as husband and wife."

"Think you'll beat me, Cooper?"

A faint voice from inside the parlor said, "Nevermore."

EPILOGUE

MICHAEL SWEPT HIS BEAUTIFUL, RADIANT WIFE INTO his arms and carried her across the threshold of their new home.

Cat kissed him soundly for the hundredth time before he set her down in the parlor. She ran a hand over the settee. "I can't believe this is ours."

To their astonishment, their parents and grandparents had given them the old Himmel spread as their wedding gift.

Michael looked around the sunny, freshly painted room. "A place to breed our own horses."

"And our children," Cat said. She placed a hand on his arm. "I guess this is as good a time as any to tell you."

He brushed her lips with his own. "Tell me what?"

"The first one is coming in seven months."

Joy lit his beautiful blue eyes from within. He took her hands in his and kissed them.

Cat said, "The night you took me back to your place after I delivered Winnie's colt? You did warn me there could be consequences."

They had shared many such passionate nights since, but Cat liked to think this precious first child had been conceived on their first night together.

Michael held her hands against his heart. "Dear God, I never dreamed I could be this happy. That my life could be so perfect." He swept her off her feet and spun her around, came to his senses and set her down as gently as if she were a rare piece of porcelain. "Tell me I didn't hurt it."

"Not a chance." She slipped her arms around his waist and held her dearest husband and friend tight. "I meant what I said that night. This baby will be a girl, and unlike her mama, she will graduate from the Chicago College of Veterinary Medicine."

One of the many schools that had refused to admit Cat.

"Our daughter will do anything she wants," Michael said with conviction.

"Daughters," she corrected him. "Three would be nice. And some boys for you."

His mouth twitched in a teasing smile. "One for each of Bounder's pups?"

Cat raised her brows. "Not *that* many!"

"At least you won't have to give them away."

His laughter died, and he released her, his eyes darkening with passion and promise. "Come, Mrs. Cooper. I've been dying to get you out of that wedding dress."

"What will happen to me when you do?"

When her lovely white wedding dress from Henrietta's lay on the floor, he showed her.